D1649799

INNERCITY GIRL LIKE ME

INNERCITY GIRL LIKE ME

SABRINA BERNARDO

HarperTrophyCanada™
An imprint of HarperCollinsPublishersLtd

Published by HarperTrophyCanada™,
an imprint of HarperCollins Publishers Ltd.

Originally published by HarperCollins Publishers in a trade paperback edition: 2008
This digest paperback edition: 2009

HarperCollins Publishers Ltd.,
2 Bloor Street East, 20th Floor,
Toronto, Ontario, Canada M4W 1A8

www.harpercollins.ca

Library and Archives Canada Cataloguing in Publication

Bernardo, Sabrina
Innercity girl like me / Sabrina Bernardo.

ISBN 978-0-00-639492-1

I. Title.
PS8603.E734I55 2009   jC813'.6   C2009-903515-4

Printed and bound in the United States
HC 9 8 7 6 5 4 3 2 1

Dedicated to those who have come and gone, and to my mother, who always believed in me.

PROLOGUE

My palms were sweaty and my heart pounded in my chest. I stood in the middle of the circle, surrounded by four people: Gina, Nathan, Darrel and an older girl named Connie. It was called four-for-five, which meant that four people could beat you up for five minutes. You weren't allowed to cry out or fall down. You had to prove to the group that you were solid, that you wanted in and that you could keep your mouth shut. This was my chance to join the Diablos.

"Are you ready?" Gina asked me with a smile.

I looked around at the other faces in the circle. All four were mad-dogging me as if to intimidate me. A crowd had formed around the circle to watch the next Diablo join the family. I gave Gina a quick nod. She gave me the honorary first punch straight to the head. I stumbled back a bit and felt the impact sting my eyes. Connie then punched me in the stomach, Nathan punched me on the other side of my head and Darrel kicked my legs. I was getting pushed, punched and kicked within that circle for five minutes, but it seemed to last forever. And through it all, I kept telling myself, "Don't fall down, not in front of all these people."

When someone outside the circle whistled, I was allowed to sit down and I quickly did so. I hurt all over, especially my head, where Gina had punched me.

The crowd cheered as I sat on the grass with my face in my hands. I was almost in tears but no one was going to see that. I felt a couple of hands pat me on the back and I looked up and saw Gina and her brother Darrel smile at me as they lifted me up by each arm. Gina then pulled a red bandanna out of her pocket and began to wipe my face. This was called "hanging," which is their process of cleaning you up. Gina then crowned me, tying the rag around my throbbing head.

"This is yours now, you deserve it," Gina said.

"Where's your smile?" Darrel asked.

I gave him a faint smile, but was in too much pain. It didn't matter, though. I felt grown up. I was a Diablo now. I was thirteen years old.

CHAPTER ONE

MY CHILDHOOD

Central neighbourhood's gang was the Diablos. From the time I was five years old I had loved Central neighbourhood—a tough part of Winnipeg. I didn't live there but my Grandma Beatriza did. She lived in a tall, red-framed house, smack dab in the middle of Central. There was this park near her house that had the biggest sandbox I had ever seen. All the neighbourhood kids played in it and I always wanted to go there, but my mom wouldn't let me.

"Those kids are dirty, their mothers are on welfare and babies pee in that sandbox," she would say while she dragged me away from it.

In my wildest dreams I imagined my parents dancing and kissing and saying "I love you" to each other because in real life they never did those things. My parents constantly bickered back and forth and for as long as I could remember they slept in separate beds. Tension between them escalated when one day I told them how Uncle John touched me when nobody was around.

They didn't know what to do about it. It was Dad who made the final decision.

"It's better if we keep this shit quiet. There's no need to shame this family," Dad told us.

Later on that evening, Mom came into my bedroom and sat at the edge of my bed without looking at me.

"Maria, it's better if you stay over at Grandma Beatriza's on weekdays and go to a school that's close by. That means you won't be going to the same school in the fall. You understand? " I told her yes and she walked out of my room. I hugged my favourite teddy bear with excitement. Not only was I excited about living with my favourite grandmother but also because I had just met a new girl named Jessica at the sandbox.

On the day I moved into Grandma Beatriza's, Dad helped me bring in my bags from the family van. Grandma Beatriza stood in the window and frantically waved at me. When I approached the door, she grabbed me and held me tightly to her chest.

"Sweet girl, sweet girl," she said contentedly. I followed her down the hall and into a spare room. The room was bare, except for a daybed and a couple of old dressers in the corners.

"It's good bed," she said while patting down the comforter with her wrinkled hand.

"Is this where I'll be sleeping, Grandma?" I asked, putting a bag full of books down.

"Yes. You sleep here, warm and nice." She grabbed a small bag of caramel candies from her housecoat pocket and handed it to me.

"I'll be back, Grandma. I have to get the rest of my stuff."
I was about to turn around but my dad interrupted me.

"I got your stuff." Dad placed the last duffle bag in a corner.

"What's wrong?" I asked, noticing his frown. He knelt down and put a hand on my shoulder.

"Be a good little girl for your grandma, okay?" I nodded yes. He kissed me goodbye and left.

I could tell my grandmother was happy to have me. She always greeted me with a smile and told me how pretty I was. Grandma was my friend. She'd tell me stories about back home and I'd tell her stories about Jessica and me. She was born in Portugal and even though she had lived in Canada for more than twenty years she still wasn't fluent in English. I knew she didn't understand most of my stories but it didn't matter. If she had understood them, I'm sure she wouldn't have let me run around as freely as I did. She asked about Jessica once and when I finally did bring her over, she patted Jessica on the head, told her she was a good girl and gave her a bunch of caramel candies to take home with her.

Jessica and I were the happiest when we were together, but the end of the day would always come too soon. She hated going home. Shortly after I turned nine, I found out that Jessica's mother, Janice, had been an alcoholic for years but kicked the habit to regain custody of Jessica. Not long after Jessica was in her life again, Janice hit the bottle and sank to the bottom.

One day, Jessica suddenly started talking about her mother.

"My mom drinks with friends, sometimes she drinks alone. She's happy at first but it doesn't take long for her to get sad again. She tells the same stories about her ex-boyfriends beating her up. She talks about my dad, the guy that would never hurt her."

"Where is he?" I asked.

"He's in heaven. He died in a car crash before I was born. Anyway, this one time she went out drinking and left me home alone. I stayed up all night worrying about her. She came home really late with a bunch of people. They were laughing really loud and yelling. I was scared to leave my room but I had to go pee. I ran to the bathroom and saw this big fat slob peeing in the sink. When he turned around I saw everything. Then I saw my mom lying in the empty tub, naked and touching herself down there. 'Get out of here, little girl!' she yelled. If child and family services find out about this, I know they'll make me go back to a foster home. Even though my mom is nutty, I'd rather live with her. How about your parents?"

"My parents are . . . okay. My dad works construction and my mom works for a temp agency. They are really busy all the time or they're fighting. I like it best when they're busy. That way I don't have to hear them scream." I shrugged. Jessica smiled at me meekly.

At school, we were surrounded by older kids; some were gang members and some not, but most of them were bad news. They used foul language in front of us with no regard and regularly offered us cigarettes and beer. They did a lot of drugs and even got us high on special occasions. They obviously didn't care that we were only nine years old. Jessica and I thought they were the coolest. We looked up to the older kids. We wanted to be just like them.

One Friday night, Jessica and I were hanging out in front of her apartment building, the tallest and scariest structure in Central, with a bunch of other neighbourhood kids. There was Nathan Troth, an aboriginal boy whose face was always dirty and who drove his BMX bike like it was a motorcycle; Francine Troth, Nathan's sister, who always had her greasy hair parted down the side; Erin Smith, a chubby native girl who hardly ever spoke; Thomas McCloud, a blond, white boy whose bark was always worse than his bite; and Jaime Briceno, a Spanish boy who didn't speak English very well and would always beat people up when he got frustrated.

"When I turn eleven, I am joining a gang," Nathan said, spinning his bike around, making the sand fly onto our bare legs.

"How old are you now?" Jessica asked.

"Nine," he said.

"Us too," I added. Jessica and I both reached down and brushed off our legs.

"Me too," Thomas said, trying to shake Nathan off his bike.

"Which gang?" Erin asked them.

"The Diablos, what else?" Nathan said, pushing Thomas away.

"Don't forget about the Street Ryders," Francine reminded her brother.

"Street Sissies? Who wants to be part of that stupid gang?" Thomas said.

"I want to join too," Jaime added.

"You can't even speak English. They won't let you," Nathan said.

"I will learn to speak good by that time." Jaime sat down beside me.

"I bet Erin can kick some ass." I tried to make Erin smile. She seemed glum to me.

"I'm moving to the North End in a few weeks. That means I won't be joining the Diablos. I'll be a Street Ryder when I grow up," Erin said as she watched cars passing us by.

"Speaking of the Diablos, look over there," Jessica said pointing across the street.

A group of teenagers and a kid our age were heading our way, all wearing red. I didn't recognize the teenagers, but I had seen the kid around. Her name was Gina McKay. She was in the same grade as Jessica and me and had a bad reputation for jumping kids for their lunch money.

"Maybe we should get out of here," Francine told Erin.

"No, if we want to be part of them, we can't be afraid of them. We've got to look cool too," Nathan rushed to say.

"What if they jump us? We're too young to win this fight," Francine said, panicking.

"Here," Erin threw her a cigarette and she lit it up. "This will make you look more tough," she said.

* * *

THE DIABLOS approached us and Nathan turned his hat around upon their arrival.

"Wait a minute," one teen said as if he were discovering something.

"What's wrong?" one of the girls asked.

She was dressed in red from head to toe with a ponytail perched on top of her head and her hair cascading over her shoulders. I looked quickly over at Jessica. I could tell she was impressed, especially by the girl's clothes.

"What's your name?" the teen asked Nathan.

"Nathan," he said in a fake gangster voice, taking a puff of his cigarette without inhaling.

"Who's your family?" the guy asked.

"Huh?" Nathan acted surprised.

I giggled to myself. I'm sure Nathan thought the guy was going to say, "Jeez, boy, you look cool, wanna join?"

"What's your last name?"

"Troth." Nathan coughed from the smoke.

"I knew your cousin Clayton Troth," the young thug bragged. Nathan's smile faded as if he was recalling a bad memory.

"Crazy what happened to him, getting killed by a bat to the head. But you know what they say, the good die young."

Nathan nodded and tried to keep his cool. The pretty girl in red took Nathan's hat off and ran her fingers through his black hair.

"If you're anything like him, you'll be a hell of a Diablo one day," she said kindly.

"I know him," Gina's voice sprang up. She walked towards us and tossed her jet-black hair over her broad shoulder. For a second I thought she was going to bully us for some money. I crossed my fingers and hoped she wouldn't.

"Let's go," a voice complained from the group.

"See you around, Nathan Troth."

Nathan and the gangster shook hands and left the park.

THE NEXT TIME I ran into Gina was in grade five. She was known as the school bully, threatening kids for their lunch money or just pushing them around for no good reason. I had gotten into trouble for swearing at my teacher and was sent down to the principal's office. I got into trouble a lot then. All the cool kids got in trouble and I didn't want to be left out. The secretary, Mrs. Fraser, told me to have a seat and as I waited to be yelled at, Gina stormed out of the principal's office and sat next to me. It was silent for a minute or two before she broke the ice.

"Are you waiting to talk to Mr. Erickson?" she asked, her face red-hot with anger.

"Yeah, I got in trouble," I said shifting my feet.

"I just hate him," Gina said crossing her thick arms.

"I don't appreciate that comment," Mrs. Fraser said.

"You're not going to hear sorry from me and the carpet in here looks like puke," Gina said stubbornly.

"You had better learn some manners, young lady, if you know what's good for you. You're in enough trouble already."

"What did you do?" I whispered.

"Put gum in all the textbooks in my math class," she said.

The principal opened his office door and called me in. I took my usual seat and kicked my feet around.

"The last time you were in here you promised me I wouldn't see you for the rest of the year," Mr. Erickson complained. Mr. Erickson was big man with a belly that stuck out over his belt buckle and whose face and arms were covered in freckles.

"Yeah, I know," I sighed.

"Well, what happened this time?" He attempted to cross his arms over his protruding chest.

"Billy called me a dyke and I threw my binder at his head," I said, noticing that his boobs were bigger then my mother's.

"Excuse me, a what?"

"A dyke."

"Why didn't you tell your teacher instead of resorting to violence?"

"'Cause that would make me a tattle-tale. I can't be known as a tattle-tale, it's not cool."

"I think you should worry less about being cool and more about your grades. You used the F word in class today, didn't you?"

"It was an accident. We always say it."

"Who's we?"

"Me and my friends."

Mr. Erickson looked disappointed. He sat at his desk and began writing a letter.

"I want you to bring this back to me tomorrow, signed. Get out of my office."

After I was dismissed Gina was still sitting there along with three boys from the neighbourhood, Omar, Nathan and Malcolm. She motioned me to sit beside them.

"Are all you guys in trouble?" I asked the boys.

"Who cares," Omar said while scratching his nappy head.

"What happened?" Gina asked me.

"Sending a letter home," I said in a carefree tone of voice. "I'll get my grandma to sign it. She can't read English anyway." I giggled.

"What are you doing after school?" Gina asked.

"Don't know," I said.

"I'm going to Burger World with these guys and some of my other friends. Do you want to come?"

Burger World was a diner across the street from school where all the popular and cool kids hung out. I had never stepped foot inside. I was intimidated, but at the same time I felt special in that moment. Gina McKay, the most feared person in our school, wanted to hang out with me.

"Okay," I said, trying not to sound too excited.

"Why don't you bring your friend with you, that blond girl, the pretty one," Omar added.

"Jessica? Yeah, she'll probably wanna come," I said.

Gina got up from her seat and gave me a little punch on the arm and said, "See you there."

AS SOON AS school was out I told Jessica about the brand new friend I had made while sitting at the principal's office.

"You mean badass Gina McKay really talked to you?" Jessica zipped her jacket and followed me out the classroom door.

"Yeah, she wants to hang out with us, at Burger World. Isn't that cool?"

"She wants to hang with me? But why?" Jessica asked as we walked outside.

"Well, Omar was the one who asked for you, but Gina was cool with it."

"Oh . . ."

"Jess, what's with all the questions? Do you wanna come or not? Because if you don't come with me I'm going without you." Jessica and I stood at the crosswalk with Burger World in sight.

"I can't let you go alone," Jessica sighed.

Jessica and I crossed the street and as we approached Burger World, she began to tense up.

"You sure we should go in there?" Jessica asked as we reached the door.

"Gina invited us," I said.

"Think she'll like me?" Jessica asked, looking into her compact mirror.

I ignored her question and opened the beat-up door.

A jukebox in the corner was blasting dance music. The cigarette smoke was thick and the atmosphere was tense. There were a lot of different groups of people in the place and everyone turned around in their seats to see who had come in.

"Oh my god," Jessica panted.

"Hey!" Gina's voice rang out. She waved us over to her booth by the back door. As we made our way, I swear I could hear Jessica's heart pound through her hooded sweater.

"What's up?" Gina asked us as she took a drag of her cigarette.

I looked at the faces of the older teenage girls and the three boys sitting beside her and I began to wonder if Gina was setting us up. That's when I really became nervous.

"Smoke?" Gina asked me.

"Yeah," I lied as I took a cigarette from her.

"You?" she asked, offering Jessica one. Jessica smiled and took a cigarette, lit it and took a quick puff.

"She looks funny when she smokes," one girl said laughing.

"She doesn't smoke much," I said jumping to Jessica's defence.

"Really? I couldn't tell," one of the girls said.

"Sit down," Gina offered.

"We have to get going anyway," another girl said, giving us a snotty look as they picked up their purses and left.

"Don't mind them," Gina told us. "They're always like that, jealous of girls that are better looking."

"And you really are better looking," Omar added.

"Are all your friends older than you?" Jessica asked bewilderedly.

14

"I got all sorts of friends, all different ages. They don't mind that I'm only ten years old." She stood up and searched for change in her pocket. Gina towered over us. She was the tallest and most husky girl in our school and didn't look like she was ten at all.

"You're so tall," Jessica commented.

"I take after my dad. He's a full-blooded Ojibwa Indian." Gina sat back down and put out her cigarette.

"Who were those girls?" I asked Gina as Jessica and I sat down.

"Girls that hang out at the junior high. They're friends with my brother."

"Who's your brother?" Jessica asked.

"Roland McKay. I thought you knew," Gina said.

This girl sitting right in front of us is Roland McKay's sister? I was only ten but had already heard of Roland's terrible reputation.

Roland McKay was one of the most infamous people in our city. He and one of his hardcore buddies, Dean O'Callaghan, had started the Diablos.

As I got older and closer to Gina I learned all about Roland McKay. He was short and stocky with dark native skin covered with tattoos of gangster words like O.G. (Original Gangster) and M.O.B. (Money Over Bitches). Roland was extremely popular with the ladies, but I was always sure it was just because of who he was. I personally never thought he was very attractive.

Gina also had a younger brother, Darrel. He was a cutie and had a sort of puppy dog look to him. Darrel had light beige skin, chiselled features, thick red lips and one dimple in his left cheek. He was a year younger than Gina, Jessica and I, but that didn't stop him from hanging around with us. Darrel was a ladies' man but had a different type of charm than Roland. It was Darrel's sweet looks that made him popular. He was twelve when he joined the Diablos. He was a gangster, a high-ranking Diablo, a good fighter and people respected him.

Roland usually had the same type of girls hanging on his arm, girls who were bad or were trying to be bad. Darrel had all sorts of girls, from in and out of the hood, who would fall head over heels for him. Even older women would admire Darrel's features. Unlike Roland, he wasn't cocky. As a matter of fact, Darrel was very down to earth. He was the type of person any girl could talk to.

By the time I was thirteen, I was surrounded on a daily basis by these tough wannabe gangster kids I thought were just the coolest. They had respect, popularity and they looked invincible. Gina had become one of my best friends and she constantly asked me to join.

"You ready to join now?" Gina would say over and over again. I'd sit there quietly and let all her gangster philosophy sink into my brain. "What are you waiting for?" she'd say.

"What if my parents find out? They'll probably take me out of school," I said. I was worried I wouldn't be able to see any of my friends again.

"If your parents really loved you, they wouldn't make you live with your grandma for most of the week. If they were worried about gangs, they wouldn't let you live in this area."

"I have to live with my grandma—there's nobody to babysit me after school. They don't know anything about gangs."

"Hellooo. You're thirteen and don't need a babysitter anymore. Maybe they just like the fact that you're never around. If you joined the Diablos you wouldn't have to worry about them not loving you. We'd love you, forever."

Even though I wanted nothing more than to belong, I kept hearing Mrs. Clayton's voice in the back of my head: "That gang is bad news, it won't get you anything but trouble," she would say. Mrs. Clayton was the one teacher at school that Jessica and I could confide in. She was one of the few teachers that cared about the inner-city youth in that school. I respected her for that. I held back as long as I could but the pressure finally got to me. I had to join.

CHAPTER TWO

GANG WARFARE

DiABLOS DESCRIPTION

I was now on a trial basis, meaning that I still had to put in work for the set—the division of the gang I was joining. Because I was young, they gave me a task that I was relatively disappointed with but that could still be dangerous. I was to go into Street Ryder territory and ruin some of their work, meaning vandalize their vandalism.

The Diablos were involved in criminal activities, which mainly focused on buying drugs from bike gangs and re-selling them on the street. Roland was a big-time drug seller and was highly respected by the bikers. He was even asked to join them because they respected his leadership skills and considered him a valuable asset, but he refused. The Diablos was his foundation.

Many people described the Diablos as a copycat gang, resembling street gangs from the United States. The way the Diablos talked, the way we dressed, the music we listened to and rules we lived by were all reflections of hip-hop culture. We dressed in baggy clothes, with bandannas under our hats or visors on our heads. Corn braids and high-perched ponytails were popular too.

We wanted the same things out of life as the American street gangs did. The Diablos wanted to be compensated for the shitty hand that life had dealt. The Diablos wanted the money, drugs and the visible power that came in numbers within gang life.

The copycat accusation was false. We had our own rules, standards and trademarks. Unlike some gangs, we always initiated our members. Our flag colour was red and we loved to set things ablaze, especially Street Ryder clubhouses.

Another unique quality about the Diablos was the powerful part women played in the sets. In the beginning, the Diablos was an all-male gang until a girl named Regina Durham, who was considered extremely solid, joined and changed it forever. The Diablos was now uniquely known as a unisex gang. Girls got "jumped in" (initiated by being beaten up by fellow gang members) just like the guys did. The girls were seen as equals in the Diablos and were not given special privileges.

I SAW members as young as ten and some as old as forty but most of us were in the prime of our lives.

As I became friends with more of the members, I learned that a lot of them had been physically or sexually abused at some point. Others were exposed to alcohol and drugs at an early age by parents who themselves were alcoholics or drug addicts. Gangs in Winnipeg have reached third-generation status, and these days, kids are exposed to gang affiliation from the very start. It's a vicious circle that never seems to be broken. Gang life is normal to a lot of us, especially when we see family members breaking the law.

In the beginning most of the Diablos were aboriginal but as we grew we became more multicultural.

The Diablos were separated into three sets. The East End Diablos were the smallest set, consisting of mostly younger members who lived in the East End. The East End Diablos were not very well organized and it seemed they had a different leader every four months. They definitely did not get as much respect as the other two sets.

"They're just bitches, they're just little kids," was a regular comment. I knew some of them would grow up to be hard and solid. They may have been a small set but they represented their crew with pride and made the East End famous.

The second-largest set was the West End Diablos. This crew was known for having people jumped in without putting in work, so a lot of them were considered bitches. The West End Diablos were the sexiest, best-dressed guys and girls and were the first to be making some major dollars from drug sales. Their leader was Darwin Johnson, a little guy who didn't look like much but knew how to hold his set down with skill.

Last but not least was my set, the Central Diablos. Our set had the most members and was the best known. We had the reputation of being ruthless fighters and just plain, low-down, dirty gangsters. Roland McKay was our leader, the originator of the Diablos. The Central Diablos had its bad side as well, and we were known to be the sluttiest and raunchiest group of them all. Rumour had it that there were several STDs going around in our set and perhaps even more serious diseases too.

The hub of our social activities was usually centred around house parties with an abundance of alcohol and drugs. Most of the people at these parties were under eighteen. Unprotected sex and multiple partners are common in gang life and so sexually transmitted diseases and unwanted pregnancies are nothing new. It's probably safe to say that fifty percent of moms in the hood carried a gang member's baby. Gangs have different types of hierarchy, with a powerful few at the top and the worker bees underneath. Break-and-enters, selling drugs and pimping out girls are just some of the ways that gangs make their money.

Gang life was not just about living it up, partying and playing games. There is a lot of hurt that can come with being in a gang. You always had to watch your back and be certain to stay away from certain areas of the city. Getting harassed or beaten up by cops was something you always had to worry about, but most of all we were on the lookout for Street Ryders, our rival gang.

STREET RYDERS DESCRIPTION

THE STREET RYDERS and the Diablos have been at war from the very start. We were two separate gangs who lived in two separate parts of the city. Each gang had different politics and different operating systems. The Street Ryders

21

had formed in prison in an attempt to protect themselves from another prison gang called the Undertakers. Their leader, William Bouchard, took the gang to another level when he got out. They jumped in their members by providing them with an initiation hit, meaning they'd give out information about an enemy to the wannabe Street Ryder and expect him to hurt that enemy badly. A lot of those hits were directed towards the Diablos and even though the Street Ryders rarely killed any Diablos, they were known for leaving their victims scarred. Darrel told me a story about how the Street Ryders put an initiation hit on one of his buddies, Germane Dawson. A soon-to-be Street Ryder stabbed Germane directly in his eye causing permanent damage. Germane then became known as the one-eyed bandit.

The Street Ryders were a gang dominated by male power and operated very much like a biker gang. They had a president, a war chief and many foot soldiers. The Street Ryder girls were never given any real entry into the gang. They were never initiated or given a voice in gang politics. They were considered to have the status of associates and had connections by going out with a gang member or through male family members. There were rumours that the hard-core Street Ryder girls were sexed into the gang, but no one ever admitted to it.

The Street Ryders were the first major street gang in the city and they considered themselves pioneers. The Street Ryder colour was black and they wore their gang's colour faithfully and usually mixed it with white. Like all gangs, Street Ryders were involved in criminal activity to support and promote the power of the gang. Their main source of income was prostitution. They called themselves Street Ryders because they'd cruise the streets in their black cars and limos, pimping out girls. That's where the so-called Street Ryder girls came into action. They usually muscled other girls into working the streets for the gang, which in turn gave them recognition.

I was taken to a building in Street Ryder territory. Connie was driving with Gina; Darrel and Omar were in the back. I jumped out of the car with my can of red spray paint and my red bandanna tied around my head and another one tied around my arm. I walked over to the side wall of a store that read SxRxP, which meant it was Street Ryder property. I took a look around to make sure there were no police nearby. I crossed out those sick words with my red paint and wrote underneath DxIxFxEx (Diablos in full effect). I stood motionless when I was finished, hoping some Street Ryders would walk by so I could show them what I was made of. But the streets were dead that night, so I hopped back in the car and everybody congratulated me on a job well done. I was now an official Diablo.

A FEW DAYS after my initiation, Gina invited Jessica and me over to her house. Gina had muscled enough money from the kids at school to get an older Diablo chick named Victoria to buy us a forty-ounce bottle of malt liquor. Jessica, Gina and I hung out in Gina's room. Gina filled our coffee mugs to the top and we chugged it fiercely. She was quick to fill our mugs up again, and before I knew it the alcohol had hit hard.

"Cute little Nathan Troth got initiated last night." Gina sparked up a cigarette and motioned Jessica to open the window. "Can't let mom smell this, she's allergic." We played truth or dare and when Gina asked me what my deepest darkest secret was, I told her about my uncle John.

"You mean he messed with you?" Gina asked.

"Yeah, and nobody did anything about it. It makes me wonder, how many more of my cousins he molested." My eyes began to sting. I tilted my head up and blinked hard, forcing the tears to go back where they came from. Gina poured herself the last bit of malt liquor. She guzzled it down and wiped her mouth on her sleeve.

"Maria, I'm giving you another name."

"Huh?" I asked.

"From now on you'll be known as G Child. Gangster child. You're the Diablos' child now. The Diablos are your new family, G Child. Nobody's gonna mess with you again and if somehow they do, I promise your new family, the Diablos, will do something about it."

I liked my new name. It made me feel safe. And being part of the Diablos gave me confidence. I was part of something powerful and I finally had a family that cared about me. I didn't need my parents anymore. The Diablos were all I needed.

CHAPTER THREE

OUR FRIENDSHIP

Being a gang member didn't change my attitude towards school in the least, and it was pretty shitty to begin with. There was only one subject I cared about and that was English. Science, math and art seemed like a waste of time for me. I wasn't good at any of them, so what was the point of even trying? Besides, if I was ever going to amount to anything, I was sure writing would be a part of it. Maybe I'd be a journalist, or a novelist, but for now I was a gang member and being with my new family was my main concern.

When Gina, Jessica and I weren't ditching class, we were hanging out in the hallway and causing a ruckus. None of us did our homework, so naturally Gina would bully some dorky student into letting us copy their work. We learned practically nothing in school. Most of the teachers didn't like me because of the crowd I hung out with. All except Mrs. Clayton. Maybe she saw something in us that the other teachers didn't.

It was the day after my initiation and Mrs. Clayton grabbed Jessica and me as we left one of our classes.

She told us that she was conducting a special field-trip to a career symposium downtown and only a select few could come.

"Why us?" I asked.

"Why not?" she responded.

"I don't know about Jessica but I don't think I'm interested."

"Okay, I'll ask again, why not?" I saw concern in her eyes and I knew she truly cared about me. I had to tell her. I reached into my pocket and pulled out my red bandanna and tied it around my head.

"Oh no," Mrs. Clayton said almost in tears. "Why did you do this to yourself?"

"I did fight it for a while but you have to understand, it's just the way it is, Mrs. Clayton. It's all around me, my friends, where I live. I can't get away from it."

Mrs. Clayton looked over at Jessica and asked her if she had joined as well. Jessica shook her head, but admitted that she was seriously thinking about it. Mrs. Clayton told us the offer to attend the career symposium still stood and that we could change our minds at any time.

Jessica and I decided to go to the symposium after all. It was held in the gymnasium at the local university. There were all sorts of older kids there, showing off projects they had made. There were kids that had made fake volcanoes with what seemed to be ketchup coming out of them like lava. At first I was really interested in the projects, but then I noticed two older girls staring at Jessica and me. They looked about sixteen. Their hair was fluffy and they had pasted makeup on like it was going out of style. They pointed and giggled while they stared our way.

"Do you know those two girls pointing at us?" I asked Jessica.

"No, but they're making fun of us and I don't like it," she said loud enough so that they were able to hear her.

"What the fuck is your problem?" I asked stepping up to them. "Who you down with?" That was an instant, reactive question but as soon as those words passed my lips, I realized how pompous it sounded.

"Who are we down with?" the prissy blonde repeated.

"She means, are we in a gang or some crap," the brunette informed her friend.

The blonde looked right at us. "No, we are not down with anyone. We don't need a little kiddy gang behind us to look good." She then asked, "Where is your project?"

"We don't have one," Jessica replied.

"Ha, I knew it. You guys are from that reject school in Central. You're here to see what rich people like us do with our time." The blonde flicked her hair.

"I'd rather be poor than have a life like yours," Jessica retorted.

"Yeah whatever, get away from us. We don't want to catch your lice," the brunette said as she turned around.

I pushed her as hard as I could and she fell into her spaceship project, knocking it to the floor.

"You stupid bitch, look what you did!" she screamed underneath all the plants and tinfoil. She jumped up and slapped me across the face. I punched her as hard as I could and she went flying into her friend, who had just gotten up from the rubble. Both went tumbling down into the mess. Jessica couldn't contain her laughter. Blood gushed from the blonde's thin nose all over her white sweater. They both started to cry and I was grabbed by an older man and held back.

When we got back to school, the principal suspended me for three days. Mrs. Clayton was the one who drove me to my grandmother's afterwards. She didn't say a word to me the whole way. When I got to my grandmother's, I tried acting like I had just had a regular day at school. But my charade ended when my father stormed into the house looking for me. He screamed for me at the top of his lungs and before I had a chance to escape, he pushed me, face first, onto the linoleum floor. I turned quickly, but he banged the back of my head into the floor and I covered my face, afraid he was going to hit me.

"Suspended from school, eh?"

My mother grabbed him by the shoulders.

"Tony, relax! We came here to talk to her, not beat her to death!" My mother distracted him long enough that I had time to escape to the bathroom. I locked the door quickly.

"Maria!" my dad shouted.

"Leave me alone!" I shouted back.

"The next time I get a call from your school telling me you're getting in trouble, I swear to god, I'll break your face." I only left the bathroom when I heard the family van pull out of the driveway. My grandmother had a worried look on her face. I wanted to comfort her and tell her I was okay, but I wasn't. I headed to my room and went to bed without supper.

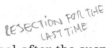

RESECTION FOR THE LAST TIME

WHEN I CAME back to school after the suspension, Mrs. Clayton still wouldn't talk to me. I guess I had embarrassed her and made her feel stupid for putting faith in me. It didn't bother me much, I was mad at her anyway.

GINA AND THE REST of the Diablo family really turned on the pressure a week after the career symposium incident, and Jessica decided to join. That same week Jessica lost her virginity at the park with a fourteen-year-old Diablo named Troy and thought that she might be pregnant. So instead of Jessica getting jumped in by the gang, Gina decided that she should start a beef with a Street Ryder girl and fight her one on one.

Jessica, Gina, Nathan, Darrel, Connie, Omar and I went to an apartment block where we knew there were Street Sissies (female Ryders). We sat on the front step of the apartment and waited for one to pass by. We spotted a Street Sissy walking towards the building. Her name was Tanya Sinclair. Tanya was our age and a real bitch who loved to talk shit about the Diablos, all the while trying as hard as she could to mess around with Diablo guys. Tanya was alone and didn't seem to be paying too much attention to her surroundings because before she knew it, she was completely encircled by Diablos.

"Hey, Tanya!" Jessica said sharply.

"Hey," Tanya said back, trying to be friendly.

"I got a beef with you, bitch," Jessica said stepping up.

"What for?"

"'Cause you're a slutty Streetwalker, that's why," Jessica said, pushing her.

"This isn't fair. Look how many of you there are. There's only one of me," Tanya said.

"This is one on one, right here, right now."

Tanya took a few steps back. "I don't want to fight you."

Jessica punched her right in the mouth and Tanya had no choice but to fight back. Tanya was a skinny girl except she seemed to have more fighting experience because Jessica was soon on the ground.

Jessica then did something extremely tasteless. She bit into Tanya's arm. Tanya let out a loud yelp and quickly got off her. Jessica took advantage of the situation, pounced on her and beat her ass to the ground. After she gave Tanya a few good shots, she gave us a tired but victorious smile.

After the fight, we all hugged her because we saw that she had struggled to get Tanya down and she fought the best way she knew how. Gina and I dusted her off and both of us took turns wiping her face with a new, never worn red rag. Gina then tied it on her head and hollered out "Diablo!"

"Let's go," Darrel said, motioning to us. We began to walk away but Jessica continued to stand in front of Tanya, who was crying helplessly. I thought she was going to hit her again, but instead she offered her hand and helped her up.

"I am sorry. It's nothing personal," Jessica said.

THE FIRST TIME we saw Violet, we were in the mall ditching our grade eight Math class. She was standing at a pay phone, wearing tight black pants and a black flight jacket with her hair pulled back in a red rag type of headband.

"Look at her, she's so beautiful," said Jessica.

"Yeah, underneath that pound of makeup," Gina replied.

"Whoa, is somebody hating?" I asked, looking through the newspaper.

"I'm not hating, I just wanna jump the bitch," Gina shot back.

"Aw man, leave the poor girl alone," said Jessica.

"What do you care? Can't you see the rag she's wearing on her head, trying to be down and shit. I swear I'll knock it off her bloody head." Gina couldn't stand poseurs. Even though I didn't think the girl on the pay phone was trying to imitate us, I did respect Gina's loyalty.

"Doesn't look like you'll have to go too far," I said, watching Violet cross the mall in our direction. She walked casually as we watched her every step.

"Excuse me, do you girls have an extra smoke?" Violet said as she held on to her shopping bags.

"Why doesn't someone like you have her own smokes?" Gina asked in a nasty tone of voice.

"Someone like what?" Violet asked.

"Rich," Gina added. Violet gave her a dumbfounded look. "You have four different bags in your hand," Gina said, pointing down at them.

"I was returning some clothes for my dad."

"Another rich bitch," Gina mumbled.

"Are you rich? Goes to show you that a girl doesn't have to be rich to be a bitch. You're a perfect example of that," Violet said, avoiding eye contact by looking through her bags.

Normally if someone put Gina down like that, they would get knocked out on the spot, but instead Gina just laughed it off.

"Got a mouth on you, eh?" Gina said, leaning over the table with a wide smile.

"Gotta stick up for myself."

"I didn't think a girl like you would stand up to someone like me."

"I don't want to be anybody's bitch. Never mind about the smoke."

"Hold on, Raggedy Ann, here's a smoke," Gina tossed it in her direction. "Where'd you learn to talk like that?" Gina asked, clearly impressed.

"You mean that bitch stuff? I don't know, just around I guess." Violet smiled, looking down at her shoes.

"Where you from?" Gina asked.

"The North End."

"You know any Street Ryders?" Gina was quick to ask.

"No."

"Do you smoke weed?" Gina offered.

"Yeah," Violet said.

"Follow us outside." Gina stood up and we followed her outside.

"She looks cute smoking up," Jessica said, giggling as Violet took a hoot. Violet looked paranoid as people watched us getting high at the bus stop.

"You ever wear that thing downtown?" Gina asked her as she pointed at her red headband.

"I don't go downtown," Violet said a bit shyly.

"Why not?" Jessica asked.

"I don't know my way around, I don't know anybody, I . . ."

"Now you do. Come hang out with us sometime. Here, this is my number," she said, grabbing Violet's hand and digging in her purse for a pen. Jessica wrote her phone number on the back of Violet's hand. "We'll all pitch in for a bottle of gin and get you drunk, Violet."

Jessica then turned her eyes towards me. "I got my period this morning, Maria. I'm not pregnant after all. I can still party!"

"There's my bus," Violet said, taking a last drag.

"Don't forget to call me," Jessica hollered after her as Violet hopped on her bus, waving goodbye.

VIOLET ENDED UP hanging out with us right after that. She was in a class of her own. She was born and raised in a part of the North End that wasn't exactly what you would call ritzy, but it wasn't the hood either. Sort of middle-class, with a few thugs thrown in.

That area was one of the most multicultural parts of the city. In the summer, the Asian teens parked outside their homes with their souped-up cars, barbecue smoke filling the air and children happily playing at their large family gatherings. At the local community pool, you would find the Portuguese boys chilling with the prettiest girls in the neighbourhood, showing off their muscle cars.

Both her parents were hard-working and law-abiding citizens who had immigrated to Canada from Italy in 1963. Violet's family owned an Italian bakery, and being the good girl that she was, she worked there part-time. The first time we visited Violet at work, Gina, Jessica and I made funny faces at her through the window and she pretended not to know who we were.

Violet's parents were really strict. They had to know who her friends were and what kind of families they came from. She wasn't allowed to have any friends that her parents didn't approve of, so we were careful not to be seen. Violet was an only child, a "lonely only," as she said.

"I am so used to being alone that it's kind of grown on me. I really value my privacy," she said.

Violet wasn't close with her parents and I think hanging out with us was her way of rebelling. I always found

Violet to have somewhat of a split personality. There were times when she'd be loud and obnoxious, and other times she would hang with us but listen to her Discman and seemed off in her own world. It was always one extreme or another with that girl.

ABOUT A YEAR after Jessica's initiation, when we were in grade nine, Gina, Jessica and I got expelled because of all the fights we had been in. A week before we were kicked out, Gina had a beef with a fat heifer named Charity Cook, who was from Gina's dad's reservation. Gina had been at a social with her two cousins when she overheard Charity bragging about how she was cool with the Street Ryders and if anyone fucked with her they were in for a beating. Gina opened her mouth and started talking her shit, dissing the Street Ryders.

"They're sissies, they're freaks!" she said over and over. Gina then shaped her hand to form the letter D over her heart.

Back at school, Gina, Jessica and I were standing near our lockers putting on our jackets and getting ready to go home when a huge native girl and three of her friends turned the corner. Gina had her back towards them as she was going on about how she was gonna sneak a forty of malt liquor into the school dance.

"Gina," I said quickly, "you know those girls?"

"Shit yeah," she said as she turned around. "Those girls got a beef with me. Get ready for war."

The three approached us. "What's up, dummy hos?" Charity said, smiling a sarcastic smile.

"What the fuck are you Streetwalkers doing at my school?" Gina replied.

"What were you doing on the rez last week at Matthew and Rosemary's social, talking your Central crap?" Charity said, stepping towards Gina.

"I wasn't talking shit. I was just stating the facts on how sissified and freaky the Streetwalkers are. They ain't shit to me or to anyone in my set, crazy Central for life."

"You think you're tough. I'm not afraid of you or any of your friends. I came here to tell you I don't ever want to see you on my reserve again."

"Fuck you, you think I'm scared of you 'cause you're a fat pig. I'll go up there any damn time I feel like it!"

"You're not even a real Indian. Your mother is a spic."

"Half spic, and proud of it, bitch. Out of my face!"

"I don't ever wanna see you up there again or I'll manhandle your Central dummy ho ass."

"I am still going up there and you can't do anything to stop me."

Just then, one of the girls with Charity grabbed me and slammed my head against the lockers. I fought her off and soon we were wrestling on the floor. Another of Charity's girls started to kick me on the side of my head, but I grabbed her foot and tripped her. The girl was obviously hurt badly because she didn't get up. I managed to get on top of her and pound her face in. I heard a loud scream from behind me. I looked over and saw Gina on the ground with the fat-ass Charity on her belly struggling to get away. Gina had ahold of her by the ankle and was stabbing Charity continuously in the leg with a knife.

I was just about to laugh out loud, when a teacher grabbed me by my armpits and screamed, "That's enough, that's enough!" I didn't struggle to get away from the teacher, but his grip was cutting off my circulation.

"Ease up, will ya?" He didn't lighten his grip. Jessica came to my defence and kicked the teacher with all her might, screaming at him to let me go. She was quickly detained by a couple of students.

The principal grabbed Gina by the arm and one of the other teachers grabbed the knife from her. She fumbled with it as though it was a gun and let out a scream when she dropped it to the floor. This time I did laugh.

"You aren't gonna talk your shit now, are you, Charity," Gina said laughing at her on the floor with two teachers holding a rag on her fat leg. "Crazy Central just whipped your nasty North End ass."

WE WERE IN a lot of trouble. Not only were we expelled on the spot, but the police came for us shortly after. They took all of us away except Charity, who was taken to the hospital in an ambulance.

We explained to the police that we were just defending ourselves because they had started the fight. But now there was the issue of the knife and that's what did it for Gina. The police let Jessica and me go, but Gina was charged with assault with a deadly weapon and was taken to juvenile hall. Because it was her first offence, she only served four months. But to everybody else it seemed like forever.

The principal called my mother at work and informed her that I had been in a vicious fight at school and wasn't welcome back. When I reached my grandmother's, I saw the family van parked in the driveway and my heart leaped in my throat. When I approached the front door, I didn't even have time to turn the doorknob. My father yanked me in by my hair and beat me up in the foyer. My grandmother and my mom yelled at him to stop but it was no use. I managed to get away from him and locked myself in the bathroom. He screamed on the other side but wasn't about to break my grandmother's door down. I had handprints across both cheeks and a cracked lip.

"Next time you wanna fight somebody, you come to me," my father said.

I heard the front door slam but didn't hear the van pull away. There was no way I was leaving that bathroom until I was sure my parents were gone.

"Maria, are you all right?" Mom asked on the other side of the door. "Maria, you could have been seriously hurt in that fight at school. What were you thinking?"

"Dad hurt me more than any fight at school. Fucking relax, Mom. Take a chill pill, would ya?"

"Who do you think you're talking too?" she asked bitterly.

"To a person that doesn't care."

"Of course I care, you're my daughter."

"By blood only."

"What the heck are you talking about? You better smarten up, young lady, or we'll make you go to a private school."

"You don't care enough about me to enroll me in a private school. Oh, and by the way, did you know it's illegal to hit your child? With this cracked lip and these welts I have on my face, I'm sure I wouldn't have a problem putting Dad in jail. What do you think?"

"Well, if that's the way you feel, we don't have to come and see you on the weekends. It'll be easy for us to pretend we don't have a daughter."

"I don't give a shit." I banged the door with my fist. Mom cursed at me in Portuguese.

A few minutes later, the van pulled out of the driveway. I opened the door and found my grandmother waiting for me. She had huge tears in her eyes and reached over to hug me.

"Mommy says you inside at nine," Grandma whispered.

"A nine o'clock curfew?" I asked, horrified. "Grandma, I'll do my best, but that's pushing it. Is that Mom's last attempt at being a mother?"

"Huh?" Grandma asked.

"It's nothing," I said, kissing her goodnight.

I was awakened that night by the telephone ringing at 2:30 in the morning. I quickly picked it up, hoping it didn't wake Grandma.

"Hello?" I whispered.

"G's up, ho's down." It was Omar. I'd recognize his deep voice anywhere.

"I already told you not to call so late," I bitched.

"Wanna come and hang?" he said over the music and voices in the background.

"No," I said impatiently.

"We'd like to smoke a joint with you. Then we'll walk you back home."

"I said no, Omar. I'm gonna hang up now."

"What's wrong, G Child? You're not acting your usual sweet self."

"Besides the fact that it's really late, my dad gave me the fucking beats today."

"What a fucking dick. We'll fuck him up, man. We'll do him in. Nobody fucks with you, girl."

"No, that's my dad."

"Are you sure? It's no problem. Not like we're doing anything important right now anyway."

"I'm sure, but thanks, though. I'll see you guys tomorrow."

"He's lucky he's your dad." He hung up.

I had a hard time falling back asleep because of the pain and debated whether to take Omar up on his offer to do my dad in. But what did *in* mean? Beat him up? Kill him?

I was lucky if my parents came to see me twice a month after that episode. Mom would attempt conversation about things she knew I liked, including books and movies. But Dad usually kept to himself and made small talk with Grandma in the kitchen.

GINA WAS OUR SOLDIER, our warrior and our leader. It was tough not having her around. She was the one who got everybody pumped up for war against the Street Ryders. Gina was the excitement and while she was gone the heart of our clique stopped beating. We still stuck together and represented Central, but it just wasn't the same without Gina.

The shit hit the fan when Gina was released. Jessica, Darrel and I hoped she was coming back a better person. Neither Jessica nor I had ever been in serious trouble before, and we were afraid to do time when we were fourteen because of all the horror stories we'd heard about juvenile hall. We'd seen some kids come out of there totally changed. Some kids cleaned up their acts—they didn't skip school anymore and stopped just hanging around, wasting their time. "I don't want to end up in a real jail," they would say.

Even though I wasn't a saint, I was secretly hoping that juvenile hall would have some sort of positive influence on my friend, but unfortunately Gina didn't come back a better person; she came back a harder one.

The day she was released, a bunch of us waited for her at Darrel's.

"What's that?" Jessica asked Darrel as he opened a big brown paper bag.

"What do you think? It's O.E., Old English malt liquor. I'm getting my sister messed up tonight."

"Wicked," Jessica said.

"Want one?" he asked me, throwing a forty-ouncer onto my lap.

"You know it," I said.

I felt and looked exceptional that day. I had my hair up in a high ponytail with red elastics holding my braid in place. I was wearing a red T-shirt, baggy jeans with red stitching and white K-Swiss kicks. I was looking dope.

"She's taking forever. I got places to go," Nathan said.

"She'll be here soon. Roland probably had a few things to do on the way," Darrel assured him.

"Roland picked her up?" Nate asked.

"Yeah, he insisted. I don't know why."

Just then Roland walked in, dressed in black and white, wearing his shades, something he never goes without. He looked like a fucking Street Ryder, but everyone knew he wasn't into sporting the colour red like we were. Roland was trying to stay low-key. The room fell silent as our godfather stepped in.

"Look at all the little kiddies." Roland smirked and shook his head at us. He took off his shoes and headed upstairs. Gina stood silent at the doorway. We stood face to face.

"Damn girl, look at you, all dressed like a badass gangster. You know that's how I like it," Gina said smiling.

I didn't know what to say. Gina looked totally different. She had butchered her long black hair. The sides of her head were shaved and the hair covering the top part of her skull from the front to the back was pulled into a tight braid. She looked like a scandalous bitch.

"Aren't you happy to see me?"

"Of course I'm happy to see you," I said, trying to shake off her new appearance.

"I know what it is, it's the hair right? Shit, I got it done today. My big brother here told me that this was my day, so he was gonna take me out. I got my hair done and got a tattoo. Check it out." Gina turned around and showed me the back of her neck. She had tattooed the word Diablos in red flamed writing.

"That looks good, suits you just right," I said, punching her on the arm.

The others watched us as we play-wrestled.

"All right," Darrel said, passing Gina the forty. She was going to open it but he stopped her. "No, hold on!"

"What for?" Gina inquired, putting her arm around me.

"Let's drink to my sister Gina's safe return to Central," he said as he held up his open forty.

"Cut the corny shit," Gina said, quickly grabbing the forty and guzzling it.

For a while, Gina was completely insane. She hated the Street Ryders more passionately than ever before. The Diablos agreed that by the time she was eighteen, she would be serving time at the women's correctional facility for first-degree murder. I just hoped she wouldn't be taking me down with her.

ON WEEKENDS we'd hang out by a downtown nightclub to have some "fun." Since we weren't eighteen yet, and none of us had fake ID, we'd go there at closing time and wait for everyone to get out. Then we'd pick fights, rob drunks, follow people to their homes and scare the hell out of them, stupid shit like that.

Gina dropped acid one night before heading out to the club and ended up having a major trip.

"Holy fuck man, I'm ready to kill," she said over and over in the back of Connie's car. I, on the other hand, wasn't into heavy drugs. So being straight, I tried calming her down.

"Just chill, it's all fun and games."

"Not tonight," Gina said.

"What does that mean?" I asked her.

"Nothing," Gina said.

We stood outside the club and waited for the perfect victims. I spotted mine not far away, a white couple heading to their car, the girl barely able to walk upright. I slowly crept up behind them. This dorky guy was about to open his girlfriend's door when I yelled out. "Hey faggot, why don't you hand over your wallet?"

"What?" he asked startled.

"Where's the money at?" I said, showing him my knife.

"The money?" he asked.

"Yeah, the money. Hand it over," I said.

"Wait, can I just put my girlfriend in the car?"

"No, give me your wallet now or else your girl gets it!" I said stepping closer.

"Okay, okay, here," he said, throwing his wallet down.

"Hers too, I want hers too!"

I was then distracted by a girl's scream that sounded like Gina's warrior cry.

"Hurry up," I told him as he fumbled to get her purse open. I heard the scream again, piercing the night air. Something was wrong, so I ran off without the girl's wallet.

"Die, bitch, die!" I heard Gina yell as I was getting closer to her voice. I found Gina in the back lane on top of another girl.

"Fuck you, you damn street hooker!" Gina dipped her fingers in the girl's blood while laughing hysterically and put two lines of blood underneath her eyes just like the natives did in the old days when they were putting their war paint on.

The girl on the ground was unconscious.

"Did you kill her?" I asked, still panting from the run. Gina didn't answer me. "C'mon, Gina, let's go," I picked her up by her arms. Bright headlights turned into the alley and blinded us.

"Get in the car!" Connie yelled at us. Gina and I both rushed into the car.

"Somebody called the cops. The cops are on the way!" Connie said, panicking.

"Bitchass cops can't touch me!" Gina screamed as we raced down the back lane and into the night.

I was worried that Gina might have killed that girl. I didn't want her going back to jail; she hadn't even been out a week. I watched the news and read the paper for the next three days. There was no word about a girl's body being found, so I guessed Gina was in the clear.

SINCE GINA, Jessica and I were expelled from our original school, we transferred to a different one in the West End. We didn't know many people there, but we were looking forward to taking over the school. We convinced our friend from the mall, Violet, to come along with us, and after days of endless whining, Violet's mom let her transfer to the school as well. This was when Violet's transformation began: the way she talked, dressed and acted were all different. She was trying to be something she wasn't; she was trying to be down. Violet obviously didn't fit in and people around us knew she was trying too hard. Violet would come to school wearing the most expensive tracksuits and the newest kicks on the market, which were, of course, purchased by her parents. It didn't take long for most of the other girls in our school to get jealous. I heard a couple of them whisper names at her like wannabe gangster, and even though I thought Violet was cool, I couldn't help but agree with them. Violet annoyed me when she tried to act hard because I knew it was fake.

"I don't give a fuck. I'm not scared of the bitch," Violet would tell us when she heard that girls were talking about her behind her back.

"The richest ghetto girl I know," Gina claimed.

One chilly winter morning two weeks before Christmas, we waited for Violet to get off her bus so we could all walk to school together. I almost had a heart attack when I saw her. She had on a new tracksuit, red from head to toe, and she had her hair corn braided with red beads at the ends.

46

"Holy shit! You look fucking good in that shit!" Gina said, touching her tracksuit and patting her on the head like a newborn puppy.

"That's a fly suit," Jessica smiled, "and your hair totally goes with it."

"Thanks," Violet said.

"Nice getup. You know what it means though?" I asked.

"What?" Violet asked.

"You're dressed in red from head to toe, you're claiming Diablos like that. Why are you down with Diablos?" I said, trying to make my point.

"Hey, she looks good," Gina said, cutting my point down.

LATER THAT DAY, Gina took me aside by the water fountain. "What's your problem with Violet?"

"There's no problem," I said. "Don't like the way she's trying to represent a gang that she knows nothing about."

"I think it's cool that she wants to be down, don't you?" Gina said.

"Sure, but there's a difference between wanting to be down and being down. You got to be careful. There's people that actually put in work and can claim that they are a Diablo. They earned that title, but her, just 'cause she wears the colour red doesn't mean she's a Diablo," I said with a stern voice.

Just then Sheryl Park and Valerie Marshall interrupted us. They were not Diablos. Sheryl's brother was a high-ranking biker and Valerie's cousin was a soon-to-be biker.

"We need to talk to you in the bathroom," Sheryl said to us.

"What about?" Gina demanded.

"In the bathroom," Sheryl insisted.

"Don't try to push us around, Sheryl. It won't work," I added.

"I don't want a problem with you. Just trust me on this," Sheryl pleaded. Gina and I cut Sheryl some slack and followed her and Valerie into the bathroom. Before any of us could say anything we heard Violet sobbing in a bathroom stall.

"They wanna kill me."

"Nobody wants to kill you," another voice said inside the stall.

"Jessica, is that you?" I asked, knocking on the stall door.

"Yeah, I'm in here with Violet."

"Yes they do. I heard them say they were going to run me out of this school. I don't know what to do."

"Who wants to run you out of the school?" I asked wondering who the tough girls were.

"We do," Sheryl said, turning around and facing me. I knew she was just waiting to see if I would rush to Violet's defence. Sheryl was probably expecting me to say, "No, you can't do that or you're going to have to get through me first, bitch."

This was amusing. I knew I could punch out Sheryl and Valerie in a heartbeat, but it wasn't my beef, so I didn't say anything.

"What's up?" Gina asked them. I could tell she was a little embarrassed for Violet. These two probably thought Violet was a Diablo, and obviously Violet was scared because she had made the Diablos look bad. Jessica and Violet came out of the bathroom stall together holding hands.

"I heard some shit the other day," Sheryl said, putting her books down by the sink.

"What's that?" Gina asked her.

"I heard that this little bitch fucked my man a couple months ago when I was out of town. Is it true?" Sheryl asked Violet.

Violet hid behind Jessica. "I don't even know who your man is."

Valerie spoke up. "That's what they all say." Valerie said, defending Sheryl, her best home girl.

"That's impossible. Violet isn't that type of girl and if something like that did happen we would know about it too. You're just making this up so you have an excuse to fight her. You did the same thing to that foreigner girl, Magda," Jessica said.

"You're a dead bitch. I'm going to get you, Violet. Don't know when or where, but I promise that your time is gonna come," Sheryl said as she stormed out of the bathroom with Valerie following.

"Why are you crying?" Gina asked Violet angrily. "Crying makes you look weak. I know you're not from around here, but you have to learn to act solid real quick, even if it's just a front, you understand?"

"I don't even know how to fight," Violet replied.

"So stop acting like you're down then," I said abruptly.

"No man," Gina said, quickly turning around. "She's got to act like she's down."

"But she's not, Gina. That's what's getting her into trouble. She's trying to be something she's not." I turned to Violet. "Stop trying to be bad."

"She's just got to prove herself," Gina said. "You have to make a name for yourself around here, that's all."

"Maybe you should initiate her," Jessica suggested.

"She made the Diablos look bad just now," I said.

"No, not yet," Gina told Jess. Gina reached into her purse, looked quickly at the door and then pulled out a little switchblade. "Here, I am giving this to you. You don't have to use it, but keep it just in case you get into a situation you can't handle."

Violet took the blade and shoved it in her purse.

I WENT HOME right after school that day. I couldn't wait to eat Grandma's homemade rice pudding: it was my favourite. I was surprised to see the family van parked in the driveway and wondered what I could be in trouble for this time. I swore to myself that if Dad tried to beat me I'd stab him with my shank that I hid in my back pocket.

Mom, Dad and Grandma were in the living room watching TV and eating rice pudding. I said hello and went straight to my room.

"Maria, can I come in?" Mom asked. She opened the door and stood at the foot of my bed. "Aren't you gonna join us in the living room? Your grandma invited us over for her famous rice pudding."

"I'm tired. I think I'll take a nap," I said, not wanting to hang out with my parents.

"I read an article in the newspaper today. It was called 'How to Spot a Gang Member.'"

"So?"

"The article even mentioned the school that you go to. The article said it was gangland. Are you in a gang, Maria?"

"No!" I shouted. "I don't know any gangs in my school."

"You don't have to raise your voice. I worry about you. Sometimes I worry a lot." Mom gave me a kiss on the cheek and left.

IT WAS judgement day for Violet a few weeks later at the roller rink. The roller rink was a happening place, especially on Saturday nights. I sparked a joint as we waited to get inside.

"Don't light that here. There's kids behind us with parents," Violet blurted out.

"So?" I said, taking a hoot.

"I smell bud!" a Diablo named Shawn Bartley hollered out, with Darrel, Omar, Gina and Jessica standing behind him.

"Hey, Maria, what's up girl?" Omar said to me. "When ya gonna let me take you out and treat you like a lady?" Omar was a sweet talker and tried to get with anyone.

"Omar, I see you almost every day. Why the fuck would you want to take me out?"

"For a good time, take you on a date and shit." Omar cracked a wise grin. "Damn girl, you know I'm only joking with you. I just wondered why you never got a man clinging to your pretty arm."

"I don't need a man clinging to my arm, thank you very much. I like to be able to swing my arms freely."

"I hear ya," Omar said.

"Yeah, well we can't stay too long," Gina interrupted.

"Why not?" Jessica said, looking disappointed.

"There's work to do tonight. Connie and her little sister Tracy got jacked last night."

"By who?" I asked.

"Street Sissies, who else," Gina said. "We don't know who did it, but I'm gonna do a couple of them in tonight."

Just then Sheryl, Valerie and a sniffed-out girl named Heather Darling stepped up to our group. Sheryl's arm was over Valerie's shoulder while Heather stood still and watched us. They were obviously drunk. Even before they managed to say anything you could smell the stench of alcohol on their breath.

"Hey!" Sheryl said, waving her hand in front of Gina's face.

"Hi," Gina said, pushing her hand away from her.

"So where's your lovely friend Violet?" she asked.

"I'm right here," Violet said, stepping towards her. I was impressed.

"I'm not letting you go roller-skating without you fighting me first," Sheryl howled.

"If you guys fight out here, then nobody will be allowed inside," Jessica said. I nudged her with my elbow and told her to shut up. A crowd quickly formed around us. Gina told everyone to back up. It was only Violet and Sheryl in the circle now. This was Violet's chance to prove herself.

"Don't let me down, Violet," I whispered.

Violet pushed Sheryl, but Sheryl pushed her back twice as hard and Violet fell on her ass. Violet stood up, and the fight now began. Punches were being thrown, one punch on Violet's left cheek, the other to Sheryl's stomach. Sheryl seemed to be getting tired and fell to her knees. It looked like she was struggling for air. Violet kicked her in the stomach. Sheryl was losing. Valerie and Heather jumped in and grabbed Violet around the neck and flung her back. I grabbed hold of Valerie and Gina grabbed hold of Heather.

"This isn't your fight, back off," I told them.

"All right, all right, just let us help her up," Valerie pleaded.

"This fight is over," Gina said.

Violet kicked her ass. Some people came to her and congratulated her on beating Sheryl down. Others claimed the only reason she won was because Sheryl was drunk and an easy target. Maybe so, but Sheryl had started it and Violet finished it.

"I'm proud of you, Violet," Gina said, passing her a joint.

"You okay?" I asked, noticing her head was a little scratched up.

"Fine," Violet said.

"I think it's time, how about you?" Gina asked me.

"I think so," I said, lighting the joint up for Violet.

Two weeks later Violet was jumped into the Diablos.

CHAPTER FOUR

HOOKING UP

Darrel McKay became a father at age fifteen. His girl-friend, Amanda Roberts, was a beautiful mulatto girl, tall, slim with long ringlets of black hair. She was the love of his young life and when she became pregnant, Darrel was ecstatic.

"My girl's pregnant," he said proudly to me over the telephone one night.

"No way!" I said shocked.

"Mom already knows about it too, and she's happy." Darrel was right. The McKays took the pregnancy well and so did the Robertses and everything was working out as planned. On April 15, Amanda gave birth to their daughter, Destiny Rain McKay. Destiny stayed with Amanda and her mother, and Darrel visited her as often as he could. Darrel sold weed so that he could buy Destiny baby clothes and diapers. He really tried his best and I admired him for taking his responsibility as a man and a father.

Four months after Destiny was born, a close friend of ours, Colin Miller, threw a block party on the street where Amanda and her mother lived. Amanda begged her mom to babysit Destiny for the night. Darrel knew Amanda would be there and decided to surprise her. He asked me to come to the street party. I snuck out of Grandma's house and met Darrel at the park.

"Thanks for meeting me here," he said, shaking my hand in a gangster fashion.

"We're not staying too long though, right? It's past two a.m. and I don't want Grandma to get worried if she finds out I'm not there," I said, trying to see his face in the dark.

"Do you still have that wacky nine o'clock curfew?" he teased.

"My parents have been putting the pressure on my grandma, telling her I should be home by nine every night, but she does let me run pretty free."

"Don't worry, I'll get you home before she notices. I just wanna check up on Amanda, make sure she's okay. She's a pretty girl, and you know how guys can get when they're drunk, all touchy and shit."

We arrived at about 2:30 a.m. and recognized a few of the faces from the street.

"Where's Amanda?" Darrel asked another Diablo.

"She's in the next room getting her freak on with Omar."

Darrel rushed to the next room and I followed. He flung the bedroom door wide open only to witness his baby's mom, the love of his life, with her legs wrapped around Omar's solid black body.

"Close the door," Omar yelled as he squinted his eyes to see who was standing in the doorway.

"Shit," Amanda whispered. When she sat up, her bare chest flashed everyone peeking into the room. Darrel stood there stunned at first, not able to say anything. With a leap, he pounced on Omar and began punching him like a madman, dragging his naked body out of the bed and giving him the beats.

Four guys held Darrel back while Omar rushed to put on his pants. I couldn't believe what I was seeing. A shamed Omar regained his balance and wiped the blood trickling down his face. Darrel and Omar had grown up together and were both Diablos.

"So what now? We're supposed to fight over a bitch? Why you hatin'? Your bitch chose me!" Omar exclaimed as he stepped towards Darrel, trying to save face.

"Darrel, I can explain," Amanda said, slipping her jeans on.

"Explain what?" Omar interrupted. "He don't need no explanation on what he saw."

"Let me go," Darrel said to the strangers as he struggled to get away.

"Let him loose," I screamed as I stood face to face with all of them.

Slowly, the four boys holding Darrel let him go, but stood near him just in case.

"I'll tell you the truth," Omar said. "I've been fucking your bitch for a long-ass time, even before you all had a baby. Who knows, maybe I'm the baby's daddy. I didn't know how to tell you seeing as you love the bitch and all."

"Fuck off, Omar, you're not Destiny's daddy!" Amanda attempted to hug Darrel but Omar held her back.

Darrel turned around and headed to the door by pushing his way through the crowd of spectators.

"He's lying!" Amanda shouted out after him, but Darrel kept on walking.

"What about Destiny—we have a daughter, remember?" Amanda pleaded once again.

"I'll go calm him down. He's my bro," Omar said, obviously feeling badly about what had just happened.

"No," I said, blocking his way.

"What? Who the fuck are you?"

"Dummy up, you know who the fuck I am," I told him straight. "You're the last person he wants to talk to. Some friend you are. You're a piece of shit, Omar."

"He's lying," Amanda said, pleading with me. "I wasn't fucking around on Darrel for all this time. This was the first time, I swear. Talk to him for me, G Child. I don't want to lose him. I want my baby to have her daddy in her life."

"Don't explain yourself to me. No explanation will make what happened here tonight all right," I said.

I went to look for Darrel. I knew exactly where he was. I knocked on Amanda's apartment door and her angry mother came to open it.

"What do you kids want from me?" Amanda's mom said, slapping her forehead, her nappy hair sticking up like a Mohawk.

"I know my bro's in here. I want to see him."

"He's with the baby. You ain't coming in," she said, one hand on her hip and the other on her chin.

"It's okay," I heard Darrel say from inside.

She looked me over, huffed and sat down on her couch. Darrel grabbed me by the arm and led me into a tiny room at the back.

"Sshh," he said, putting his finger to my lips. I looked up into his eyes and saw how red they were and couldn't help but feel sorry for him. We both looked over the cradle and watched little Destiny sleep, as she lay cozy underneath her yellow blanket.

"My sweet little girl," he said as he ran his fingertips gently over her delicate forehead. "I know she's mine. She has my dimples." Darrel picked her up and gently rubbed her back. I watched him and was touched at how really loving he was. All I really wanted was to wrap him in my arms and tell him that everything was going to be okay, that every girl wasn't a scandalous whore.

"Hey," Amanda's mom said in a grouchy voice as she turned on the bedroom lights. "It's too late for visiting. You kids go party next door." Darrel seemed to be choking back tears and did not answer her.

"Darrel, what is going on?" Amanda's mother demanded to know.

"I caught her with someone else tonight," Darrel said, kissing his daughter.

Just then, Amanda burst through the door.

"There you are!"

"Stay away from me!" Darrel said.

"No, don't go. I can make it better, I promise," she begged holding on to his sleeve.

"Leave me alone, slut," he moaned as tears began to roll down his cheeks.

"Look at our Destiny. We don't want you to leave!" Amanda grabbed Destiny out of his arms and held her up to his face.

"You did this to yourself," he said as we left the apartment.

DARREL WAS SILENT on the way home. I was just about to hug him goodbye when Omar appeared down the street. He was frantically waving and begged us to stop. He finally caught up, and it took him a few moments to catch his breath.

"Darrel, listen, man, I'm sorry. I meant no disrespect, bro. I'm tripping out on acid."

"It takes two," Darrel said solemnly.

"I didn't fuck her. We didn't fuck a lot. Only tonight, tonight was the only time, bro. I feel like such an ass."

"Well, you should," I said. I couldn't help but interfere.

"You know what, Omar? You're a guy, I'm a guy, guys think with their dicks. But Amanda, she should have known better," Darrel said.

"Dicks before chicks?" Omar asked him.

"Bros before hos," Darrel said.

"G's up and hos down," Omar concluded. They exchanged the Diablos' handshake. I stood back feeling sick.

Darrel remained in contact with Destiny and dropped off money for her every two weeks. One time we were about to go on "the hunt" (picking beef with Street

Ryders), when Darrel asked us to make a stop at Amanda's aunt's house to drop money off for Destiny. We waited in the car for him as he walked up the driveway and rang the doorbell. He was surprised to see Amanda open the door, holding Destiny in her arms.

"My aunt couldn't be here, so I came to get the cash from you," Amanda said, opening her hand in front of his face.

"Whatever, here's fifty bucks."

"We have to talk," she said as she took the money and stepped closer to him. Darrel obviously didn't want to listen and was preoccupied with another problem. We were on the hunt for a guy named Armando James, a Street Ryder who fucked around with Nathan's sister Francine.

"It's about Destiny," she said.

"What about her?"

"Hurry up. We're gonna miss him!" Gina hollered from the car.

"Can we do this some other time?" Darrel said as he held up his hand, motioning us to wait.

"Your friends are more important than your daughter?" Amanda said.

"No, I gotta do something. You know how my life is."

"You don't care about Destiny, you . . ."

"I'd jump in front of a bullet for her. You know that."

"I'm not asking you to jump in front of a bullet."

Gina leaned on the horn. She had no respect where Amanda was concerned.

"I'll call you in a few hours, okay?" Darrel said, walking away.

"Don't bother, you selfish asshole. You won't be seeing her anymore."

DARREL RECOGNIZED that Amanda was trying to blackmail him, as in "If you don't wanna be with me, then you can't see your daughter."

Darrel didn't give in to her tactics. In fact, he and his mother, Lenore, took Amanda and her mother to court, and the two families eventually came to a verbal agreement. Darrel was to see his daughter every other weekend.

Roland, the original gangster himself, sympathized with his brother, and in an effort to cheer him up he offered to pay for Darrel's first tattoo one night when we were over at Gina's, playing poker.

"There's one condition," Darrel replied to his brother. "Gina and G Child get one too." I turned around to face Darrel and blew my cigarette smoke in his face.

"Who said I even want one, Mr. McKay?" I said batting my eyes playfully at him.

"You're not scared are you?" Roland teased.

"Who, me? Never."

"Well, prove it. I'm paying anyway." Roland winked at me. I agreed.

"Right on!" Gina hollered. "From now on anyone who's over sixteen has to get a tattoo representing Diablos. What a perfect way to show your loyalty. Thanks for the idea, Roland."

"How about Violet and me?" Jessica asked. "Roland, are you gonna pay for our tattoos too?"

"Since I'm feeling generous, why not." Roland winked at Violet.

"I DON'T KNOW, man. Tattoos are supposed to hurt," Connie said as Darrel, Gina, Violet and Jessica hopped out of her car and walked towards a tattoo parlour the following day.

"Mine tickled," Connie said.

"Yeah, stop being such a pussy," Gina teased.

"Tattoos are forever though," Violet said.

"No shit, Sherlock. What are you trying to say?" Gina asked while putting a cigarette behind her ear.

"Nothing," Violet said, looking away.

"What's wrong with your friends?" Darrel asked me.

"Nervous I guess."

"Little pussies," Darrel said, pushing Violet playfully. Everyone laughed except me. I was nervous too.

We stopped at the underground tattoo parlour Roland had recommended. Inside, Connie and Darrel kept themselves busy looking at the samples on the wall while Jessica and Violet stayed firmly planted by the door.

"Will you guys get in here?" Gina said. "You guys should be happy. You're getting inked up to represent who you really are: Diablos. This guy's really good at lettering. You should have gotten your ink done a long time ago." A big guy came down a flight of stairs and stood glaring at us.

"You Gina McKay?" he asked crossing his arms.

"Yeah," Gina said, standing up to face him.

"Hi, I'm Pep," he said, shaking her hand. "Roland told me to cut you kids a deal."

Darrel flexed his muscles. "Who said we're kids?"

"Who wants to go first?" Pep asked, ignoring him.

"She can go first," Gina said and pointed towards me.

"All right, follow me," Pep said. He led me to a small room that was closed off with a black curtain.

"Sit here," he said, pointing at a black leather folding chair. "Ever get a tattoo before?"

"Nope," I said.

"Some say it hurts but I like the way it feels. I hope you had something to eat before you came down here. I had a little guy come in here who didn't eat anything this morning and he turned green by the time his tattoo was done. What will you be getting?"

"D-i-a-b-l-o-s across my arm," I said, lifting up my sleeve.

Pep's eyes widened; he laughed and shook his head. "If you want, I can add something to make it a bit more interesting, like barbed wire or intertwined flames."

"Do it up," I said nervously.

My friends sat with me the whole time. Darrel kept cracking jokes, I'm sure to help get my mind off the pain.

"You gonna be okay, youngs?" Gina teased.

"Don't youngs me. I'm two months older than your ass," I said between clenched teeth.

64

"Hurts like a bitch, eh?" Gina asked as she watched the tattoo gun pierce my skin.

I closed my eyes and tried not to think of the sharp needlepoint going in and out of my skin, over and over again.

When it was done, forty-five minutes later, Gina's eyes brightened with happiness.

"You did it, looks awesome!"

It took practically all day for everybody's tattoos to get done. Violet's took the longest, just because she kept on stopping Pep in between sketching. Afterwards we all headed up to Central Park and showed off our work to our friends. In the midst of our gloating, I noticed Violet sitting on a swing by herself. I walked up to her and handed her a beer.

"Here you go, champ," I said

"No thanks," she said, wiping a tear away.

"You still in pain?" I asked.

"No. It's just that . . . I knew I shouldn't have got this tattoo," she said, showing me her ankle. She had gotten a violet flower tattoo with the word Diablo in a darker purple across it.

"So why did you then?" I asked, a bit annoyed.

"Because I had to or else Gina would have rolled me out."

Gina stepped out of nowhere and wrestled me to the ground, knocking over my beer. "You knocked my drink over, stupid."

Gina laughed and helped me up. "What's with the long face, Violet?" Gina asked.

"Oh nothing, my ankle is a little sore."

"Maybe we should pour some beer over it, numb it out a little."

"No way man." We laughed and Violet never mentioned the tattoo again.

WHILE DARREL was preoccupied with Amanda and Destiny, the rest of us were having our own fun.

Jessica and I have always had the same taste in men. As teenagers, we would go to the mall to see how many boys' phone numbers we could collect. As young adults, we'd do the same at the bar. Yeah, we liked them thugged out—we especially liked them from Central.

When I say thug, I mean guys who had been tagged with a few assault charges or were dealing some kind of drug. Weed was a given, crack was an extra.

Over the years, Jessica gained a bad reputation in Central. She was known as the "party whore," an unfortunate handle that stuck for a long time. Even after the name-calling and all the fights that she had gotten into because of jealous girlfriends, she still was determined to find her ghetto prince.

"I'll know him when I see him," she would say. "He'll be native, with dark, smooth skin and long black hair. He'll be just a little bit taller than me and he'll have an incredible smile. He'll treat me right and then I can forget about all these punks."

GINA WAS never really interested in guys but she would get hers here and there. Gina was funny when she got laid, which wasn't too often. She would style the boys, just like a player, and toss them out like they were bitches.

"I fucked that boy good," she would brag. One guy, Reese Kelly, claimed that Gina was one of the lousiest lays he'd ever had. She punched him out when she heard what he had said about her.

There was really only one guy I remember Gina taking seriously. His name was Anthony Peters. It was the day after we got our tattoos done, and Gina and I were taking the bus, heading to a brand new tanning salon downtown. We'd heard that they had the strongest beds in the city and were excited to try them. We hopped onto a packed bus and Gina raced over to the only seat left. Gina plopped herself down, then grinned up at me, short of breath. The guy beside her tapped her on the shoulder and asked her if she had a lighter.

"What for? You can't smoke on the bus," I said. Gina handed him a lighter regardless.

"Sure you can," he said as he grabbed her lighter, lighting up a cig and blowing the smoke in his lap.

"So, what area are you from?" Gina asked.

"Bag Town," he said.

Bag Town was in the North End, but it was the projects for low-income housing complexes. Hanging around Bag Town was almost like being in your own little world. All the neighbours knew each other; there were parties all the time and everybody in Bag was invited. Bag Town was also home to a number of Street Ryders.

"Anthony," he said, sticking out his hand. "I just moved here from Toronto. I'm staying with my cousin and her kids."

His hand was still held out, but Gina didn't shake it.

"Okay," he said, sitting back. "Guess you're not too friendly. How 'bout you?" He looked up at me.

"Who is your cousin down with?" Gina asked seriously.

"My cousin isn't down. She's thirty-two years old with four kids," he said as he let out a little laugh. "Why, who you girls down with?"

"Diablos." We showed him our tattoos simultaneously.

"Thug girls," he said with a smile.

"They don't come much harder than this," Gina said proudly.

"Hey," he said changing the subject. "Do you know where Maryland Street is? That's where I have to get off."

"Hell yeah, that's my part of town. It's coming up real soon," Gina said.

"You can show me where it is then, maybe even walk me out?" he asked her with a wide smile.

"Why, you scared?" Gina asked.

"I wouldn't say scared, but I guess I would feel safer with a thug girl like you by my side."

"Shake it off, buddy. This is Maryland right here. It's your lucky day, dude. This is our stop too."

We stepped onto the street and stood on the corner.

"So this is Central, eh?" Anthony asked. There wasn't much to see, only beige buildings and poor people making their way to the soup kitchen nearby.

"Sure is. Boy, where you got to go?" Gina asked while tugging on her braid.

"Meeting a couple friends. Where do you live?"

"What's it to you? You better not be a Street Ryder," Gina said suddenly.

"Street what?" he asked. "What the hell is that?"

"Don't act like you don't know," Gina said.

"I really don't. I'm from Toronto, remember? You got beef?"

"Hell, yeah. We got beef," I jumped in. "We got beef for life with those clowns."

"Take it easy, Al Capone," Anthony said, getting a bit uneasy.

"You just don't understand," Gina said.

"Is that a gang?" he asked me.

"A pretty goofy one, but yeah it is. That's the rival gang of Central."

"Am I going to get myself shot at because I'm talking to you girls?" Anthony asked sarcastically.

"Street Ryders know better than to come into this area 'cause they know they'll get blasted out of here. As for Central, I am the one who does all the shooting, me and my dogs."

"Yeah?" Anthony said, smiling and covering his mouth.

"You don't believe me?"

"It's not that I don't believe you. It's just that I never met a girl like you before. You're fucking ruthless."

"You'll never meet another one, remember that shit," Gina said. Then she surprised me by adding, "Sorry about the thing on the bus."

"What thing on the bus?" the guy responded with a smile.

Gina held out her hand and the two of them finally shook.

"My name is Gina, and this is my best friend, G Child. "

"It's nice to meet you guys," he said. "What do you think of hanging out later?"

"Depends on what you have in mind," Gina replied.

"Dunno, thought about smoking some bud with you over in my hood."

"No way. You wanna hang and smoke, then you chill with me in Central."

"Here's my number anyway." He grabbed a pen from his pocket and wrote it on Gina's hand. "You better give me a call, I'll be waiting."

They both turned back and smiled at each other as we went our separate ways.

GINA AND ANTHONY didn't hook up that night, but they did the night after, and the night after that and so on. Gina made me promise not to tell the other girls anything about him, but they were all curious to find out who this mystery man was.

"What does he look like?" Jessica asked as she combed her hair, getting ready to go on a date of her own.

"He's white, tall, with a shaved head and goatee," Gina said, fixing her hair as well.

"Is he hot?"

"Kind of," Gina said.

"He's hot," I added.

"Is he a gangster?"

"No, but I think he's down with a gang back in Toronto. He was claiming some set the other night on the phone but it wasn't anyone from here. That's cool with me, as long as he ain't no fucking Street Ryder."

"No doubt," Jessica said as she shoved all her makeup into her purse.

We were happy that Gina liked someone. We had never seen her in this state before. She would actually get dolled up before she'd go out and meet him, which was a first. You'd never catch Gina wearing makeup except for the odd time she'd put on a little lip gloss or mascara, but that was it. Gina had been getting into too much trouble these days and a guy who wasn't hardcore was something I thought she needed.

Unfortunately this thing didn't last very long because Anthony's true colours shone through one night, literally.

They both agreed to start seeing each other on a regular basis. Anthony had kicked it in Central Park with Gina a couple times, so he thought it was only fair that she came to his area to lounge with him there.

"I'm not going there alone, G Child," she said over the phone to me one night.

"You're not scared, are you?"

"What the fuck? Dummy up, will ya? I know who I am, Gina motherfucking McKay, and so does everybody else. That's Street Ryder territory. I'd be stupid to go alone."

"Ask one of the girls to go with you, or your brother Darrel." I yawned.

"I don't want them. I want you, my sidekick."

"Gina, my grandmother has a really bad flu. I don't wanna leave her alone tonight."

"So you're choosing your grandmother over your blood."

"She is my blood." Gina could be so pushy sometimes, which really ticked me off.

"Fuck . . ." There was a moment of awkward silence. If I didn't go with her, I knew I'd never hear the end of it.

"I'll go with you, Gina, but I can't stay all night. Grandma is really sick."

"Thanks, I appreciate it."

Gina and I made the trip to Bag Town by bus. Gina carried Darrel's .22 calibre gun with her, just in case. Anthony was waiting for her by the bus stop. He greeted her with a warm hug but looked surprised to see me standing beside her.

"I hope you don't mind, I brought G Child." We headed back to the complex. He walked a bit ahead of us.

I leaned over to Gina, "All these houses look the same," I said, noticing the never-ending pattern of duplexes.

"What do you expect? It's welfare housing," she said.

"Looks like nobody's ever heard of garbage bags either." Trash was scattered at practically every corner.

"Where're your relatives?" I asked Anthony as we approached his pad.

"They went up north to see some preacher."

We stepped inside and took off our shoes. At least it's clean in here, I said to myself. Anthony took us into the living room, which was around the corner from the front doorway. Gina and Anthony couldn't keep their eyes off each other.

"Kinda feel like a third wheel. Got any friends?" I joked.

"Sure, but I doubt they'd be your type." They sat next to each other on the couch and began to cuddle. I stood against a wall, feeling intrusive.

"Don't worry, we won't have sex. We'll all watch a movie or something," Anthony assured me. He got up and searched through a stack of VHS movies, but a heavy knocking on the window behind the TV interrupted him.

"Shit, hold up, all right?" Anthony said. There were three different voices and I was curious to know whose. Gina got up from the couch with a worried look on her face. She peeked around the corner to see who was at the door and quickly motioned me to follow. They were Street Ryders. All of them were dressed in black; one sported a white bandanna and the others had white hats. Anthony exchanged the infamous Street Ryder handshake with the sissies. Gina's face was beet red with anger. She was about to pounce on them but I held her back.

"No," I whispered. "We don't know how many are out there."

"This guy was trying to set me up this whole time," Gina whispered back. I let her go and she reached into her jacket pocket and held Darrel's gun close to her heart.

"Oh my god, Gina, what are you going to do?" She didn't answer me; we continued to watch.

"Coming out today, Anthony?"

"No, got company," Anthony said, leaning against the door.

"Your girl over?" one of the other voices asked.

"Yeah, I was actually kind of busy."

"We'll be coming by later, got things to do tonight, dog."

"For sure," Anthony said. They exchanged another handshake. The Street Ryders took off and Anthony closed the door behind them. He walked into the living room and Gina's first reaction was attack. She surprised him by grabbing him by the throat, placing the gun to his temple.

"Motherfucker, you trying to set me up?"

Anthony took a step back and I stood near the window to make sure we weren't being surrounded by Street Ryders.

"I was gonna tell you I was hooked up, I swear," Anthony said.

"You weren't gonna tell me shit. You were going to set me up," she said, pushing the barrel deeper into the side of his head.

"No, I wasn't going to do anything like that. I was going to tell you. I just didn't know how you were going to react." Anthony's tone was calm, I don't think he believed Gina would shoot him.

"This is how I was going to react," she screamed. "You should have told me the truth the first day I met you on the bus!"

"Gina, put the piece down. Let's talk about this," Anthony pleaded.

"Do you know how sick I feel? I let a Street Ryder kiss me, hold me and . . . Get away from me!" Gina said as she pushed Anthony away from her.

"It's not that big a deal. You take this gang stuff way too seriously."

"If there's one thing I can't stand, it's phony gangsters. This is my life. I hate your kind and I will always hate your kind, got that? Let's go," Gina said, motioning me to follow her out.

Anthony yelled after her, "Gina, hold up. I really do care about you. Nobody has to know about us!"

"Fuck you, Street Sissy!" she hollered back.

ON THE WAY back to Central Gina panicked.

"G Child, listen to me. You got to swear to me, better yet swear on your flag, that you won't tell anyone what happened tonight," she demanded as she pounded her fists into the bus seats.

"You mean you don't wanna retaliate? Gina, c'mon, we can't let him get away with this. We know where he lives and everything!"

75

"If Roland ever finds out that I fucked a Street Ryder he'll knock me out. Everybody will lose respect for me. Omar, Malcolm and Nathan will never respect me again. I should have seen this coming. G Child, you can't tell anyone."

"If that's what you want but . . ."

"But nothing. I'll just tell the girls that I dumped him, he was cramping my style or some shit. I dunno, I'll make something up. He's damn lucky I didn't blast him in the fucken head. G Child, we're gonna forget this ever happened. We're never speaking about this again." And we never did.

CHAPTER FIVE

THE VIOLENCE HEATS UP

As the four of us approached sixteen, we became obsessed with gang life. Petty crimes such as shoplifting or jumping people for their jackets or shoes became more serious. That led to B & Es (break and enters) and eventually having so many enemies you'd have to watch your back constantly.

I started to feel the weight of being a female gang member. I had to think twice before going out to eat with the girls or waiting for a bus outside Jessica's apartment or even going to the drugstore to get tampons. I knew the Street Ryders would get me sooner or later. Some people thought I was just being paranoid.

One night after supper, I met up with Connie and Omar in the park. We stood around, a bit bored and smoked a joint.

"Why don't we check out that new gangster flick?" Connie asked me.

"It's an independent film and it's only playing in select theatres," I said.

"So?" Omar asked.

"The only one that's remotely close by is the Play-house Theatre in the North End." I passed Connie the joint and lit up a cigarette.

"You saying we can't go?" Connie passed the joint to her brother.

"There's only the three of us. That's just asking for trouble, Connie."

"This isn't fucking Los Angeles," she snuffed.

Maybe she jinxed us that night because the streets showed us differently. I was waiting at her little run-down house when all of a sudden a group of Street Ryders barged in. It was judgement day. Connie was older and had been a Diablo longer than most of us. She had been on the Street Ryder hit list for a long time.

There were seven of them and only the two of us, so naturally we ran. My first reaction was to head to the back and rush out the door. But when I was about to open it, a large rough hand flung me back inside. I tried to pull away but he had a tight grip on my shirt. My shirt tore away, leaving me with only my bra on. That didn't faze me as my only goal was to get the hell out of there. I ran up the stairs as fast as I could with a face-less Street Ryder close behind. I ran into the first room I saw and managed to close the door behind me and push a dresser against the door. The Street Ryder began to barge his way in.

There was only one other place to go: out the window. I jumped and landed on hard concrete in my barefeet, my knees buckling on impact. I was in terrible pain but was still so scared, I just wanted to get away from there.

I got up, not looking back, and started hopping down the street wearing only a bra and black hip-huggers.

My ankle screamed at me to stop. The pain actually turned my stomach. I couldn't take it anymore and sat down on the curb.

A passing car slowed to a stop where I was sitting.

"Hey, you hurt?" an old man asked me as he rolled down his window.

I nodded and he motioned for me to get in. He drove me to the emergency at a nearby hospital and once I was inside, I limped over to a pay phone in the hall. I tried getting ahold of Gina but her cell phone was off.

"Fuck," I swore to myself and hopped to the emergency room.

WHILE MY FOOT was being X-rayed, I worried about Connie and hoped she had gotten away. I started feeling like a bitch; I hadn't even tried to fight back and just left my friend behind. I knew those Street Ryders weren't there to make a social call. They meant business and they were going to give two gangster girls the beats to put us in check. Those Street Ryders caught us off-guard, they caught us slippin.'

It turned out that nothing was broken but I did have a badly sprained ankle and torn muscles. I needed crutches to hobble out of there and a bottle of painkillers to boot.

The next time I tried Gina, she picked up. Connie had already phoned her and they had people looking for me.

I waited outside the hospital for about ten minutes before Gina roared up with Connie in the back seat of Darrel's Honda.

I got in the front, shut the door and stared Gina in the face.

"Holy fuck, we thought you were still in the house!" Gina said.

"How did you get out?" Connie asked me.

"I jumped out the window," I said, pointing at my ankle.

"Man, that's a high jump. Did you break your leg?" Connie asked, putting my crutches in the back.

"Might as well have. What happened to you"? I asked her.

"I got knocked around but I ran out the front door before they could really hurt me."

I looked her over. She had a scuffed-up face with a lump in the middle of her forehead and what appeared to be the start of two nicely blackened eyes.

AFTER THAT DAY, it was back and forth with the Street Ryders. We jumped them and they jumped us. This war went on for a year and now that I think about it, that was the first sign that gang violence was becoming a serious issue. This was punctuated by the death of Jeremiah Thompson.

JEREMIAH WAS just the cutest little wannabe gangster. He was a year younger than we were with a small stature, but did he ever have a big mouth on him! Sometimes he acted too large but I guess the kid was trying to make a name for himself. Jeremiah was Métis, half native and half French, with puppy-dog eyes, a sweet, innocent smile and these puffy cheeks that girls loved to pinch. We were all friends with him but he was one of Violet's best friends. Violet first heard about Jeremiah at Brittany Kent's place. We were on our way to a party, waiting for Brittany to get dressed and being nosy, as usual. Jessica began sifting through Brittany's things on top of her dresser.

"Who's this cutie?" Jessica asked Gina as she passed her a Métis status card.

"That's Jeremiah, Brittany's little stepbrother"

"Let's see," Violet said, taking the card out of Gina's hands.

That night Violet went on and on about how darling Brittany's brother was. So one day Brittany brought him to Central Park. Violet pinched his cheeks all night and the two were like gin and juice after that.

Not too long after, Violet and Jeremiah began to hang out on a daily basis. She'd sneak Jeremiah into her house at night and they would smoke joints in her basement. Violet loved to terrorize him, tickle him, steal his hat away from him and pinch him until he bruised. In return, he'd steal her makeup, throw her purse across the street and pinch her ass. It was a weird way of showing affection, but that was how it was with those two. Violet acted like a little girl around him, something she wasn't able to do with us. Rumours flew around for a while about their relationship.

"She's sucking him off," Omar told me.

"He eats her pussy every night," Nathan said.

"That's so sick, it's ridiculous!" Violet said defensively. "Those rumours are just not true."

People just couldn't understand what Violet and Jeremiah could ever have in common. Violet may not have been sexually involved with Jeremiah but she sure did love him; she didn't have to tell us, we just knew. Violet told us about how he would ask her to tell stories about the way she grew up over and over again. He'd ask her to hold him and rock him when he would cry and made her promise never to stop being his friend.

"He's really just a little kid underneath that ghetto shield," she said as she pulled out something from her backpack and handed it to us. "This is an Ojibwa dream-catcher. It keeps bad dreams away from you when you sleep and only lets good ones come in."

"It's pretty. Where did you buy it?" Jessica asked, touching the soft red feathers.

"I didn't buy it, Jeremiah made it for me," Violet said.

"Jeremiah makes these things?" Jessica asked.

"He's a smart and talented kid," she said.

A FEW WEEKS after Jeremiah and Violet started hanging together, I went over to Jessica's with Gina and Darrel.

Violet and Jeremiah were sitting together and we caught him saying, "Yeah, so I fucked that bitch right up."

"Who? Where?" Gina interrupted.

"You know Keely Taylor?" he asked Gina.

"Who's that, a gangster?" Gina asked.

"No."

"Then I don't know her," Gina said, suddenly not interested.

"Anyway," he said rolling his eyes, "Keely Taylor, I fucked her shit up right."

"You mean you had sex with her?" Jessica asked in shock.

"Yep, and her friend Tracy too."

"Tracy Williams?" Jess asked, interested in the gossip.

"Yeah, Connie's younger sister."

"And that's not the latest," Violet added.

"I heard that Shauna is pregnant with my kid and the rumour is that Michelle is too."

"You're a straight-up player, aren't you," I commented, surprised at how many girls this little kid had been with.

"More like a dog," Jessica said disgusted. "Ever heard of abstinence?"

"You should talk," Gina said, kicking her feet up.

"Don't be so mean to the little guy," Violet said, holding Jeremiah close. "He's cute, he can do anything he wants."

Jeremiah thanked Violet for her support and promised to come and visit her again within the next couple of days. I followed him outside and grabbed him by his jacket.

"You make me laugh, son," I said.

"Why?" he asked, fixing his jacket collar.

"Everybody thinks you got the hots for Violet. If that's true, you're not gonna win her over by telling her your sex stories."

"Actually, I got more than the hots for her but I'm not good enough. She comes from a good family, and she's a good girl, ya know. Someone like me would only corrupt her. I wouldn't only wanna fuck Violet, I'd wanna have a relationship with her. But I wouldn't be able to bring her to my house to meet my parents; they're fucking drunks, man. Maybe I'll change my mind sometime but until then I'm happy being friends with her. Why you tripping?"

"Nobody's tripping. Like I said, you make me laugh, son."

SOON AFTER, Jeremiah got caught stealing a car with a few of his careless buddies and was sent to the youth centre. His friendship with Violet was temporarily put on hold, at least in a physical sense. Jeremiah, the cute little wannabe gangster, was shaking it rough in jail.

Violet did something very special for him. She went to Father Joe, a priest at her church, and begged him to go and visit Jeremiah in jail. Father Joe agreed and went to see Jeremiah on a regular basis. When it came time for Jeremiah's court date, the judge was impressed with the relationship that the two of them had formed, so Jeremiah was let out on good behaviour.

One Sunday, when Violet and her family were on their way to church, Violet spotted Jeremiah walking in the same direction. She knocked frantically on the window but he didn't hear her. She thought Jeremiah had forgotten about her because he didn't even call her when he got out of jail. Her parents parked the car and Violet told them she'd come inside in a minute. She waited in the car for Jeremiah to pass by, but instead of walking on the sidewalk, Jeremiah crossed the street and walked through the church parking lot. Violet jumped out and startled him.

"Oh hey!" Jeremiah said, smiling ear to ear.

"Why didn't you call me?"

"I came here to surprise you. I promised Father Joe I'd start coming. You don't look too happy to see me."

Violet realized her mistake and gave him a huge hug. "You finally got out!"

"Yep, here I am. I wouldn't be here if it wasn't for you."

Jeremiah promised he would accompany Violet and her family to church every Sunday.

The next weekend Connie's parents went away to the Dominican Republic, so naturally she decided to have a little party. There was a lot of anticipation before the party for all of us—and for different reasons too.

Jessica was excited because she knew that many of the Diablos from all three sets around the city were going to be there. Gina and I were excited because we had set up a couple of girls from school who we were planning to punch out. And Violet was excited that she was going to spend time partying and drinking with her best boy, Jeremiah.

The night was rich with gangsters, hoods, wannabes and thugs, all up in the same room. I felt the tension in the air.

"I wonder where the little man is?" Violet said, coming up to the table where Gina and I sat playing cards with the boys.

"I fucking suck at this game," Omar said, shaking his head at his cards.

"You got to step up," Nathan said while taking a long drag from his cigarette.

"He hasn't got here yet?" Gina asked Violet as she slammed an ace of spades on the table.

"No, I talked to him this morning. He said he was going to be here early so I could blaze this joint with him but it's twelve-thirty already and he's not here."

Just then the front door opened wide and little Mike Gross stormed in with tears rolling down his cheeks.

"They shot Jeremiah! They shot Jeremiah!" The commotion in the room got thick, and all the happy faces turned sour.

"Who did?" Violet cried out grabbing ahold of Mike and trying to calm him down.

"Street Ryders!"

"No way!" Gina said, stepping up to Mike. "Where is he?"

"His sister Brittany told me that he was at City Hospital and that's all she knew."

The girls and I rushed to the hospital with Violet. We

weren't surprised when the nurse wouldn't let a bunch of bucks and white-trash kids in to see him.

"Family only. You'll have to wait outside."

We had no choice, so we did as we were told. We waited for an hour outside the emergency room trying to get word on how our little buddy was doing. A half hour later the nurse came by and told us that Jeremiah was dead.

"What?" Violet asked in utter shock and disbelief. "Are you sure?"

"Yes, he lost a lot of blood. There was nothing the doctors could do for him. It's better if you kids just go home now."

"No! I want to see him. Let me see him," Violet screamed.

"You have to go or I'll call the police."

"Let's go, Violet," Jessica said, rushing to her side. "There's nothing you can do for him now."

"It's not fair—I want to see him. I didn't even get to see him for one last time!" she sobbed as we huddled around her and tried to comfort her.

"What's the problem here?" a plump nurse came and asked the other nurse who wouldn't let Violet in.

"I've told these kids to get outta here already. They're making too much damn noise."

"What is it that you want?" the large nurse asked Violet.

"Our friend has just been shot, and his girlfriend here wanted to get one last look at him," I said, stretching the truth a little.

"Oh, his girlfriend," the second nurse said. "Let me see what I can do."

She came back a few minutes later and told Violet that Jeremiah's parents were fine with it. Violet followed the nurse and disappeared down the ward. The rest of us sat in the waiting room.

"What a shitty night," Gina said, picking her nails.

"Why would anyone want to hurt Jeremiah? He wasn't even a Diablo," Jessica said.

"This is crazy," I murmured, more to myself than anyone else.

"What do you mean?" Gina asked.

"Jeremiah . . . dead? Man, I talked to him a couple of days ago. We were laughing, joking around like always. I didn't think it was going to be the last time I'd see him. It's almost like, I don't know how to put it, a waste of a life."

"Just what are you trying to say G Child?" Gina asked with an annoyed tone in her voice. Before I could answer Violet came around the corner and told us she wanted to go home.

JEREMIAH'S FUNERAL was packed, not only with friends and family, but also with plenty of outsiders we were sure he didn't know. His murder was all over the media.

The police questioned Violet about Jeremiah's friends and enemies and who she thought would do such a thing. Violet told the police she didn't know anything and that everyone got along with Jeremiah. Violet was lying and we all found out the truth about what happened that night.

The story was that Jeremiah was on his way to Connie's party when a minivan pulled up and stopped him only a block away. A Street Ryder named Marvin Dallas rolled down a window and began to question him.

"Who are you down with?"

"Diablos in full effect, crazy Central for life," Jeremiah said, proudly making a sign of the letter D over his heart.

Then Chase Brookes, who was also in the van, pulled out a gun and shot Jeremiah in the face.

It took police several weeks of investigating to find out what had happened. Chase Brookes, who was nineteen at the time, was charged with first-degree murder and sentenced to twenty-five years in prison. Marvin, who was fifteen, was given six years with eligibility for parole in three. Jeremiah was also only fifteen when he died.

Jeremiah's death completely changed the way the police dealt with street gangs in Winnipeg. Before his death, police took gangs too lightly, not realizing the violence involved or the ties to the bikers and organized crime. After his death, they realized that street gangs posed a serious problem. They created a gang unit, a section of the police force that specialized in gang-related issues. We got to know that section of the police department very well over the next couple of years.

CHAPTER SIX

JUVENILE CENTRE

Jessica, Violet and I graduated from grade ten. We were proud, not because we passed with flying colours but because we were the only Diablos left in school. Gina dropped out three months prior to graduation due to lack of interest. Jessica and I boasted that the only reason we still went was to sell weed to the kids at school. Violet's parents forced her. I knew it was really all about the money for Jess, but I still cared about my English classes and when I had a moment to myself, which was hardly ever, I'd write a story or two.

After we cleaned out our lockers on the last day of school, Jessica suggested that the three of us treat ourselves to the Chinese buffet across the street.

"You two go. I have bad period cramps. I'm just gonna go home and sleep," Violet said.

"Whatever you want, V," Jessica said.

We sat at a booth much too big for just the two of us and waited to be served drinks.

"Are you going back next year?" Jessica asked me.

"I don't know, we'll see," I said eyeing the buffet. "Man,

I'm really starving. It's been a long time since I've been to a restaurant."

"As soon as this slowpoke waitress takes our drink orders, we can help ourselves," she said giddily. I tried waving the waitress over for the second time but then caught sight of two guys who walked in, and my heart leaped in my throat. I coughed.

"What's wrong?" Jessica frowned.

I pointed towards the entrance. "You see those two people that just walked in?"

"Ugly, aren't they?" Jessica whispered.

"They're Street Ryders. They were there that time Connie and I got jumped at her house. I think the fat guy's the one who chased me up the stairs . . ."

"What should we do?"

"Pounce." I leaned forward and told Jessica my plan. We waited until the two Street Ryders were in the buffet line. They passed the giant pot of wonton soup and stood by the salads. That was our cue. We pushed our way through the line and grabbed the wonton soup and struggled as we carried it over to them. Praying they wouldn't turn around and discover us, we dumped the entire pot of near-boiling soup over their heads. The soup was hot, really really hot. Some of it splashed on me burning a part of my hand. They immediately crashed to the floor and screamed in agony. Everybody screamed. Both of us kicked at them and shouted, "That's what you get for messing with the Diablos! Crazy Central for life, assholes!" Jessica and I bolted for the door but were stopped by a flank of police officers. Unbelievably, I had forgotten there was a police station right next door.

OUR PARENTS were called immediately. I pleaded with my mom to pay my jail bond. She refused and told me if I went to jail it would be my own fault. I then called my grandmother. I tried to explain to her that I was in jail and needed some money to be able to get out, but as soon as I said the word *jail*, she freaked out and began to cry.

"Sweet little girl, in the jail? Jesus, help you." She was beginning to frustrate me, so I told her I'd call her later. Jessica's mom had spent her welfare cheque on booze; we were shit out of luck. Both of us were charged with assault causing bodily harm. We were sent to juvenile court the next day and got what seemed to be a lenient sentence of two months at the youth centre and two hundred hours of community service.

After a sleepless night in jail, Jessica and I were shackled up in the back seat of a cop cruiser and taken to the youth centre.

"I can't believe I'm going to jail," Jessica said worriedly.

"It's not real jail," I said trying to cheer her up. "And the community service isn't so bad, picking up trash in Central Park."

"But still, we're gonna miss the whole summer." She looked out the window.

"Jessica, I'm sorry I got you into this. It's my fault.

I should have called Gina when I saw those two Street Ryders. Gina would probably be excited to go to the youth centre."

"Don't even apologize to me, G Child. You would have done the same for me."

I HAVE TO ADMIT, the first couple of weeks in the youth centre were scary. There were a number of large Street Ryder girls who liked to push their weight around, and unfortunately for us, there weren't many Diablos. There were only three other Diablo girls in, besides Jessica and me—Nancy Isaac and Desiree Diamond, two black chicks who represented the East End Diablos, and a white badass named Melissa Scott, who was also from the same set. I had heard of these girls throughout the years but didn't know any of them on a personal level.

"Don't you girls bang Central?" Nancy asked me at lunch.

"Yep, we kick it with Gina McKay," Jessica said.

"That's Roland McKay's sister, huh?" Desiree asked.

"Yeah, that's our girl," I said.

"We've heard a lot of stories about her," Melissa said.

"Oh yeah, like what?" I asked, making sure they weren't going to talk shit about her.

"We heard she's solid and that she beat up three Street Ryder guys at once," Nancy claimed.

"That's true," I said.

"I'd like to meet this girl one day," Melissa said.

"All in good time," I told her.

"How come you don't like East End girls?" Desiree asked nonchalantly.

"Who said that?" Jessica asked.

"Nobody said it, we can just tell," Nancy said aggressively.

"Let's clear that up right now," I said, matching her aggression. "There is no beef between Central and the East End."

"Says who?" Melissa asked with a weird look.

"Says me," I replied firmly. "Listen, I don't give a fuck what's going on in the streets. I care about what's going on in here, right now. If you girls haven't noticed, we're kinda outnumbered here. We aren't your enemies, they are," I pointed at a group of girls playing cards, all Street Ryders. "Now is the time for us to be sticking together."

"One of those girls tried manhandling me already," Desiree said.

"We can't let that happen, we have to stay together."

The East End girls did as they were told and we kept together in a pack even though we were outnumbered. Not only were there a lot of Street Ryders in the youth centre at the time but there were also a lot of girls who weren't gang affiliated. I saw that I had no choice but to get things into action. I needed to make the Diablos bigger, a force to be reckoned with, so I began recruiting members. I told the other three what I planned to do, and they agreed that this was a perfect opportunity.

I initiated ten girls, some of whom were from the North End but weren't affiliated with the Street Ryders.

"If you want recognition and the protection of the gang outside these walls, you have to prove yourself in here," I told them.

"But how are you gonna jump us in?" one of the civilian girls asked. "There's guards everywhere, they'll catch on."

"We're gonna go to war with the Street Ryders in here. That will be your initiation. Remember, we're all gonna get more time for doing it. So if you're brave enough to attack the Street Sissies and you're willing to give up months of your life for the Diablos, then you're good enough to get in."

The girls were excited and felt the power that obviously comes in numbers, and together we made a plan for attack. We rushed the Street Ryder girls at gym one evening with me ahead of the crew provoking the fight. I rushed Lexis Valentine, a Street Ryder bitch who was pulling weight with her girls. I attacked her from behind and jumped on her like I was riding a horse in the rodeo. Six of her girls tried to jack me up, and out of nowhere came my girls fighting with a razor-sharp edge representing our set. It was crazy: guards were trying to pull us apart and break up the brawl as we yelled and swore at each other. I got about six death threats right there but I wasn't afraid.

"Bring it!" I said, encouraging the Street Sissies. Six of us spent time in the hole while the other four got two more months of time, Jessica and I included.

I HAD one month left to go. I hadn't spoken to my grandmother or my parents since I'd been locked up. I was kinda pissed at my parents for not paying my jail bond, but I decided to put it past me and call them up. The first number I dialled was Grandma's. I wanted to tell her that I loved her and would try my hardest not to get in trouble. I wanted to tell my parents that I wouldn't be out in time for school but they didn't have to worry; I'd catch up quick. Nobody answered on either end, and so, feeling lonely, I went back to my room and sat on the bed. I picked up a book that one of the guards gave me to read. It was *Charlotte's Web* and the cover had a picture of a little girl and a pig underneath the title.

A counsellor came into my room and handed me a couple of letters. "You got some mail but before you open it, I want to have a talk with you," she said and closed my door.

"What about?" I asked.

"Your time is almost done here. What have you learned while being in here?"

I hated nosy bitches like this. "Nothing," I said.

She folded her arms across her chest. "Did you enjoy your stay?" she asked.

"You make this place sound like a vacation spot or something. No, I didn't enjoy my stay here. I hope I never come back to this place."

"That's what I want to hear," she said, turning around. "Behave, keep off the streets and you'll never have to step foot in here again."

After she left, I opened one of my letters. It was from Gina and it read:

> To my partner in crime,
>
> Wuz up dawg? Damn you've been in that place for a while. I just thought I'd write you this corny letter and let you know that I haven't forgotten about you. I wish I could tell you about my plans but I know that your eyes won't be the only eyes on this paper but I will tell you to hurry the fuck up, me and Violet miss you! Oh yeah, Darrel misses your ass, so do Connie and Francine, they told me to tell you hi. There is a girl that was in there with you, I met her yesterday and she told me about what happened in the gym. That was the bomb! I'm very proud of you, looks like I taught you well. I heard you have to stay in there a little bit longer but don't worry, it's cool. Anyhow, I got to go to the mall with Darrel and look for a new watch for Mom, it's her birthday tomorrow but you know, keep your head up and I'll be seeing you when you get home.
>
> Your home girl,
> Gina McKay

I had a big smile because writing letters wasn't Gina's style. Even though it wasn't very long, I appreciated the fact that she went out of her way to send it. Gina's letter made me feel that the extra months were well worth it; she made me feel proud of what I did.

The next letter was sealed in a violet envelope. It read:

> Hello friend,
>
> It's been a while since we spoke. I hope you're not upset that I haven't written you sooner, I've been really busy. I actually got suspended from school last week for fighting and when my parents threatened to take me back to Italy, I got so mad at them that I didn't go back to school anymore. They kicked me out, and now I'm staying with Gina and her family. It's okay here but I feel like an intruder. Gina's mom, Lenore, said I was welcome to stay as long as I wanted, all I got to do is help her clean up and do some chores around the house. She also made it very clear that she was not responsible for me and that she wasn't about to tell me how to run my life and what to do with it. Basically meaning that she doesn't care what time I come home or what time I leave. I like the freedom I have here but I feel alone, more than I did before. I miss my parents but they hate me now, there isn't anything I can do.
>
> Besides that there have been a lot of parties, really good ones. I've been drunk at every single one. Darrel and Omar got jumped a few days ago, they had to go to the hospital and

get stitches but they are okay. Nobody knows who did it. Connie's cousin Victoria is pregnant, can you believe it? She doesn't know if she's keeping it or not. There is lots of things I want to tell you but I know I can't so I have to wait to see you again.

I miss you, gangster, it's just not the same without you around. Please be good in there so you don't have to stay any longer, that way you can come home.

Sincerely,
Violet Marino

I put the letters down, laid on my rock-hard bed and stared into space. Violet's letter touched me in a different way than Gina's. Her letter made my heart feel heavy; it made me miss home. I began to think of my parents but when I realized what I was doing, I quickly turned my thoughts back to Violet. She wasn't afraid to show her emotions. The rest of us had been trained over the years to hide them so well. I often wondered if we had any compassion or concern left in our bodies or brains. For Violet it was okay to feel lonely, it was okay to cry; it was human nature to feel some emotion.

Being a gang member, surrounded by the kind of people that I had around me, made being human extremely difficult. The only way we could survive in our world was to show few of our real feelings. I respected Violet in that sense and even though sometimes her emotions got in the way, they kept her innocent and pure. No matter how down she wanted to be or how down she became, she somehow kept her values alive.

THE DAY BEFORE I was released I tried calling my family again. Nobody was picking up at my parents', so I tried my grandmother's.

"Hello?"

"Grandma, it's me. I'm coming home!" I said happily.

"You no come home. You no come home no more. Here, here is Mommy," she said in broken English.

"Hello?" my mother said sternly.

"Mom, what is Grandma trying to say?"

"She doesn't want you here anymore. I don't blame her either. You use people."

"What are you talking about?" I asked, raising my own voice. "I live there!"

"Not once since you've been gone did you call me or her, not even once."

"I did try calling but you weren't there. Why didn't you come to visit me?"

"It's not my job to reach out to you after what you did. You should reach out to us and beg for forgiveness."

"That's something I'll never do, Mom. I did something wrong and I did my time. I don't need to be forgiven."

"I can't believe my own daughter is so cruel. You dumped boiling soup over a man at a restaurant. You obviously wanted to kill him."

"The soup wasn't boiling; he wasn't a man; he was a punk kid and if I wanted to kill him I would have used my hands, not a pot of soup!"

"You can come and get your things out of here and do what you want with your life. Don't even think about trying anything funny while you're here. The police will be escorting you out. When you clean up your act and leave those idiot friends of yours, maybe you can come back but until then good luck." And with that she hung up. I wanted to cry but I held it in.

"I couldn't help but overhear," Jessica said out of nowhere. I turned around and found her biting her nails.

"How long were you standing there?" I asked.

"I wasn't eavesdropping, I wanted to call home too. G Child, you don't have to worry. You know you'll have a place to stay. You can stay with me and my mom. I know it's not much of an apartment, but Mom would like to have you. She knows we've been friends forever."

THE DAY Jessica and I got out, the set celebrated our return with the usual party, complete with drugs, alcohol and sex galore. I didn't feel up to it, and sat in the corner of the room and drank to ease my head.

"What's wrong with you? Don't you wanna smoke?" Darrel asked me over the blaring music.

"No, I just want to relax," I said, putting my feet up on the table. I had been locked up for four months and nothing had changed. I didn't know what I expected to be different; after all, four months isn't that long, but I still felt disappointed. Maybe I was downhearted because I got kicked out of my grandmother's. I wished my mom would just leave me alone and let me live my life the way I wanted.

"Did the youth centre fuck with your head?" Gina asked, smiling down at me and stumbling a bit with her drunkenness.

I got up and acted the same way I did before, but that was exactly what I was doing, acting.

CHAPTER SEVEN

A REAL JOB AND LOVE

The next three years were filled with partying and gang-banging (hanging out with gang members and putting in work). Jessica got pregnant three times. The first time was by Omar, which nobody was surprised about. They had been sleeping together off and on but Jessica never took him seriously. It was a difficult decision but in the end she decided to abort the baby.

The second time was by Shawn. They both got extremely drunk at a party and the next morning neither of them could even look at the other because in real life, and without alcohol screwing with their senses, Jessica and Shawn hated each other. Jessica had an abortion without hesitation.

The third time she got pregnant was with Troy Davenport. Troy's father was Jamaican and his mother was pure Mohawk Indian from Minnesota. Troy had an exotic look to him, with chocolate brown skin, slanted eyes, high cheekbones, thick lips and a big heart. This pregnancy was not an accident. She had always had a crush on Troy and wanted to be his girl, not just a bed buddy.

Troy was the careful type so he insisted on wearing a condom but Jessica coaxed him into doing otherwise.

"Don't worry, I'm on the pill. I won't get pregnant."

Troy was absolutely furious when he found out that Jessica was pregnant. He claimed he got information from an outside source that Jessica was never on the pill and that she was trying to trap him. Jessica denied it.

Two months later, Jessica woke me up in the middle of the night complaining of terrible stomach cramps. She moaned and hunched over.

"Jessica, look!" I screamed. A bright red patch of blood was spreading over her cotton pyjama pants. Jessica had a miscarriage and Troy could not have been happier.

GINA GOT SENT to the youth centre every year. She was busy recruiting members in what we now referred to as the crib, the youth centre's new nickname. She even told me that she'd rather be in jail than on the street.

"At least there are people that are real solid in here who are just dying to be down with us," she'd say in her letters.

Gina was disgusted by how some of the Diablos were turning out on the street. Connie, for example, had joined the Diablos before me, but decided to settle down. She got married at eighteen to a trucker from Ontario and moved away with him.

"What a traitor. He's not even a gangster," Gina said.

Troy decided to finish high school and went off to college in Quebec to become an engineer.

"If he wasn't planning on being a Diablo for life, then he shouldn't have joined at all," Gina complained.

Our old friend Victoria got pregnant and moved to Vancouver to live with her grandparents. "What a fucking skinner," Gina said.

Whether Gina liked it or not, kids in gangs eventually do get older. The overwhelming majority stay in the same way of life, either ending up in jail or dying early. But some of them actually do change and go down a different path. The straight and legit lifestyle was not on Gina's agenda, though, and she didn't expect it to be on anybody else's either.

Turning eighteen didn't change Gina's fighting spirit; she was still as hard as day one. She breathed, lived and dreamed as a Diablo, twenty-four–seven. As for me, I was happy for those friends who were bettering themselves. I wished I had something positive going on too. I wished I had paid more attention when I had been in school. Maybe I could be going off somewhere to study just like Troy. That would have made my parents happy.

They still weren't talking to me. I tried telling myself I didn't care about them anymore and I reminded myself of how they did nothing to protect me from my uncle when I was a kid, but I still felt sort of like an orphan. I missed living at my grandmother's. I lived with Jessica now. Every night I pulled out the futon and woke up with button marks on my back in the morning. Jessica's mom wasn't always a picnic either. She'd come home drunk, bang around and sometimes pass out on the floor beside me. At least I had a place to stay. It could be worse.

THEY SAY what doesn't kill a person makes them stronger. I always hoped this saying would hold true for Violet. Not speaking to her parents really got to Violet. They were mad at her, she was mad at them and she really felt abandoned. Where was this so-called unconditional love that Violet's mother claimed to have for her only child? Violet felt misunderstood and there was an empty void in her life we couldn't fill.

She also always seemed to be in the wrong place at the wrong time. Violet never did any time in the youth centre, but she was always caught in situations that affected her life for the worse, especially after she was a witness to a gruesome murder.

Louise Parker was murdered right in front of Violet one night at a local bar. Suzy Keith and Karen Anwar, both unknown to Violet at the time, got into a scrap. Louise, being a good friend of Karen's, tried to break it up. Suzy ended up slashing Louise's throat with broken glass. Louise bled to death before the ambulance arrived.

Louise Parker's murder seriously impacted Violet's life for the next year. She was constantly interrogated by police and was forced to show up in court as a witness. She became an emotional wreck. The day before the trial began, Violet was at Jessica's stoned out on Lorazepam, which the doctor had prescribed to calm her anxiety.

"Hey," Violet said looking at us with fear in her eyes.

"What?" Jessica asked.

"I want to tell you both something but I'd prefer if you wouldn't tell Gina."

"We don't like keeping secrets from each other," I said.

"It's not a secret. I just don't think she'd understand."

"What?" I asked.

"I feel like I'm not cut out for this kind of life. Do you know what I mean?" Jessica and I looked at each other, then shook our heads no. But deep inside, I knew how Violet felt, I knew exactly how she felt.

MONEY WAS GETTING REALLY TIGHT for me. I never did end up going back to school, so I didn't have as many customers to sell joints to. I was starting to feel like a bum. I was nineteen and had never had a real job before.

"Jessica?" I said, trying to get her attention as she read through a copy of *Cosmopolitan*.

"Huh . . . ?" she asked, looking up at me.

"I think I wanna get a job."

"You mean like a normal job?"

"Yeah, the weed business has really dried up for me."

"What would you do?"

"I was thinking retail. They're hiring sales associates at Queen's Jeans."

"I love Queen's Jeans. I steal from there all the time. Hey, maybe I can come with you. Mom would be so proud."

Jessica and I applied at Queen's Jeans the next day and got hired on the spot. We worked the day shift, starting at nine and ending at five. It was a pretty standard job, showing people to their change rooms, putting clothes away and doing inventory. I hated working the cash register. All those buttons and impatient people made me nervous. I was exposed to tens and twenties on a daily basis. I wanted to grab it all for myself, but I kept on saying over and over in my mind, "This isn't your money to take. It's the company's." I was trying to set that legit mentality in my head and while I was struggling with my conscience, I met the man who would change me forever.

JESSICA AND I were folding a bunch of men's tank tops when I caught sight of him. He casually strolled towards us, pretending to be interested in the tank tops, but he wasn't fooling me—I knew he was interested in me.

He held the tank tops towards his face. "Which one would look better? Black or grey?" He stood tall next to me, about six feet. He was lean and dark and his nose looked like it had been broken a few times.

"Go with the grey," I said, thinking it would make his hazel eyes stand out. He didn't bother trying it on. He paid for it quickly and headed back to the table.

"My name is Jay, by the way."

"Hi." I giggled.

"Listen, I don't usually talk to strangers but I'd really like to take you out sometime."

"How 'bout now," Jessica broke in. "She's on her lunch break in two minutes!"

I flashed her a look of disbelief, but she just shrugged her shoulders and winked.

Jay took me to a Vietnamese place across the street and was kind enough to order for me.

"You look familiar but I can't remember where I've seen you before," he said, rubbing his goatee.

"Couldn't have been at Queen's Jeans. I just started working there. Maybe we know some of the same people. Do you know any of the McKays?" I asked. Jay spat his drink across the table, nearly hitting me in the face.

"Gina, Darrel and Roland McKay?"

"That's them. They know everybody." I handed Jay a napkin to wipe his face.

"I used to live beside them on Alexander Street. The four of us used to play war and build these wicked forts. Is Gina McKay still crazy?"

"Crazier than ever. We're best friends."

"So . . . you're a Diablo . . ." he whispered.

"Yeah . . . I am."

"You don't look it. I don't mean that in a bad way. You're too pretty. All dressed up, working at Queen's Jeans . . ."

"Gotta grow up sometime," I said, taking a bite out of an egg roll.

"Yeah but it's hard. How did you do it?"

"Do what?"

"Pull yourself together like that."

"I don't know. I didn't realize I was pulled together."

"Oh . . ." He leaned closer and put his lips to my ear. "You're put together baby, in all the right places."

I COULDN'T WAIT to get to Gina's and tell her about Jay. Man, was he funny. He made me laugh the whole lunch hour, plus he was street smart too. Even though he wasn't a Diablo I could respect his thinking. He believed that a real man walks alone, not with twenty warriors behind him.

Jessica and I barged into Gina's bedroom and found her asleep. I flickered the lights on and off and then jumped on her.

"Fuck off," she said grumpily. She sat up and rubbed her eyes.

"Get up, it's past six," Jessica said. Darrel and Violet walked in carrying McDonald's bags. Violet threw Gina a cheeseburger.

"If I knew you guys were coming over, I would have bought you some too," Darrel said, sitting on a nearby chair.

"G Child's not hungry. She had a lunch date this afternoon," Jessica announced.

"A date?" everyone asked simultaneously.

"It wasn't really a date, Jessica," I said shyly.

"It was a date. He's handsome too. He looks like one of those Indian actors in those Pakistani movies."

"What a geek," Darrel said.

"Remember Jay Sidhu, Gina?" I asked.

Gina looked at her brother and they both laughed in unison.

"Please don't tell me that's who you're drooling about," Darrel teased.

"I'm not drooling," I said, checking my chin in the mirror.

"That guy's a little bitch, man. Fuck, buddy, if you go out with that guy you'll be the laughing stock of the entire town. The guy's such a bitch that his nickname used to be Jay Bitch."

"That was a long time ago," Gina said.

"Not only that but he's dirty, he fucks hookers and shit. Everybody knows that. He's a crack fiend too. Do what you want G Child, but don't say I didn't warn ya."

"Darrel, why don't you go fuck a tree or something. I wanna speak to the girls alone," Gina said, getting up from bed.

"Bitches." He mumbled on his way out and shut the door.

"G Child, don't listen to my brother. He's probably just jealous," Gina said.

"Why is everyone making a big deal out of this? It's not like I'm gonna marry the guy," I said.

"He's nice," Gina pronounced. "As long as he ain't hooked up with no Street Ryder set, you're allowed to go out with him."

Allowed? I wasn't asking for her approval in the first place. But wisely I kept my mouth shut.

* * *

A LOT OF PEOPLE expected Jay and me to hook up sooner or later. It was a pretty well-known fact that Jay had a thing for me but I refused to get involved with him in that way. I hated to admit it but Darrel ruined it for me when he told me all those nasty things about him. Whenever he'd lean in to kiss me, I'd pull away thinking about all the hookers he had kissed.

I had been working at Queen's Jeans for about a month. It was my first day off since I started and I decided to spend it with Jay. He took me to a matinee. I wasn't interested in the movie, only in him. I couldn't hold it in anymore. I told him everything I had heard about him and demanded to know the truth. He told me how he used to hang around a dude named Randy Richards. The two of them had never smoked rock before but did one night as a result of a stupid dare. Right from the first toke, they were hooked on the evil drug. Jay and Randy began to rob 7-Eleven stores for money to get their fix. Randy and Jay really struggled with their addiction. The first time Jay got locked up was for robbery but Randy remained out on the street, still getting high. Jay took programs in jail to deal with his addiction and he claimed they helped him out a lot.

"The programs helped me think straight. I was even thinking of going legit."

Of course he didn't go legit but he did manage to stay clean for good. The hooker thing he denied.

"Is that why you won't be my girlfriend, G Child? Because of my past?" I couldn't answer him. I asked him to hold me tight and he did.

As we walked out of the matinee together, Jay had a sombre look on his face.

"You got some time?" Jay asked.

"All day."

"I wanna pawn this watch that I stole from a party last month," he said, pulling it out of his pocket.

"Where was I?" I asked, insulted that he hadn't invited me.

"I didn't know you."

"Ohh." Jeeze, I was getting jealous.

As I reached to open the door of the pawnshop, it flung open unexpectedly, hitting me in the face.

"Fuck man, watch what you're doing!" I said to the guy without looking at him.

"Your face looks all fucked up now, worse than before. I didn't think that was possible," Jay joked.

"Shut up you fucking sniffer," I said, holding my nose. But Jay had stopped laughing and was gazing down the street.

"That guy looked familiar. He looked like Randy."

"You mean the Randy we were just talking about? Are you sure?" I asked.

"Yeah, yeah, did you see his face?"

"No, I had a faceful of door at the time."

"Which way did he go?" I asked. "There he is!" I pointed across the street.

"Never mind," Jay said. "That can't be him. But let's go find out for sure." Jay grabbed my hand as we ran cross the street. "Randy!" he yelled out.

The dishevelled figure continued looking in the

opposite direction. Jay approached him and grabbed him by the shoulder. A very tired and hungry-looking face stared back at Jay.

"Hey, what's up buddy?" Jay said smiling, but his face quickly turned ashen. It was Randy, who didn't smile back or even answer. "What the fuck is wrong with you?" Jay asked, raising his voice.

Randy looked down at his worn-out shoes. "When did you get out?" he said, still looking away.

"Three months ago, man. Where the hell you been? You're still fiending out, aren't you?" Jay said, shaking his head. "What the fuck, Randy, this ain't no way to live."

"I know but this is my life now, not too much I can do about it."

"Sure there is. You can get your fucking act straight, you can get help. Whoa!" Jay fanned his nose with his hand. "You stink. When was the last time you took a bath? Listen, Randy, why don't you come to my place for a bit? You can take a shower. I'll give you some clean clothes, get you something to eat, c'mon, buddy."

"I can't do that."

"You were my bro. Wouldn't you do the same for me?"

"Probably," Randy said, pinching his nose.

"Here's my number," Jay said, handing him a little piece of paper he pulled from his wallet.

"Your bus is here," I said, interrupting.

Randy hopped on the bus and didn't turn around. Jay stared at the bus, then turned to me.

"Fuck, I wish I hadn't followed him. I hate seeing him like that. I've never seen him this bad!"

"Just a quick question—why did you have a piece of paper in your pocket with your number on it?"

"I have a whole bunch," he said, giving me a handful of torn-up little papers with his name and number. "Just in case I meet some hot chick and neither of us has a pen."

"You're desperate," I said, giggling.

"No, just always thinking ahead," he corrected me.

"Wait a minute. How are you flirting and hanging out with me all the time but still have time to think about hooking up with some other ho."

"Don't call yourself that," he said, stepping closer to me. "You didn't seem interested. I made all the advances, you just never responded."

I grabbed him as hard as I could and kissed him until my lips hurt.

"Does this mean you're my girl?" He asked, looking into my eyes.

I kissed him again.

MY JAY. He was an instigator, always plotting, planning and playing with something. He showed up at Lenore's door the following day looking for me, with a great big smile on his face. "Come outside," he said.

"You come here," I said, opening the screen door.

"No, trust me girl. Get your ass out here."

"Okay," I said, trying to put my hair in a ponytail.

"With what I got under my pants, I swear your pussy's gonna get wet just looking at it," he said excitedly.

"If you're going to show me your dick, I'll pass."

"Oh, I guess that sounded sort of bad. It's not that but if you want . . ."

"Jay, please!"

"When I saw this, I swear my dick got hard in two seconds. I had to have it."

"Hurry up," I said, getting impatient.

"This is my real girlfriend," Jay said, slowly pulling a sawed-off shotgun out of his pants. I quickly looked around to see if anyone saw it.

"You're walking around with that?" I said, grabbing ahold of it myself.

"Why not? I had to walk with a limp. I just pretended I had a metal leg."

"You're an idiot. Is it loaded?"

"Yep," he smiled.

"Fuck, you're stupid, walking around with that shit, especially you. The cops just love you, don't they?" I said, handing him the gun.

"I told you I was crazy."

Jay didn't give a fuck about anything; he was really careless. He lived a dangerous life but that was all part of his charm.

A week later, Jay stood me up. He didn't meet me after work like he always did. That night, as I was getting ready for bed, Jessica pounded on the bathroom door.

"The phone's for you. It's Jay."

"Tell him I'm brushing my teeth and I don't talk to people that stand me up."

"I think you better take the phone, G Child." There

was a tone in Jessica's voice that I didn't like. I quickly opened the door and grabbed the cordless phone out of her grip.

"Jason, where are you?" I called him Jason when he ticked me off.

"I'm at the remand centre."

"What? What the hell are you doing there?"

"I robbed the 7-Eleven by my house."

"The same 7-Eleven that you robbed the first time?" I asked in disbelief.

"Yeah . . ." His voice sounded sad.

"Why in the hell would you rob the same store twice, Jason, what the fuck?"

"I wanted to get caught. I need help, G Child. I didn't want to tell you but I've been using again."

"Jay, how could you?" Jessica stood by me and put a hand on my shoulder.

"I'm surprised you never noticed."

"I wouldn't know what to look for," I said, holding back the tears.

"I might get three years, G Child. Will you wait for me?"

"What do you mean, wait for what?"

"I love you girl. I'm sorry I fucked up, but from now on I'll be good. I promise."

"Of course you'll be good, you'll be in jail."

"Don't fall in love with anyone else. Fuck once in a while if you have to but don't fall in love, okay?" I didn't answer him. "I know you love me. Your kiss told me so."

"Jay, don't do this to me now."

"Promise me you'll write me, okay? C'mon, promise me!"

"I promise!" I cried.

"I gotta go. I love you."

I stood silent and stunned.

"G Child?" Jessica put her hand on my shoulder.

I forced myself not to cry. I was hurt. I trusted Jay not to go back to doing drugs again. I felt betrayed but I still cared for him.

CHAPTER EIGHT

MOVING ON UP

It was October thirty-first, my birthday, and I was headed over to Gina's after my work shift. I turned twenty that day but I wasn't happy. Before the end of my shift at Queen's Jeans I called my parents, thinking they might want to talk to me on my birthday. My mother told me to forget about them and hung up. I stood there stunned, still holding the phone to my ear. I hadn't been a perfect daughter, but why did they hate me? Were they still upset about the whole thing with my uncle?

As I made my way over to Gina's, I couldn't stop thinking about all the obstacles I faced, and not only my own but everyone else's problems as well. Violet tried on numerous occasions to speak to her parents again only to have the door slammed in her face. Jessica was becoming lonely and was losing faith that she would ever find her ghetto prince. She wanted a boyfriend so badly but could never find one that would stick around for more than a week. She was convinced she was destined to be unhappy. I told Jessica to be patient but being patient was something Jessica wasn't very good at.

Gina was usually happy, especially when she was putting in work for the set or getting even with our enemies. But she had been acting grumpy. Two nights earlier, Gina was on her way to buy a gun from a biker. She stood in an alley and waited for her so-called biker friend. A ghost car (an undercover cop car) pulled up to her and before Gina realized what was going on she was pulled into the cop car and they brutally gave her the beats. Gina's biker friend had set her up. The cops broke her nose and wrist.

It was about 6:00 p.m. when I knocked on Gina's door.

"Who is it?" Gina asked. Her huge eye stared at me through the peek hole.

"It's your mom," I said jokingly.

"Fuck you," she grumbled and opened the door.

I entered the house and Jessica hurried to greet me.

"We were wondering when you were gonna show up." I dropped my jacket to the floor and plopped down beside Violet. "I was on the phone."

"You're late," Gina continued grumbling. "I should beat you for making us wait, but since it's your birth-day, I won't."

"Doesn't look like you're gonna beat anyone up for a while," Jessica joked as Violet giggled aloud.

"You're not funny," Gina said as she made a fist with her unharmed hand.

Violet quickly changed the subject. "There's a street party on tonight."

"I wanted to go to the club tonight," I said.

"We can't do that, we're all broke," Violet said.

"You and Jessica are the ones with jobs, G Child. You guys should have some money," Gina coaxed.

"I might have a job but I'm as broke as anyone right now. Most of the money I make I give to Jessica's mom for letting me stay there. Plus, my shifts are getting cut."

"It's true," Jessica added. "We only make $7.50 an hour and we work so damn hard."

"Well, it don't really matter." Gina sat down on the floor next to me. "My big brother offered me a kickass job last night."

"Oh, yeah, what's that?" Jessica asked combing her hair.

"A runner." She widened her eyes at us.

"A drug runner?" I asked.

"Yeah, I'll be making two hundred a night guaranteed, and that's just for starters," she said with a tough voice. "I think it's about time I got into that business. Practically everyone's selling rock nowadays. Shawn, Omar, Troy and Darrel have been doing it for a while."

"People get shot all the time over things like that," Violet said sharply.

Gina lit a cigarette. "Yeah, but those people are just clowns anyway."

"Serge wasn't a clown. He got shot once," Jessica insisted.

"Are you kidding?" Gina said disgusted. "Serge is a bitch. My brothers rolled him out, and besides you never hear of anything happening to girls. My brothers will make sure I'm strapped."

"I don't know any girls who deal," Violet added.

"Listen to her, eh?" Gina said, smiling at me. "They're around, just not big-time."

"Are you gonna do it?" I asked, not concerned about the others and their hang-ups.

"Yep and you girls are gonna do it with me. C'mon, think about it. You'll be making good money working for Roland. Imagine money never being an issue again. Violet, you're always complaining about how lazy you are. Hustling rock is the easiest job in the world! Jessica, think about the respect you'll get after becoming one of the city's successful female dealers," Gina said, raising the Diablos gang sign in the air. "Everyone in the hood will look up to you. Don't you want to be a hard-core motherfucker?" She looked over at me. "I know I don't have to tell you what it's about. You were made for this. You're just down like that."

"But I don't know anything about slanging rock," Violet said.

"Not a problem," Gina said, sitting straight up. "I know everything there is to know about it. I've been watching my brothers go at it for years now. They're gonna hook me up with a car and everything. All I got to do is get a crew set up. When our shift is over, yours and mine," she pointed at me, "that's when Jessica and Violet will go on. It's so simple."

Growing up in Central exposed me to drugs and drug addicts. I knew crack was the type of drug that took over people's lives. I'd seen addicts jonesing for a fix; they act all excited and alert. Their pupils become dilated and they look sweaty. One day, out of curiosity, I asked a crackhead what it felt like to be high on crack.

"Like heaven on Earth," she said, showing me her rotting teeth. "Sucks, though, it only lasts for a few minutes. Then I get depressed and paranoid but I gotta get high again, man."

A lot of Diablos were selling rock. I even knew some that were smoking it from time to time, but I hadn't thought about getting caught up in that myself. Dial-a-dealer drug selling just didn't really appeal to me. I thought it was boring. Driving around all day long, going from house to house selling crack just wasn't my bag, but at the time, we weren't in the position to be choosy.

Money had always been an issue for us. Of course we could always do some B & Es or sell stolen goods, but not a lot of people were into just stealing anymore. Especially because we were all over eighteen and we would do real time if we were caught. Out of the four of us Gina was the only one who didn't care whether she went in or not. Being over eighteen never stopped her. For a few moments, we were silent, lost in thought. Finally, Jessica said, "I'm up for that. I've been planning to quit Queen's Jeans for a while now."

"You sure?" Gina asked, not knowing if Jessica was being serious or not.

"Yeah, I think it might be a good idea."

"You know, if you don't like it after the first couple of days, you can just quit," Gina said. "So Violet, what's it gonna be?"

"As long as you show me what to do, I'm cool with it," Violet's voice was still a bit uneasy.

"What's up with you, girl?" Gina asked, putting her arm around me.

"Well . . . the pay at Queen's Jeans is pretty shitty. I think it's time to make money."

AS TIME went on, I came to regret those words. I wished we hadn't accepted so quickly—should have at least slept on it. But in the beginning, we were excited about this change in our finances. The four of us worked under Shawn, who worked, of course, for Roland, who bought crack from the bikers. Gina was upset with her big brother because he had told her she would have her own crew and be in charge, the way she likes it. But Roland changed his mind and thought it was better to keep us in training, Gina included, for the first few days.

We caught on quick to the crack game. Ultimately Shawn decided that Gina should be in charge of our crew. We got set up with our own phone, which was always ringing off the hook with people in need of their fix, and we got our own car. It was a shitty little Mazda but it did the job.

It took us two weeks to save enough money to move out and choose a place that was straight-up ghetto. The neighbourhood was full of welfare houses, young gang members and a couple of crack houses. We moved into a typical beige Central apartment in an extremely rough-looking building. The front door had no window, plus there was no lock on the door, so anyone off the street could just walk in anytime. There was an elevator, decorated inside and out with graffiti. We'd come home sometimes to find a homeless person sleeping in one of the hallways. Shawn, Darrel and Omar were our next-door neighbours.

"Welcome to Langside Arms," Darrel said as he helped me carry some of my stuff into the block.

"Gangside Arms, you mean. You know I asked a cab driver to bring me to this building once and he wouldn't do it."

"Ha, he didn't feel safe," Darrel snickered. He stacked the bags in the elevator and said, "Not half bad here. I know everybody in this building. Some are actually customers of mine. There's this one guy on the first floor named Ozzy. He came knocking at my door one night asking for crack. I told him if he ever did that again I was going to bust his head wide open, that fucking heat score."

We approached suite five, and my heart sank a little more as I saw a mouse run past the apartment door.

"It's okay here, as long as you don't mind those West End Diablos, especially the one that keeps asking about you," Darrel teased.

"What for?" I asked with my guard up.

"They think you're hot!" He looked down at my bags. "Need help with anything else?"

I opened the door. "Naw, I can handle it." The last thing I wanted was to get myself involved with a bunch of gangbanging drug dealers who sometimes wanted sex in exchange for drugs.

"Come check me out later," he said as he disappeared around the corner.

JESSICA'S MOM bought us a tacky old maroon-coloured couch that she found at Value Village, complete with cigarette burns. She also gave us some scratched-up end tables and a coffee table that was falling apart. The other stuff we managed to buy on our own, second-hand of course.

The first few months of dealing drugs were a blast. I did nothing but smoke weed and make money. Any hang-ups lurking in my conscience went out the door after I saw the cash fly into our pockets.

Unfortunately, Jessica had a bad first week of slanging. Shawn and Darrel were training Jessica and Violet. They made a stop at a motel near the airport and as Shawn turned into the parking lot, he was pulled over by the cops. Jessica was holding all the tinfoil-wrapped crack rocks.

"Swallow it, before the cops get out of their car," Shawn hollered at her.

"You want me to swallow this?" she asked with a disgusted voice.

"Hurry up," he said.

Jessica did as she was told and swallowed five rocks.

The police searched the car and didn't find anything, but they seized the car nonetheless because Shawn was driving without a valid licence. Gina and I, of course, killed ourselves with laughter when Jessica and Violet came home and told us about their shitty day.

"Now you'll have to wait until you shit it out!" Gina giggled.

"And if you're brave, you can pick it out yourself," I added.

"Why do you think I bought Ex-Lax?" Jessica said, reaching into her purse and throwing the box at us. "I wanna shit these crack rocks out ASAP!"

AFTER THE TRAINING period was over, we were under Gina's command and we started to make serious cash. Gina bought a big-screen TV; Jessica bought a DVD player along with a bunch of movies. Violet and I went halfers on black leather couches. After we got all those things together with a few other little accessories here and there, our pad looked pimped out. Violet complained that it was heat score to have all these nice things in such a grungy apartment but we didn't listen to her.

One night we decided to have a little gathering at our place. Well, you know how it is, you tell one person at the bar that you're having a little get-together and everybody shows up! Violet was upset when forty people crammed into our little run-down apartment.

"This is bad. One of the neighbours is going to complain for sure," she said.

"Damn Violet, nobody cares about that around here," I said, opening a beer and handing it to her.

She refused it and kept on bitching. "Sure they do. People need their sleep, you know. What if the cops come here and find all our crack? Look at all these Diablos. Almost everybody is wearing their bandannas—the neighbours are gonna think this is a crack house!"

The noise from the party was making it difficult to hear, so I raised my voice without caring who heard it. "The cops are not going to come here and if they do, they can't search the place without a warrant."

"Yes they can," Violet yelled back. "If they have reason to believe there are drugs here, they could barge in at any time! At least tell these guys to take their bandannas off just in case they do come. I don't understand why they still wear them. That's so childish."

"You're giving me a headache. Stop being so paranoid," I ended the conversation with that.

She stomped away and locked herself in the bedroom like a grouch.

I joined Jessica, Gina and the other drunks in the living room. I wasn't going to let Violet's paranoia or shitty attitude stop me; it was time to party! I was sipping on my vodka and orange while Jessica was drinking her Budweiser, and Gina, of course, was chugging away on her O.E. I never understood how Gina could still drink that crap. The only reason I drank it back in the day was because it was cheap—only five dollars back then. When

I teased Gina about it, she would just say, "I'm from the old school sista!" I always thought she watched *Menace II Society* one too many times.

The night was filled with smoke and drink and dancing, and I was getting a kick out of people's reactions to us. In Central there was something called "hat tipping." You know, like the cowboys used to do to greet one another in the Old West. Well, in my hood, the cowboy hats are replaced with baseball caps and tipping a hat is a sign of respect. Mainly OGs (original gangsters) would get hats tipped to them. Gina had it done to her many times but tonight was my night! Two Diablo studs tipped their hats to me and the feeling was awesome because I had never felt respect with such honesty; the respect felt real that night.

Omar and I downed another vodka and orange juice; the room began to spin and I needed to sit down. Gina kicked some hood rat off the couch so I could pass out, but Jessica wanted me to keep her company.

"No, don't pass out yet. C'mon, have another drink." She put her arm around me and shoved a beer in my face.

"Stop it," Gina demanded, taking the beer away from her. "The girl is tired, leave her alone."

"No, I want her to stay up with me." She shook me a couple of times but I pretended I was asleep. Jessica suddenly gasped for air and then jumped up, pulling on my arm. I had no choice but to open my eyes.

"Who is that?" Jessica asked as she pointed across the room towards the door. Two guys stood in the hallway. The shorter one had a shaved head and reminded me of

Doctor Evil from the *Austin Powers* movies. The taller one was dark skinned with long hair pulled back in several elastics working down to a ponytail. His jacket hung open and a bright red T-shirt peeked through. Portrait-perfect Indian, as Jessica would say.

"Holy fuck, that's Tyson. Tyson! Tyson!" Gina hollered across the room, waving him over.

"Tyson, is that his name? The one in the red shirt?" Jessica asked.

Gina ignored her.

"You can let go of my arm now," I reminded Jessica. I had a feeling she had forgotten she was still holding on to me. She dropped it instantly as the two strangers approached us.

Gina greeted Tyson with a big hug. "Tyson, I haven't seen you in years. How the hell are ya doing?" she asked him.

"Not bad, hardly recognized you with your hair like that. You're all thugged out and shit," he said with a great big smile.

"Nice teeth," I whispered under my breath. He introduced his friend Alfred to Gina. They shook hands; Alfred then plopped himself on the couch beside me and I moved over as far as I could, trying to eavesdrop on their conversation.

"This is my good friend Jessica," Gina said, pointing at Jess. Tyson eyed Jessica appreciatively.

"Sexy friend."

"How come I've never seen you before?" Jessica asked nervously.

"I've been living on the rez for the last four years," he said.

"Did you live in the city before?" she asked.

"I lived here for a while but decided to move back home for a bit."

"A bit? You missed a whole lotta shit, cuz. You might as well have been in jail," Gina said.

"Cuz?" Jessica asked confused.

"Yeah, we're cousins," Gina added.

"You're a McKay?" Jessica asked excitedly.

"Proud to be one. Are you from this hood?" Tyson said, getting closer to Jess.

"I grew up here, with Gina and this girl right here," she said, turning to face me.

"Why didn't you tell me you had such a pretty friend? I would have come back a lot sooner," Tyson teased.

"He likes those white girls," Alfred said, turning to face me.

Yuck, this guy stinks, I thought as I moved farther away from him.

Tyson grabbed hold of Jessica's hands. "Tell me, beautiful, you got a boyfriend?"

"No, I don't," Jessica said, looking mesmerized by his dark eyes.

I just knew what Jessica was thinking: this is him; this is my ghetto prince; he's the one for me. She was such a dreamer.

"It must be my lucky day," he said, leading her to a corner of the room.

The two continued their conversation with their eyes

fixated on each other. Gina sat down next to me and put her arm around my shoulder.

"How you feeling?" she asked.

"Fucked up," I said, still watching Jessica and Tyson.

"Tyson was down with the Diablos when Dean O'Callaghan was still alive. My Aunt Rita begged him to come back to the rez before he got himself killed," Gina whispered.

"Was he hard-core?" I asked somewhat interested.

"He was alongside Roland in everything," Gina said as she got up.

DEEP INTO the wee hours of the night, I was awakened by Violet screaming, "Get the fuck out!" She was pissed at some girls who were being too rowdy. Gina climbed on top of our coffee table and started running her mouth about whatever and whomever she didn't like. The other drunks were like an audience to her, clapping and cheering her on. Violet attempted to go back into the bedroom but began to argue with Jessica, with Tyson still at her side. Both their arms were raised, fingers pointed at each other. Violet once again stomped away angrily towards the couch and sat down with a disgusted look in her eye.

"What happened?" I asked, not really caring but feeling it was the right thing to say.

"Jessica and that guy kicked me out of the bedroom 'cause they want to be alone," she said.

I struggled to lift my head up and the room began to

spin again. I saw Tyson lead Jessica into the bedroom.

"Fucking slut," Violet grumbled. "What's wrong with you, drink too much?"

"Yep," I said, putting my head in her lap. "It's not about flying colours or running Street Ryders out of your hood. It's about dollar bills, yo."

"G Child, what the hell are you talking about," Violet said with a giggle while stroking my head.

"Don't listen to me, Violet. I'm drunk."

"You know what they say: the truth comes out when you're drunk."

"Maybe so." I dozed off.

THE NEXT MORNING I had a wicked hangover. My body ached from head to toe and I found it almost impossible to move. I heard giggling coming from the bathroom. Tyson must still be here, I thought.

"What a mess," I heard Violet say as she whizzed passed me with a mop and broom. When she saw that my eyes were open, she ordered me to follow her into the kitchen. I struggled to get up and as I did I felt the hangover fill my body like a cloud of poison. My jaw hit the floor when I saw our brand new microwave on the floor with a huge crack right down the middle.

"Oh, shit," I said, leaning against the wall.

"Yeah, that's what I said too. We can't have parties like this anymore."

Violet just stood and stared at the floor with disgust.

We heard the bathroom door open and Jessica came out wrapped in a towel with Tyson fully dressed behind her.

"Did you see this?" Violet asked but Jess ignored the comment.

Jessica walked Tyson to the door and they stood together like two lovestruck fools.

"When are you gonna call me?" she asked, rocking back and forth.

"As soon as I get home," Tyson reassured her as he gently rubbed her arms.

Jessica giggled like a little girl and wrapped her arms around him.

"Then I'm gonna pick you up, so get ready, okay?" he said, patting the back of her head.

"Yeah for sure," Jessica said, planting a big wet kiss on him.

"See you in a bit," he said as he closed the door behind him.

"Ah!" Jessica screamed in delight. She grabbed Violet by the arms and spun her around.

"Wait, wait, look over here," Violet said, interrupting her dramatic love rush. She pointed at the microwave on the floor but Jessica didn't acknowledge it, even though she was the one who had bought it.

"Who cares, I'll buy another one," she said nonchalantly. "Did you see him?" she asked me.

"I saw him, I saw him," I laughed.

"This is him. I know this is him," Jessica said, running circles around Violet.

"What's wrong with this fool?" Darrel asked, stepping into the apartment and sitting at the kitchen table counting his money. He winked at me.

"I'm in love!" Jessica panted as she sat beside Darrel and pinched his sweet cheeks.

"With who?"

"Your cousin Tyson," she said proudly.

"My cousin Tyson?" he asked in a shocked voice. "That asshole was here last night?"

"Yeah, he was with me most of the night," she added.

"Fuck that guy, man. I don't like him," Darrel said, shaking his head.

"Why?" Jessica asked disappointed.

"He may be family but the guy's a goof. Just wait, you'll see." He turned to me, "You look sick."

"I am sick," I said, holding my stomach. "Why weren't you here last night?"

"I went somewhere else," he answered.

"Where?" Gina interrupted as she overheard us in the next room.

"Never mind," Darrel replied, clearly annoyed.

"Why are you calling Tyson an asshole?" Gina asked, her hands on her hips.

"It's a personal beef between me and him. But don't you remember what he did to that girl Felicia?"

"Yeah but that was between them," Gina said.

"I want to know what happened," Jessica said, still hyper.

"He beat a girl up so badly she had kidney failure,"

Darrel said, shaking his head. "Not only that, I heard he was a joneser."

"A crack fiend? No fucking way." Jessica panicked.

"It's just a rumour," Gina assured Jessica.

"I saw the girl. She was in rough shape."

"I don't want to hear any more about it. Nothing is going to change my mind about Tyson. I'm gonna stick with him," Jessica said, grabbing ahold of Violet's hand.

FOR THE NEXT two weeks Tyson was with Jessica twenty-four–seven. He even went on the road with her and helped her sell crack.

"It's supposed to be Jessica and me, not Jessica, Tyson and me," Violet complained. She told me how they would make out all day long and that she got sick of seeing it. "One time they even tried to pull some funky shit in the back seat but I threatened to kick them out if they did," Violet said.

Personally, I couldn't have been happier for Jess. Tyson was the type of guy she had always been looking for from the time we were kids; it was about time she found him. That comment Darrel had made about Tyson being a goof stayed in the back of my mind, but I didn't really let it get to me, nor did Jessica. The only part I didn't like about the whole thing was that we would see less and less of her as she'd spend all her spare time with Tyson. She spent way more time at his place than at our apartment.

ONE MORNING after Gina and I came back from our shift, we were surprised to find Jessica sitting on the couch going through an old picture album. The album was full of photos of us back in our Central Park days, being drunk and looking it, too.

I looked at a picture of Jessica and me hugging. "You're never home anymore," I said. Jessica didn't answer. "That was a good night," I said, pointing at a picture of Gina and me struggling to grab ahold of Shawn's nine-millimetre gun.

"It was," she said quietly.

"What are you doing here?" Gina, who was already in a bad mood, didn't wait for an answer but headed for the kitchen. We hadn't sold our usual amount of rock, which meant we didn't have our usual amount of cash.

"What does it look like I'm doing?" Jessica snapped.

The fridge door slammed shut. Gina came back into the living room and stood in front of Jessica with a beer in her hand. "Who pissed in your throat this morning? I asked you what you were doing here."

"What am I doing here? I live here, don't I?" Jessica said annoyed, keeping her head down, away from Gina's eyes.

Gina tore the photo album away from her. "Listen, if you were anybody else, I would have punched you out by now, but since you're my friend, I'll tell you to straighten the fuck up. Don't fucking come in here with your bullshit attitude and try to act all tough 'cause your going with Tyson. You wouldn't be shit if it weren't for me. Remember that the next time you wanna talk back to me because next time I might not be in such a good mood." She threw the album across the room. "I'll be next door," Gina mumbled, slamming the door.

"What the hell's wrong with you?" I asked her, pissed off that she had talked to Gina that way.

"It's Tyson," she said.

"You guys break up?" I asked, knowing that if they did, it would have been the end of the world for her.

"No," Jessica said, looking away from me.

"He's cheating on you?"

"No," she shook her head.

"He's going back to the rez?" I asked, not knowing what else to say.

"No, he's . . . he's pimping out a couple of girls."

"Pimping girls? So what is he, a Street Ryder now?" I asked jokingly.

"C'mon," Jessica whined.

"So what?" I asked raising my palms.

"What do you mean, so what? He's a pimp!" Jessica said.

"Not like you've never met a pimp before. Omar was pimping Helen Reed and Becky Courtland out. You didn't seem to have a problem with that."

"I wasn't going out with Omar, was I?"

"Yeah but you fucked him and so what? Would you rather Tyson be a hit man?"

"No . . ." She stopped for a minute, then said, "I just don't like the fact that my boyfriend is a pimp. It makes me look like his whore."

"Are you turning tricks for him?'

"No."

"Then you're not his whore, you're his girlfriend," I reassured her.

"No, no, no . . ." Jessica repeated to herself. "He's so much better than that."

"Is he?" I asked.

"What?"

"Jessica, the guy is a thug and worst of all he's a McKay—did you forget that? What did you think?"

"I understand all that, but it's just so . . ."

"Low?"

"Yes, it's gross."

"You think we're high class? We ain't high class. We're on the bottom of the scale. We're what society thinks of as low-lifers. I thought you knew that."

Jessica sat back, crossed her arms; tears filled her eyes.

"Cheer up, Jess. Whatever happened to thug love?" I said, giving her a nudge with my elbow.

"I still love thugs. That will never change," Jessica buried her face in her hands. "Tyson means everything to me."

"I know, don't let something like this ruin it," I said, patting her on the back.

"Before he came into my life I was only pretending to be happy, but I really wasn't at all. He takes care of me, he doesn't judge me and he really does love me. I wouldn't want to imagine life without him. Maybe I'm overreacting."

"Think of it this way: We sell crack to a lot of prostitutes that are addicts. They go out and sell their bodies to get their next fix. After they come down from the high they go out on the street again. Like it or not, Jessica, we're part of the cycle too."

Jessica paused for a minute. "I never looked at it that way before—that makes me feel sick, not better."

"Why?"

"It makes me feel guilty. Do you ever think about all the people that we hurt? We provide such a bad service, you ever think about it?"

"No," I said.

"I do, but then I see all that cash and I think well, they want it, I give it to them and they love me for it."

"Point is, don't judge Tyson for what he does if you don't want to be judged for what you do."

Jessica sat straight up. "I'm going next door to apologize to Gina. I shouldn't have talked to her that way."

"That would be nice. Gina's the last person you would want as an enemy," I reminded her, "considering all the shit that she's done for us."

"You're not kidding. Hey, this is sort of off topic but have you seen my initiation rag?" Jessica asked.

"Your bandanna? No, I don't think so."

"I think I lost it when we moved here, might as well have, eh?" Jessica turned around and was about to leave the apartment.

"Jessica, what did you mean by that?" I asked, curious.

"It isn't about representing the Diablos anymore. It's about filling your pockets, right?"

"Yeah . . . right." Jessica had the courage to say what I had been thinking for a long time, but could only admit when I was drunk.

CHAPTER NINE

ON THE ROAD

Since Gina and I were partners on the road, we spent a lot of time together. I wouldn't have it any other way. I cared about Jessica and Violet, but when I was thuggin', I loved kickin' it with my girl, Gina. She was fun to be with on the road because she hardly ever let it get boring. She actually hooked up this hidden microphone in the car but took it out after our shift. She didn't want Jessica and Violet using it stupidly and then having it taken away by cops. We'd be cruising down the street and we'd yell profanities at people over the mic.

They'd jump in fright and look around, but we'd already be driving past them, laughing hysterically. I had tried to quit weed for a couple of weeks but one night I couldn't resist taking a hit from Gina's joint. The high was so intense that it amplified everything tenfold. We drove past one of the city's casinos and saw an older aboriginal lady dressed totally in purple. I started singing the *Barney* theme song.

"I love you, you love me, we're a happy family!" She looked around and couldn't figure out who was doing it. I rolled the window down. "Over here, Barney!" I hollered.

She looked at me and started towards the car but we rolled out.

"Love your show!" I yelled.

One thing that did bother me about being on the road with Gina was the way she treated customers. Sometimes it was comical but most of the time it was too harsh. Once in a while, a customer might be a few dollars short, and Gina would shit on them so bad that they stopped calling her and would only call me.

"You have to be nicer to them, even if they are jonesers," I told Gina.

"They know how much the stuff is. They should come with the right amount."

I wouldn't go out of my way to be rude to jonesers the way Gina did. I remembered what Jessica told me about how we were providing such a bad service. I felt sorry for them and tried to cut them some slack. Jonesers were even funny to me sometimes because when they didn't have enough money for a rock, they'd give us stuff worth a lot more than forty bucks. It wasn't unusual to get everything from brand-name perfume to jewellery to laptops and CD players. Once I even got a PlayStation and since I was never really into video games, I gave it to Destiny, Darrel's daughter.

One night we stopped by a house to see one of our customers named Rebecca. She had been smoking rock all night and it was the third time she had called us in two hours. Gina and I pulled up outside her house and she walked up with a worried look on her face. We saw a police car pull up behind us, so we told Rebecca to get into the car so she didn't look like a heat score. We drove away and pulled into the back lane.

"How many?" Gina asked Rebecca as she sifted through the crack rocks in her hand.

"No wait! Look at what you gave me last time!" she said, handing Gina a piece of foil.

"It's just an empty piece of foil," Gina said.

"Yeah, you didn't give me anything."

"Fuck you, Rebecca. I wrap these up myself—I know what I gave you.

"No, it was empty. I swear there was nothing in there," Rebecca insisted.

"I'm not stupid!" Gina said angrily. "Are you gonna buy another rock or not?"

"You ripped me off!" Rebecca cried.

"No, we didn't," I spoke up. "And if you're not going to buy another piece then get out!"

"No, please just give me another one. I'm a good customer, I give you girls a lot of money!" Rebecca said, tugging on her hair.

"Time for you to go, Rebecca," Gina said, revving the engine.

"I'll do anything," Rebecca pleaded.

"I warned you," Gina said, getting out of the car. She opened the door to the back seat and pulled Rebecca out. Out of nowhere, Rebecca pulled out a knife and pointed it at Gina.

I got out of the car and knocked the knife out of her hand. Gina rushed her, giving her two punches to the face.

"You stupid, stupid bitch!" Gina yelled angrily. "You aren't going to get any rock with no money. I don't care if you do have a knife."

Rebecca pleaded with Gina, begging not to be hurt. Gina kicked her in the face and swore that she was going to kill her one of these days. And with that bit of ugliness done, we drove away.

After that episode, Gina and I were hungry and ended up in the drive-through at McDonald's. We parked in the lot and began to chow down.

"I'm gonna kill that joneser," Gina said, her mouth full of fries.

I shook my head at what had happened.

"Know what?" Gina asked, "if it weren't for you and me, those two girls wouldn't have made it."

"Who?" I asked. Gina always jumped all over the place. She expected me to read her mind.

"Violet and Jess," Gina said, taking a sip of her drink.

"You think so?" I asked. Gina truly believed she was everybody's protector.

"Hell yeah, I mean think about it, how many people talk shit about those two."

"True, but I think people are over that kind of stuff. Ya know it's all about making money now."

"Yeah, yeah," Gina said, wiping her mouth.

"I've been meaning to ask you, G Child," Gina said, swallowing noisily and looking me straight in the eye, "how come you don't wear your bandanna anymore?"

"I don't know. I think I stopped wearing it when I started over at Queen's Jeans."

"Time for you to pull it back out, don't you think?"

"It's not really my style."

"That's where you're wrong, G Child. It'll always be your style."

"It seems kinda childish to me. I don't have to wear it to know who I am."

"I still wear mine. I'm not childish."

"Depends who you're asking," I joked, hoping she would change the subject.

A part of me always believed Gina refused to grow up. She was still very much into gangbanging and representing colours when the majority of us couldn't care less about that anymore.

"Jessica's been acting weird lately," Gina continued. "I swear I was so close to punching her out the other day. She borrowed a bunch of my things, my hair spray, my shirt and a butterfly knife that I had stashed. I didn't mind but when I asked for it back she denied taking it. I saw Tyson the other day and he told me he found my knife in his house. What the hell's up with that? Was she trying to steal my things or what?"

This was news to me. "I think she and Tyson are having problems," I said, trying to make sense of the situation.

"Still don't mean she has to act like a bitch all the time. Here, have one," Gina said as she passed me her bag of fries. "Look at us, we're making easy money, having the time of our lives. I love my life, for real."

"This is what it's all about, bling bling," I said, holding up my gold chain.

"I always knew you were a downass bitch," Gina said, smiling her gangster smile.

WHEN DARREL'S DAUGHTER, Destiny, turned four, there was a party for her over at Lenore's house. Lenore was the opposite of her daughter, Gina. She was a gentle woman amid the madness all around her. Lenore was passive but she knew what was going on in the streets. I heard stories about her younger days when she would go to parties with her husband, Ed, and nobody would pick fights with her because Ed was known for being ruthless. I often wondered what attracted her to Ed in the first place. Lenore met Ed when she was fourteen and she had a hard time seeing him because her family knew she was too young to be getting involved with guys. The worst part was that Ed was full Ojibwa Indian; Lenore's parents wanted nothing more than for their only daughter to marry a Latin man from Central America, but that was not the way it turned out. Lenore hid the relationship for two years but when she became pregnant with Roland at sixteen, her family kicked her out. They ended up living on Ed's reserve up north for two years, got married when they were eighteen and moved back to the city.

"I should have listened to my parents," Lenore told me as I helped her put up decorations for the party.

"Why would you say that?" I asked, looking around, hoping Ed wasn't there to hear that comment because I knew what would happen to her if he did. Ed was known to be physically abusive.

"Ed was always in jail and I was stuck raising the kids alone for the longest time," she said, looking up from the pile of goody bags she was filling. "Now he's out and I'm still all alone, and when he is here, I feel as if I'm walking on eggshells."

The birthday party was a big one with many of Gina's relatives there. Destiny was turning out to be an adorable little girl. She had her mother's nappy hair and Darrel's creamy mocha skin with cute little dimples that popped up every time she smiled.

Amanda chatted with Lenore most of the evening. I caught her giving us the evil eye a few times. She thought she was better than us because she worked at the casino and wasn't dealing drugs. Amanda was engaged to some goof who also worked at the casino. According to Darrel, she loved to rub it in his face.

"He always wears these classy suits. He has his whole life mapped out and money in the bank," she'd tell him over the phone. Ever since Amanda started waitressing and dating this preppy, she stopped calling Darrel for things. Before she went all high class, she would constantly bug him about dropping money off, needing clothes or diapers or whatever. Darrel did the best he could and dropped off money for his daughter every week. Now Amanda was making it difficult for him to see Destiny.

When we arrived, Violet instantly went over to Roland, who was busy counting money in a corner of the room. I figured that since Violet used to lived with Gina and her family for a while, she and Roland must have become somewhat acquainted. Violet later announced that she and Roland had some business to take care of and were going to leave early. I wasn't quite sure what kind of business that would be—getting laid maybe? Not that I would blame Violet. Every girl needs a little thrill every once in a while. But why with Roland McKay? What was she thinking? Maybe I was making too much of the situation, and anyway, it was none of my business.

Darrel sat happily on the couch, holding Destiny in his arms.

"What's wrong with you?" he asked Jessica who was sitting on a chair with her hands covering her face.

"Just tired, some fiend gave me a hard time today."

"Shouldn't even serve a fiend that stresses you out," Gina said, holding on to Destiny's hand.

"Jonesers stress me out, 'cause you never know what they'll do," Jessica said.

"Stop talking about that crap in front of my daughter!" Amanda said, raising her voice, shooting Darrel a dirty look.

"Calm down," he said without looking at her. "She doesn't understand what we're talking about anyway."

"She understands more than you think—give her here!" Amanda stood straight up, glaring back at Darrel.

"No, I want to spend some time with my baby girl on her birthday."

"Darrel!" Lenore called out warningly.

"What?" Darrel said angrily as he looked back from his mother to Amanda.

"Destiny, come here," Amanda called. Destiny wiggled out of her daddy's arms and ran over to her mother.

"Fuck, I want to punch out that bitch. If she wasn't my baby's mama . . ." Darrel whispered to me. I looked at him as if I didn't know him for a second. I couldn't see Darrel being violent towards women. But people said a lot of things they didn't mean when they were mad.

"Presents now!" Destiny said, hitting Amanda on the leg.

"Okay, let's open presents," Darrel said, scooping up his baby girl and heading towards the present-laden table. Darrel gave Destiny a little box wrapped up in shiny blue metallic paper. Destiny ripped the paper open but fumbled with the box. Gina took her from Darrel's arms so he could help. He pulled out a flashy gold chain with a dollar sign hanging from it.

"Isn't that pretty, Destiny?" Darrel asked as he dangled the shiny chain in front of her eyes. Destiny nodded her head yes and her eyes sparkled as she stared at her gold necklace.

"What kind of gift is this?" Amanda said as she stood up, yanking it out of Darrel's hand.

"What's wrong with it?" Darrel asked as he took the necklace back and clasped the necklace around Destiny's neck.

"As if Destiny is really going to appreciate this. C'mon why didn't you get her some toys or clothes?" Amanda said, rolling her eyes.

"I got another present for her too," Darrel said, handing a package over to Destiny but Amanda yanked the package away from him and opened it up herself.

"A tracksuit? You got our daughter a red tracksuit and a gold chain for her birthday?"

"What the fuck, it's the right size and it's her favourite colour. I got it from Gap Kids!" Darrel said.

"You're trying to make her look like a Diablo. That's what you're trying to do!"

"Are you ever a bitch!" Gina blurted out. "Don't talk to my brother like that!"

Darrel grabbed the tracksuit from Amanda and faced his daughter on his knees.

"You like what Daddy got you?" he asked.

"Yes," Destiny said, squishing her daddy's face between her little hands and giving him a kiss on the mouth. Amanda sat back down and just watched.

By nine o'clock that night, Destiny had become cranky and wanted to go home. Amanda called her fiancé and waited patiently to be picked up.

"When's the next time I'll be seeing her?" Darrel asked, pinching his little girl's cheeks.

"Not for a while," Amanda said, zipping Destiny's jacket up.

"Why not?" Darrel asked.

"I'm moving out of the province, with my fiancé."

"I don't care about that. I asked you when you were dropping off my little girl," Darrel said.

"She's coming with me," Amanda said, holding onto her daughter's hand.

"Like hell she is," Darrel said with disgust.

"Yeah, what you gonna do about it?"

"Take you to court," he replied, handing his daughter her gloves while Amanda laughed aloud.

"Take me to court? Fuck, Darrel, grow the fuck up will you? Who do you think the judge will favour? A nineteen-year-old woman who has a job and a lot of money saved, who's gonna marry a suit, who also happens to love Destiny like she was his own, or you, a nineteen-year-old gang member who sells crack for a living and puts everyone first and his daughter last?"

There was honking outside and Amanda headed out the door but Destiny didn't follow her.

"C'mon, we gotta go," Amanda said, waiting for her little girl.

Darrel crouched down by Destiny. "Hey, little girl, give Daddy a kiss."

"I love you, Daddy," she said, giving him a hug.

"I love you too, baby. I'll see you soon, okay?"

"Destiny, hurry up now. We have to go home," Amanda said opening up the car door.

"We're not done talking!" Darrel hollered after Amanda but she didn't turn back.

Destiny pressed her face against the car window and waved goodbye to her dad. Darrel watched the car leave, then shut the door and looked up. I'm sure everyone in that room saw the same hurt in his eyes that I did.

Lenore came over to him and put her hand on his shoulder. "It'll be okay, son. We won't let her take Destiny away."

"She's right, Mom. Maybe I am a bad father. What kind of life can I give that little girl?"

Jessica walked over to Darrel and took ahold of his hand.

"I don't know anything else, this is my life," Darrel said as he pulled away from Jess and ran upstairs.

A FEW WEEKS later Gina and I were on the road with a black chick from the West End named Jasmine Walters. She was never a Diablo but was still cool in our books. It was about three in the morning and Jasmine got a call from her friend Carla Brian. Jasmine told us that Carla had been beaten up by her boyfriend and was begging to get picked up on a street corner right by our place.

Since Gina had a thing about guys beating girls, she agreed to pick her up. We drove towards home to find a shivering white girl whose mascara was smeared all over her face. Carla was crying uncontrollably.

"Why did he do this to you?" Jasmine asked.

"He . . . he put a gun to my head," Carla managed to say.

"What?" Gina asked.

"He tried to kill me," she sobbed.

"I'm turning the car around. I'm gonna kill this son of a bitch," she said, clutching the wheel.

"No wait," the girl said, pulling on Gina's shoulder. "He's a Street Ryder."

"What the fuck are you doing with a Street Ryder? You don't look like no gangster," Gina asked in shock.

"I'm not. Please just leave it alone," Carla begged.

"Fuck!" Gina yelled, hitting the steering wheel with her hands. "I don't like it when girls get beat up. Are you sure you don't want me to get him? I ain't afraid of no Street Sissy."

"No, it's okay. I just won't talk to him anymore," Carla reassured us.

"Hey wait a minute," Gina said. "You're down with the Street Ryders?"

"No, I . . ."

"You fucking with one makes you down with them, you bitch. Get the fuck out of my car before I blast you out of here myself."

"Gina," Jasmine pleaded. "She's a good kid. She just got mixed up with the wrong guy."

"I don't give a fuck. I don't want a Streetwalker in my car."

"Gina, she ain't like that."

"What's this Street Ryder's name?"

"Hugh Sheppard, you know, he's down with Roland and shit," Jasmine said.

"My brother is not involved with any Street Ryder," Gina said, staring straight ahead to the street.

"Yes, he is. Hugh's, like, twenty-seven, he's not into gangs no more, and he works for Roland, so does Vaughn Baxter."

"You mean to tell me that Vaughn Baxter, that little bitch from Jig Town, works for my big brother? Why don't I fucking know about this shit?"

"I don't know," Jasmine said, sitting back.

"This is bullshit. I am taking you home and you can take your lil' bitchass Street Sissy friend with you. I

154

don't ever wanna see your face again, you got that? The nerve you have bringing Street Ryder trash in my ride! Actually get the fuck out right now!" Gina demanded.

Without hesitation both the girls got out and ran down the street. Gina began to pick up speed and chased them down with the car.

"Gina, lighten up," I said, grabbing ahold of her arm but she ignored me and kept going.

"Watch this," she said, rolling down the window and reaching into the glove compartment. She pulled out her gun and screamed, "Hey, bitch!"

The girls both screamed frantically and cried out for help. Gina laughed hysterically and sped off but I remained quiet. Gina was insane; nobody pulled shit like that anymore.

"What's wrong?" Gina smiled at me. She was obviously proud of herself.

I looked out my side window. "I don't think that was necessary."

"Fucking bitches, man," Gina said. "If I ever catch that Jasmine slipping, I'm gonna give it to her raw 'cause I'm still banging. What the fuck is your problem? Hope you're not going soft on me."

"No, I'm not going . . ."

"Good!" Gina hollered.

WE MADE our way back to the apartment to reload. Gina waited in the car while I went inside to get the stuff.

Violet was there alone, getting dressed up in the washroom. She was wearing a sexy little black dress that I hadn't seen her in before.

"Where's Jess?" I asked, passing Violet on my way to the bedroom.

"With Tyson."

"Of course. Where are you going all dolled up?"

"I'm meeting Roland."

"What for?" I asked.

"For coffee."

"Right now? It's four in the morning."

"It's okay. We've been talking for a while. It's not a big deal."

"Sure, sure, you just want to get your pussy licked," I teased.

"You're sick—he's just taking me out. I would prefer if you didn't tell too many people about it. I don't want anyone to get the wrong idea."

"Yeah, what's really going on?'

"Nothing right now. We'll see what's up," she said.

"I know you're lying but don't worry—your dirty little secret is safe with me," I said, grabbing five rocks out of a hole in the wall.

"Gee, thanks," she said sarcastically, leaving the bathroom.

"Here's a jimmy," I said, throwing her a condom. I grabbed the crack rocks and a letter that Jay had sent me from jail. Jay wrote me a poem and it comforted me when I was frustrated. I stuffed everything in my jacket pocket and left the apartment.

AFTER A FEW DAYS, Roland picked Gina and me up from Lenore's. As Gina got into his car, she asked him if what Jasmine had said was true. Much to her amazement, it was: Roland had taken a few Street Ryders under his wing and had them selling drugs on the street. Gina was outraged.

"What the fuck are you doing?" she asked him.

"Hey, listen," he pointed his finger in her face. "Don't tell me how to run my business. I know what the fuck I'm doing."

"You're making a big mistake!" she pleaded from the back seat. "Street Ryders are dirty bitches that can't be trusted!"

"If you don't like it, you don't have to work for me. I don't need you telling me how to run my shit. You're just along for the ride," Roland said angrily as he turned the wheel.

"You did not just say that to me," she said, her eyes filling with rage.

"Easy," I told her under my breath.

"Past is the past, Gina. It's time to bury it."

"No! It will never be over. I won't accept this! Stop the fucking car!"

Roland slammed on the brakes and Gina stormed out with me behind her. I caught up to her and grabbed her from behind.

"Hey!" I said, shaking her.

"No, no, no . . ." she said, sobbing, hardly able to stand.

"Pull yourself together."

"This is the end of the Diablos. We can't let him do this!" she screamed.

Since our car wasn't running, we took a bus home. Gina was quiet on the way there except for a little outburst of screaming and kicking the seat in front of her. She wiped the tears from her face and mumbled to herself, "He thinks he's the leader? I declare myself the leader from now on."

WORD ON THE STREET was that the Street Ryders and the Diablos didn't exist anymore. A few months earlier, a number of Street Ryders were convicted of a range of charges and all the major players were now locked up. That left only the little kiddies on the streets. Most of the Diablos were slanging rocks now and others went on to different things. Like the Street Ryders, all that was left were little kiddies claiming, "I'm a Diablo, crazy Central for life!"

It made me laugh to think that was me not too many years back.

Gina lied to Roland about how she would accept the way he was doing things; what she was really planning was to take over the Diablos herself. There were only a few Diablos that were upset with the new order but the most influential of those was Shawn. He had unconditional hate for the Street Ryders and he, too, secretly refused to surrender it. Gina and Shawn started hanging out together. That bothered Jessica.

"I don't understand why Gina would hang out with Shawn. He's such a prick. His baby was my first abortion, remember?" she asked.

"That was so long ago, man," I said as I stretched myself on the sofa. Gina could hang out with whoever she wanted, as far as I was concerned.

"Yeah, but a girl never forgets her first abortion," Jessica said sitting next to me.

Over the next few weeks, Jessica, Violet and I were sure that Shawn and Gina were planning a conspiracy to set up Roland. This was a plan heading for disaster and if Gina thought this was the way to make the Diablos strong again, she was wrong. It would only make them fall apart. It's true, Gina had a lot of respect from people, the most I've seen a female gangster have, but the level of respect Roland had was incomparable. If she was planning to do her own brother in, it could be her demise as well.

One morning Jessica handed me a letter from Jay. "I went to the mailbox this morning."

My letter had already been opened. "Jessica, didn't your mom ever tell you it was rude to read other people's mail?" She had always been too curious for her own good.

"It was an accident. I thought it was for me. I'm sorry, G Child."

"I don't believe you but . . ."

"Why would I lie?" Jessica coaxed.

"Could you leave me alone for a minute?" I asked her as I pulled the letter out. Jessica nodded and closed the door behind her. I was always excited to get a letter from Jay. It was almost like getting a Christmas present.

Dear G Child:

Great news! I'm getting out in a few weeks! I have to spend a year in a halfway house but at least I'll be out of this place. I love my lawyer, he's the shit. I can't believe the way I was thinking before. Being in here made me really think about stuff. I'm never going back to doing drugs again. I'm gonna change my ways, people will be seeing a different kind of person when I get out, everybody's gonna love me again. No, no, no, it's not just jail talk, I really mean it this time. I'm allowed visitors at the halfway house, so please stop by. You know the one, right on the corner of Selkirk and Main Street. Visiting hours are between 6:00 and 10:00 p.m. I'll call you when I'm out. See you soon!

Jay

CHAPTER TEN

THE BEGINNING OF THE END

A month passed after Jay's letter without a word from him. Darrel had a friend who was doing time with Jay and had recently been released.

"Colin told me Jay got out before he did," Darrel said when I finally told him about the letter. I phoned the halfway house and the lady over the phone told me Jay was a resident there. I was stunned. Why hadn't he told me he was out? I knew one thing for sure: Jay was always full of surprises. Maybe there was one in store for me. I couldn't wait until visiting hours to see him. But what if he wasn't there? I took my chances and headed out to the halfway house.

When I got there, I expected at least to have to ask for him but there he was, sitting on a leather couch going through his pager. He didn't notice me at first. I cleared my throat to grab his attention. He looked up, startled at first but quickly regained his composure.

"How's it going?" he asked me.

"Not bad," I said, looking him up and down. He was

wearing new clothes. I wondered when he was going to give me a hug.

"Got a couple outfits yesterday," he said, looking down at his tracksuit.

"Jay, why didn't you tell me you were out? I was waiting for you to call, you know."

He shrugged.

"Are you coming out for a bit?" I asked, trying to make him talk.

"Naw, I'm just gonna chill here," he said, looking around. "Visiting hours are at six, you know."

"Why don't you wanna come and see everyone?" I said, ignoring his comment.

"Sorry I wasn't out for your birthday," he said, ignoring my question. "Happy belated." He finally stood up and hugged me. "You're still as cute as ever. Sorry for disappearing."

"I was getting scared you were cracked out again."

"I've been doing good for myself, hear you are too."

"Yeah, I got things going good right now. Jay, why don't you just come and chill with me and the girls for a bit?"

"I got other priorities right now." His voice sounded agitated.

"You haven't gotten laid yet?" I asked, thinking that must be it.

"Actually no, that's not my first priority." He sat back on the couch.

That's a first, I thought to myself, remembering all the dirty sex secrets that Jay had told me over the phone.

162

Not to mention his little fantasy of buying me some purple vibrating underwear and him taking control of the switch.

"Then what?" I asked, annoyed with his secretivness.

"I should keep this to myself," he said, looking past me.

Now I knew there was something going on that wasn't cool. Jay always trusted me and now all of a sudden he didn't.

"You used to tell me everything," I objected.

"I can't tell you this," he said, grabbing his pager. "Don't tell anyone that you saw me, okay? Don't tell anyone I'm here either. It's best that we act like we don't know each other anymore."

He stood up and said he had a quick phone call to make. I wasn't about to stick around to get into an argument so I lied and told him I had a car waiting for me outside. He shook my hand goodbye and I left, pissed off to the max.

I stomped away as hard as I could, crushing the snow beneath my feet as though it were Jay's face. This is what I get, after all the letters I wrote him, all the collect calls I accepted—this was the fucking treatment? There weren't many people I opened my heart to; Jay was one of them. We had such a strong friendship. How did he just turn to shit? What in the world did I ever do to make him so ashamed of knowing me?

Another thought came into my mind. Jay said he was doing well for himself and that only made me think he was selling crack. He wasn't working for Roland, so he had to be working for somebody else, Street Ryders, maybe? Stupid Jay, I didn't care who he was working for because I wasn't like the other dealers out there. I wasn't into jacking anyone just because they didn't work for Roland. Fuck that noise, I just wanted to do my own thing and worry about my own ass.

But something shady was in process. To make matters worse, there were a couple of Street Ryders, Silas Flett and Dan Russell, crossing the street and heading towards the halfway house. They didn't know me but I sure as hell knew them. Silas and Dan were big into pimping girls. As they walked past, Silas looked up; not only did he not recognize me, the moron tried picking me up.

"Hey, baby, why don't you let me get that number."

I wanted to bark at these bitches but knew I was outnumbered, so I acted like a civilian and didn't say a word back. Silas put his head down and kept on walking. I turned around and watched them enter the halfway house.

THREE WEEKS later, Jessica skipped work to get a pap smear done. She coaxed me into coming with her. After her appointment, we came up to the apartment to get our laundry. We were forced to take it to her mother's house as somebody in our building had thought it would be funny to smash all the washers and dryers in the laundry room.

We stepped inside and heard deep moans coming from the bedroom, one voice was female, the other male. At first I thought of Violet and Roland but realized that he would never come to our place alone, so it had to be Gina and someone else.

"Gina actually gets laid?" Jessica asked me.

"How do you know it's her?" I whispered.

"Violet is too modest to bring anyone here."

"So she really is a freak!" I giggled.

"Fuck, I got to get some of my clothes from that room," Jessica said.

"Go knock on the door," I said, giving her a little push.

"No way, you go," she said, pushing me in return, making me stumble into the door.

"What the fuck was that?" I heard Gina say from within the room.

We had to cover our mouths in an attempt to silence our laughter.

"Hey, it's just us," I managed to say, not able to contain my laughter any longer.

"How long were you out there?" she asked.

"Long enough . . . we have to get some clothes out of there. Can we come in?"

"Just wait!"

A couple of minutes later, she opened the door with Shawn leaving the room behind her.

"What the fuck?" Jessica asked me as she picked up the hamper in our room. All I could do was shrug.

Gina came into the room and closed the door behind

her. "Don't even ask," she said, grabbing her red track-suit from the closet. I could tell she was upset with us for interrupting her love session.

LATER THAT DAY Jessica and I went shopping for some new spring jackets. We were in a sports store and I was about to buy a bright red windbreaker when my cell phone rang.

"Yeah," I answered, seeing Shawn's number on the call display.

"What are you doing?" Gina asked me.

"Shopping, what's up?" I said, handing the cashier some money.

"Is Jay still staying at the halfway house?" Gina asked. She panted breathlessly and I wondered what could be wrong.

"Jay?" I asked.

"Jay Sidhu, remember?"

"Sure I do. No, I don't think he's at the halfway house anymore. I'm pretty sure he's done all his time, why?"

"So he's at his mother's then?"

"I guess so. What's going on?"

"Do you remember where he lives?"

"Yeah, I know where it is."

"See you soon." She hung up without giving me the chance to ask what was going on.

When the taxi driver dropped me off, Gina and Shawn were standing on Jay's front steps. I should have known the new dangerous duo were up to something, something no good. I opened the gate and waited to be formally greeted.

"That's a slick jacket you got there," Gina said, smiling as we exchanged a Diablos handshake.

"I got it today," I said, turning around like a runway model. I was nervous about this whole thing but I tried my best to keep my cool.

"Nice," Gina said, touching the material.

"What are we doing here?" I asked, changing the subject.

"Waiting for Jay, that fucking goof," Shawn said as his eyes scanned the streets of Central.

"Why, is he gonna roll with us tonight or something?" I asked wanting to sound innocent but knowing they were here for a beef.

"I thought you knew," he said. "He backstabbed us. He went to work for the Street Ryders."

"What?" I said almost losing my balance. A tight knot formed in my stomach. The suspicions I had about Jay hooking up with the Street Ryders were true after all.

"He's trying to take some of our customers with him too."

"Nice friend he turned out to be. He switched on us."

"I thought the Street Ryders didn't exist anymore," I said.

"They still do and that's why tonight is very important. We got to show them that the Diablos are still alive. We got to make them remember that!" Gina added.

"Haven't you noticed that Jay hasn't been kicking it around no more?" Shawn said.

"Yeah but . . ."

"Didn't you go visit him at his halfway house when he first got out?" Shawn asked me.

"Yeah, yeah," I said, trying to sound very casual. I didn't like the direction this conversation was going in.

"Did you know about this shit? If you did, you're just as much of a snake as he is." Shawn was really angry at me now.

"She didn't know about it. He didn't even want to kick with her when he got out," Gina assured him.

"Motherfucker was hooked up with those guys back then," Shawn said.

"Know who I heard he chills with?" Gina asked me.

"Who?"

"Those two little jerkoffs, Silas Flett and Dan Russell."

I almost fainted when I heard those names. Silas and Dan were the two Street Ryders that passed by me as I left the halfway house that day. Now everything was falling into place. True, I had suspicions that Jay was dealing with Street Ryders but I would have never thought it to be Silas and Dan. Fuck, was Jay ever a scumbag!

"How did you guys find this shit out?" I said, my blood beginning to boil.

"I went to visit my cousin in the North End and guess who happens to be walking down the street right beside Silas and Dan, Jay the joneser. I wanted to give it to him right there but decided to wait until the time was right," Shawn answered.

"What are we going to do?" I asked.

"Kill him," Gina said, clenching her fist in her hand.

"No really . . ."

"You think I'm joking?"

"He's our friend."

"Jay is now a Street Ryder and he ain't no friend of ours. If you live by the sword, you die by the sword," Gina said passionately as she looked into my eyes.

I sat on Jay's porch and collected my thoughts. I hated Gina at that moment. Why did she call me here in the first place? She knew how close Jay and I had been. At the same time, my anger slowly turned into understanding. Gina called me here because she loved me with all of her heart. I was her better half, the one who fully understood her. Gina thought if she was upset over this, then I must surely be upset since he was such a close friend at one point in my life. Gina had never killed anyone, but I could see the intensity in her eyes. Tonight was the night, and Gina wanted me, her best home girl, to join in her victory.

As we waited for Jay, I became more nervous by the second. I felt betrayed as a Diablo and I felt betrayed by him as his friend. I even felt stupid for believing promises he'd made to me in his letters. Jay had lost my respect and trust but I still didn't want him dead.

The minutes ticked by, and Gina and Shawn became edgier and edgier. They both paced around like they were having anxiety attacks. I was secretly hoping Jay wasn't going to show up or that Gina and Shawn would get tired of waiting. Then I saw Jay coming out of a neighbouring house and my heart just about stopped.

He was holding hands with a pretty blonde, his dark skin clashing with her powder white face. The others had seen Jay as well and both stood like statues eyeballing him. Jay and the blonde were laughing away; they obviously hadn't noticed us yet. They approached the gate and Jay's eyes met mine. He had a nervous look on his face but cracked a crooked smile at me anyway. I stared back at him, trying to signal him to run, to never come back to this place. Jay seemed to be getting the message but Shawn quickly took over.

"What's up?" Shawn barked.

"Not too much," Jay replied.

"Where the fuck have you been, man? You disappeared for a while." Gina said to him.

"I was in Calgary."

"Yeah, sure."

"I was."

"What were you doing tonight?" Gina asked, stepping a little closer.

"Hey, am I on trial here? I was chilling with my girl, this is . . ."

"I don't give a fuck who the bitch is, man," Gina said, stepping up to his face. The blonde began to fidget.

"What the fuck?" Jay said, grabbing ahold of his girlfriend.

"Did you think we just came here to kick it like old times or something? Why aren't you out selling crack for your new friends?" Gina asked him.

"What?" Jay tried to walk past Gina, still holding his girlfriend's hand.

His denial seemed to enrage Shawn even more. Shawn grabbed Jay and slammed him down into the snow. Jay's little girlfriend fell down as well. It was surreal, like a scene from a bad movie. Gina instructed the girl to get lost and the blonde bolted down the street, disappearing around the corner.

Shawn held Jay down with one foot on his chest and Gina had hers on his knees. She then stomped the hell out of him, over and over again on his skinny legs. Jay screamed in pain.

"Did you think you were gonna get away with this without getting pounded out?" Gina hollered.

"I was never a part of you guys. What the fuck did you do with my girlfriend?"

"Answer me, you dumb fuck!" Gina screamed.

"Where's my girl?" Jay yelled back.

"Are you deaf?" Shawn said and then kicked Jay in the mouth.

"Okay, what do you guys want from me?" Jay pleaded.

"I want you dead, you fucking traitor piece of shit!" Gina hollered.

"What did I do to you?" Jay asked helplessly.

"You switched on us, bitch. You work for the Street Ryders, don't you?" Gina screamed, spitting in his face.

"No, no, I'm just doing my own thing. I swear," Jay said, trying to convince us.

"It's time to drop a dime, Jay. Who the fuck are you down with?" Gina asked, trying to get Jay to tell the truth.

"Nobody!" Jay screamed, looking at me.

I knew in that moment that Jay thought I had betrayed him. He must have figured that I told Gina and Shawn about his dealings, although he actually never told me himself. I wanted to let him know that it wasn't me, that I didn't do this to him: he did it to himself.

"And you're not stealing customers either," Shawn said sarcastically.

"I am not stealing customers . . ."

"You lying bitch," Shawn grunted as he began kicking him in the face with all his strength.

"Take it easy, Shawn," I called out but he just went harder.

I fought inside myself. I wanted to leap on Shawn and pull him back, but I knew I wouldn't hear the end of it if I did. I stayed firmly planted where I was.

Shawn's nostrils flared, his teeth clenched and his hands shook with madness.

"Hey, motherfucker!" Shawn yelled out but Jay only moaned while blood gushed from his mouth.

"C'mon," Gina told Shawn and me as she dragged Jay towards the back lane, a bloody trail left on the snow behind him.

I grabbed hold of Gina. "Enough!" I told her.

She couldn't believe it. Her face registered severe shock. She pushed me away and I tumbled into some garbage cans.

"What the fuck is wrong with you? Don't you feel betrayed?" Gina yelled out to me.

I heard Jay moan and spun around to see Shawn stabbing him in the chest.

"No!" I yelled, but it was too late.

Gina took out a chrome flask and was about to dump gas all over Jay and set him ablaze but bright headlights from the back lane got all of our attention.

"Hey," Gina said, running to me, "I see cops down the street!"

"Where's my knife, where is my knife?!" Shawn panicked.

"Let's go," Gina pleaded. "They're just around the corner!"

We bolted down the back lane and crept back to the car without being seen.

I SAT in the back while Gina drove and Shawn sat in the passenger seat.

"Lost my shank, shit!" Shawn yelled.

"Are you sure you don't have it?" Gina asked, looking around.

"No, I dropped it!"

"Chill, you were getting down like a gangsta," Gina said, trying to cheer him up as she sped through the city.

"You knew about this. I saw the way he looked at you!" Shawn said with his adrenaline still running high.

"Fuck you, asshole!" I said, wishing I had his knife on me so I could have stabbed him with it.

"Stupid disloyal bitch!"

"How the fuck was I being disloyal?"

"Bitch, you didn't even want us to kill him. You were in on this shit."

"Both of you shut the fuck up, right fucking now! I'm just mad that I didn't have enough time to burn him alive, Diablo style!" Gina said.

"Where are we going now?" I asked Gina as she pulled up to our apartment

"Get out," she said calmly.

"Who are you talking to?" I asked her.

"I am talking to you."

"I thought we were going on the road. This phone's been ringing all night," I said.

"We're going on the road, you're not," Shawn said. "Pass me the phone."

"Fuck you, Shawn. Who the fuck do you think you are?"

"You pulled dummy tonight—all you did was stand there and watch. If I wanted an audience, I would have sold tickets and made money from that motherfucker!"

"Fuck you!" I told him. "What do you want from me, congratulations on a murder charge?"

"Fuck the charge!" Gina said, cutting the air with her solid voice. "I don't give a fuck. He's a traitor and he got what he deserved."

"You're a clown," Shawn told me.

"Watch your fucking mouth," I said to him. Before I could stop myself I reached over and hit Shawn in the head. He leapt at me from the front seat. I fought him as

174

hard as I could. Gina jumped out of the car and dragged me outside and threw me to the curb.

"Don't trust her!" Shawn said, screaming from within the car.

"This wasn't why I asked you to meet me tonight. I thought you were down!" she said.

"I am down," I said, defending myself, "but I wasn't down with killing Jay. Goddamn it, Gina, do you realize what you've done?"

"He might not be dead but I hope he does die. And, yes, I know what I've done if we did kill him. Tell me you're not in on this shit too. Tell me you ain't hooking up with no Street Ryder set," she said defiantly.

"Gina!" I screamed, feeling like I was going to lose my mind. "This fucking goof's getting to your head. It's me, don't you know who I am?"

Gina's eyes began to water; she walked to the middle of the street. "Look around you, little girl. Take a good fucking look!"

A car was coming down the narrow street but Gina would not move out of its way.

"Get off the road!" I told her but she just stood there waiting for the car. The car stopped and honked its horn, but Gina still would not move out of its way.

"What's your problem?" a guy asked, rolling down his window.

"This is mine!" Gina said, raising her arms to the sky. "This is all mine!" she said as she spun around like a foolish ballerina.

"You're crazy!" the driver said as he backed his car down the street.

Gina turned my way, her eyes filled with tears. "Read the walls, man. Don't forget where you're at," she said, pointing at graffiti that was sprayed on our building. "Roland made it so we could walk around Central with our heads held high, with pride in our hearts. He was tired of that dirty North End gang coming here and trying to poison us. Roland formed the Diablos and since then the Street Ryders have never been the same. Now he's letting those maggots join our side and make money with us. He's been corrupted, but not me, not me ever!" Gina slowly walked towards me. I watched her, realizing that Gina McKay lived in a fantasy world and refused to see how things in life are bound to change. She stopped in front of me. "Here you are, a girl that was down with Central from day one, defending a Street Ryder like Jay."

"It ain't about flying colours anymore. It's about making money."

"Bitch," she said, grabbing me by the throat. "Remember that tattoo you got on your arm? Doesn't that mean anything to you anymore? Tattoos are for life, just like gangs are for life! It might not be about colours to you, Jessica, Violet, Connie, Troy or even my brother, but it will always be about colours to me. It's about respect!" Gina screamed before finally letting go of my throat.

I reached into my pocket and threw the phone at her. "Go ahead, go with Shawn on the road. I don't give a fuck." I turned and opened the apartment building door.

"I'm not finished talking to you!" Gina hollered.

"Oh yes you are," I hollered back.

I WALKED into our little rundown apartment and took a good look around. The place was gloomy even though we had a high-end entertainment unit, a leopard throw rug and black leather couches to boot. Our coffee table was covered in scraps of tinfoil, weed and magazines. I went to the kitchen and saw that the dishes were stacked a mile high. We still hadn't picked up a new microwave; our fridge was bare except for an old bag of KFC, and a deflated air mattress sat in the middle of the hallway.

I headed to the bathroom, closed the door behind me and stood staring at my reflection in the mirror. My hair was all scraggy and it felt and looked dry and thin. The extensions I had put in for corn braiding had done serious damage. I touched the skin on my face, which was unnaturally dark from the tanning beds and not as smooth and supple as before. I kept looking in the mirror, staring at my lifeless eyes. People had always complimented me on my eyes but looking at them now I could see they'd lost their sparkle. I wanted to look at my body, so I took off my clothes. My body didn't seem too bad but I had gained weight since I started dealing drugs because of all the fast food I was eating. I didn't have time to work out anymore. I was either sitting in a car, sleeping, shopping, tanning or partying.

I showered and watched the water fall from the rusty

showerhead onto my body and over my tattoo. I took the bar of soap and lathered it over the ink. I began to rub the tattoo harder and harder, hurting myself, wanting it to wash off. It was stuck, just like I was, in this miserable life.

Afterwards, I walked out of the bathroom, wrapped in a towel and was surprised to see Violet in the living room straightening up the coffee table.

"Hi," she said as she crumpled the scraps of tinfoil.

"Have any cigarettes?" I asked her as I sat on the couch.

"Nope," she replied, continuing her cleanup. "Hey," she said, facing me with a hand on her hip, "why aren't you on the road?"

"Don't want to talk about it." I put my feet up on the coffee table and made myself comfortable.

"Oh, okay," she said in a quiet voice.

"Why aren't you out playing with Jessica somewhere?"

"I'm hardly ever with Jessica anymore, just when we're working, that's it.

"So where do you go all the time?"

"With Roland."

Roland this, Roland that. I was sick of hearing his name from Gina's psychotic mouth; now I had to hear it from Violet's.

"We're still seeing each other," she said.

"No way."

"It's getting serious now too," Violet added with a smile on her face.

"Roland doesn't seem like the type," I said, getting up and heading to the bathroom to brush my teeth.

"That's what everybody thinks. Nobody knows the real Roland. They know him as a gangster but not as a man." Violet followed me into the bathroom and sat on the toilet seat. "He told me he loved me the other day."

"Are you sure he's not just trying to get you in the sack?"

"Well . . ."

"Don't tell me you guys slept together."

"Yeah, we've been sleeping together for a while already."

"Listen, Violet. Roland is a very dangerous guy to be hanging around with these days."

"Why?" Violet asked me in a childlike way.

"Trust me, getting involved is just gonna cause a whole lot of drama for you."

"I am involved, I'm a fucking dealer."

"No, it will cause drama between you and Gina," I corrected her.

"She doesn't have to know. You won't tell her, right?" Violet asked.

"I hate keeping secrets but no, you don't have to worry about that."

"I care about him a lot," she said, sitting next to me.

"Well, I am not hating on you but I just don't want to see you hurt."

"Don't hate," Violet joked.

"I don't hate, I participate."

We both giggled.

"Like I said, people don't know the real Roland," Violet stood behind me and wrapped both her arms around my shoulders. We both stared at each other's reflection in the mirror.

"He and I actually have a lot in common. We want the same things in life. Did you know Roland was fluent in Spanish?"

"No, I didn't know that."

"He wants a normal life—a house, a wife, kids. He wants to be happy."

"Isn't he happy now?"

"He's been unhappy for years. He's felt empty for so long."

I went into the bedroom, pulled my pyjamas on and plopped into bed. "And then Violet came along," I said, burying myself underneath the blanket.

"Actually there's something I want to tell you, I'd like it if you would keep it to yourself."

"Excuse me?"

"You want to hear this or not?" Violet asked, annoyed.

"Do I have a choice?'

"Fine, I give up," she said, getting up.

"I was just kidding. Come back here, come talk to me."

She sat down again.

"I'm gonna have a baby," Violet said, closing her eyes.

"What? You're keeping it?"

"You know I don't believe in abortions. Could you at least try to be happy for me?"

"Violet, I am not unhappy for you, just shocked. Are

you sure you want to do this? Having a baby is a huge responsibility. It will change your life."

"This is going to change our lives, Roland's and mine, for the better."

FOR THE NEXT WHILE, things between Gina and me were uneasy to say the least. I was still dealing crack with her at night because I felt I had no other choice. Even though we spent hours together making money, we exchanged few words. Gina didn't look at me the same anymore; her crazy mind didn't let her, and I didn't look at her the same either.

Two days later Gina and I stopped at a 7-Eleven near our place to get some coffee. I noticed some kids huddling around the cash register, with the cashier leaning over and looking at the newspaper they had in their hands.

"I think I've seen that guy before—in here, as a matter of fact," the cashier said.

I was curious to see what the fuss was all about so I bought a copy and read the headlines: "Gang Member Stabbed Outside Home: In Critical Condition."

I headed out to the car with the paper and stuck it in Gina's face.

"He wasn't a gang member," she said as she started the car. She grabbed the paper and threw it out the window.

"I was going to read that!"

"Pick it up if you want."

"You're pissing me off, Gina." I jumped out of the car, picked up the paper and quickly skimmed through it. Thank God he was still alive.

ABOUT A MONTH and a half later Violet insisted on taking me out to lunch at her favourite Italian restaurant. I was excited to have this quiet time with Violet. It was a nice change after having to put up with Gina's shitty attitude.

"I hope it's a girl," Violet said. "I'm looking forward to it." She looked down at her tummy.

"I guess you and Roland are planning to be together for a long time?"

"We're going to have a baby together but we'll see how our relationship goes. I'm not going to be raising the baby alone. Roland will always be a part of the baby's life, but only on one condition."

"What's that?" I said. Violet's soap opera life was a welcome distraction.

"He's gonna have to change the way he makes money and all that gang bullshit."

I almost choked when I heard her say that. I gulped down some water. "Violet, are you kidding me? Roland's not going to stop doing what he does. Fuck, girl, what the hell else does he know how to do but ball and make babies?"

"That's not funny. I think he will. Like I said before, I know a side of him not many people know."

"Violet, get real, he's a big-time drug dealer, connected to the bikers. Even if he does get out of the game, he's marked for life. Enemies aren't gonna disappear just 'cause he's a dad."

"When are you going to hook up with somebody?" she asked, changing the subject. "How's Jay doing? Did you visit him in the hospital?"

"No. I'm probably the last person he wants to see."

"But it wasn't your fault. You didn't know that was gonna happen, right? Honey, you need someone in your life." Violet smirked and looked down at her lap. "You're gonna kill me for saying this, but I know who would be perfect for you: Darrel McKay," she whispered.

"Violet, that's . . . sick!"

"Don't tell me Darrel's not cute. Everyone knows it."

"Darrel is nice-looking but he's . . . Darrel! It's never going to happen. Darrel isn't interested in me like that."

"Don't be so sure. Want to come with me to my parents' for a bit?" she asked changing the subject again.

"Your parents? I thought you didn't talk to them."

"I've made up with them. They asked me to stop by sometime this weekend. No better time than the present. If you don't feel comfortable, we won't stay long."

"Okay I'll go," I said, not really wanting to go but knowing it would mean a lot to Violet if I did.

VIOLET'S PARENTS lived on a quiet cul-de-sac. Their white bungalow was still laced with Christmas lights.

"Before we go in, I better warn you, they like to embarrass me in front of my friends. So just go along with it and laugh at the jokes even if they're corny," Violet said as we stood in front of her parents' door. "One more thing, no swearing, gang or drug talk. They don't like to hear about it and I don't like to tell them."

"Yeah, okay."

"C'mon, I'm being serious, do you understand?"

"Yes, I understand. Let's go in already."

We rang the doorbell and waited to be greeted. Violet's mother came to the door and gestured for us to come in. She was quite attractive, a bit on the plump side with curly red hair. She greeted Violet with a hug and me with a handshake.

"Where's Dad?" Violet asked.

"He's not here, but he should be back in a bit. Please make yourself at home," she said as I took off my shoes.

We sat in the living room and Violet's mom put on a home movie of a very young Violet at one of her ballet recitals.

"I didn't know you were in ballet," I said, mocking her.

"Violet is very talented," her mother said.

"What's with the 'fro?" I asked, taking note of her short curly hair.

"Bad perm," Violet said.

After the video, Violet gave me a little tour of the house, which was carpeted in a light velvet grey colour and decorated with black and white furniture. I found one room particularly interesting. It had a large shrine dedicated to Jesus Christ and a little altar with candles in all different shapes and sizes.

"Nice," I said, observing the shrine and all the religious statues in the room.

"This is my favourite piece," Violet said, picking up a little statue of a beautiful woman in a blue veil and robe standing barefoot on a pillow of clouds. "That's our Madonna. Some people call her Lady of Lourdes, and others call her Lady of Fatima. This is Jesus' mother, the holy virgin. Roland and I agreed to baptize the baby in a Catholic church, since we were both baptized as Catholics."

"Why would you ever want to leave a place like this?" I said as she lit several candles. "You have two parents that love you a lot. You have a beautiful house in a rich area . . ."

"I was lost. I didn't know where I belonged."

"Time to get unlost, Violet. This is where you belong. You look at peace here."

We made our way to the kitchen and Violet's mother offered me some tea.

"Violet tells me they call you G Child," she said, crossing her chubby arms.

"Yeah, that's the name I go by," I said, figuring my name must have sounded odd to her.

"Is that the name you were given at birth?"

"It's the name I was given by my peers at a different birth."

"Are you a Diablo as well?"

I remembered Violet's warning but she wasn't coming to my rescue. I didn't want to lie to her mom.

"Yes, I'm a Diablo."

"Mom, you're making her uncomfortable."

"Did you know that Violet was pregnant?"

"She was the first to know, Mother."

"I don't know how she got herself caught up in this mess; she's far too young. There are many contraceptives out there. It should not have happened."

"Mother, what's done is done. I can't do anything about it now."

"Unwanted pregnancies are something that shouldn't happen nowadays."

"With all due respect, Mrs. Marino, I'm twenty and Violet is turning twenty-one soon; she's hardly a baby anymore. I don't think she's too young."

"You sell drugs?" she asked me with a bewildering smile.

"Mom, that's none of your business!" Violet exploded.

"I don't know why you girls live such secretive lives. This isn't the mafia."

"We have to get going," Violet said, rescuing me.

While Violet called a cab, I went down the corridor to the front door, putting my boots on as fast as I could. I heard footsteps and I wasn't sure if they were Violet's or her mother's, so I put my head down to tie my shoes. A gentle hand touched my chin and lifted my face. I was now making eye contact with Mrs. Marino.

"You like Italian bread?" she asked me.

"Yes," I replied, looking down at the brown bag in her hand.

"Take this home then," she said, placing it in my hand and I smiled at her. "Take care of my daughter," she said sincerely. "I can't help her now."

Violet and her mother said their goodbyes and we left.

Once outside Violet apologized. "I'm sorry about the way my mother was acting. She didn't mean any harm by it."

We saw the cab turning onto the street and walked down the driveway to meet it. I was truly happy for Violet. She needed her parents. I was also envious of her; I needed my parents too. I turned around and took one last look at the house before getting in the cab. Mrs. Marino was watching us from the window. She waved and I waved back.

CHAPTER ELEVEN

THEY'RE OUT TO GET US

Violet and Roland broke the news about the upcoming baby to everybody in the hood about two days later. People were shocked that they were even a couple but the whole baby thing was a killer. Violet and I would be at the store or a gas station and people would ask her if it was really true.

The police even found out about it. Two cops seemed to pop out of nowhere one day to confront Violet and me as we headed into a tanning salon.

"You girls are coming with us," said a blond female cop, grabbing Violet's arm and twisting it back.

"Ow!" she hollered.

A male officer grabbed me and did the same.

I had had a bad feeling just before Violet and I left the apartment. Violet insisted that we walk to the salon, which wasn't far from where we lived. I didn't like walking around during the day. There were too many cops around who knew me and some of the other dealers in the area.

"Nothing bad is gonna happen. It's a beautiful day outside. Let's go, please?"

That was all I could think about as the two officers pushed us into the back of their cruiser, our hands cuffed behind our backs.

"I heard you and badass Roland McKay were an item," the blond cop said to Violet. "Isn't that cute, a modern day version of Bonnie and Clyde."

"I don't know what you're talking about," Violet said.

"That's right, play innocent but that's not going to work. Where is he?" she said, raising her voice.

"I don't know where he is," Violet said, now becoming nervous.

"I'm gonna nail your boyfriend on so many charges he won't know his dick from his ass."

"He's not my boyfriend."

"Yeah, and you're not pregnant either."

Violet looked away and began to cry.

"Aw, you ain't so tough now are you, little girl?" the female officer said, mocking her.

"Where's Gina these days?" she said, turning to me.

I knew I had run into this cop before but I just couldn't remember where or when.

"I don't talk to her anymore."

"You dropped Diablos?" she asked.

"No," I said.

"Still running the streets, eh? Shame on you. Where is Gina McKay? I know you know where she is!" she yelled at me.

"I don't know," I said again.

The other officer started the car and drove down the street but I was too afraid to pay attention to where we were going. This did not look good. The next minute, the blond cop said in a hard voice, "It's too bad that I'm going to have to do this to you. I liked you. I really did."

Violet gasped with fear.

"Hey!" I said firmly. "Do whatever you want to me, but leave her alone because she really is pregnant!"

The male officer parked the car outside an apartment block. The female officer then got out and jerked me out of the car. I fell onto the pavement and heard one of my ribs crack. The cop then began kicking the shit out of me as I lay there helpless, secured by handcuffs. I had never been beaten up by a cop before but Gina, Darrel and the other Diablos had told me about it. I had always wondered when it was going to be my turn.

I felt the first blow to my face from her steel-toe boot. I took myself back in time to when I was initiated into the Diablos. I was just as scared then but I didn't cry out and I didn't tell them to stop. I took the beating and to me this was the same. After the blows to my face stopped, the bitch cop uncuffed me and then I heard a car door slam and Violet's whimpering cries. The police car rolled away and I felt the warmth of Violet's hands on my face.

"Oh my god, you're bleeding! We should go to a hospital," Violet said.

"I'll be okay," I said, trying to open my eyes but my right one was swollen shut.

"Did those pigs do anything to you?" I asked her as I tried to lift my head.

"No, I'm fine," she said, helping me up. "Let's get you home."

I LAY in bed the rest of that day and most of the night. I was done in and Violet was right; I probably should have gone to emergency, but I had come to hate hospitals and refused to go. My right eye had swollen to the size of a plum and I had cuts and bruises all over my face and body.

"I'll slang with Violet tonight," Gina said, looking me up and down as I lay in bed. "You're in real rough shape, man. Get some rest and if you're feeling better, you can come on the road tomorrow night. Violet told me they were looking for me and Roland."

"Yeah, they definitely asked about you guys."

I couldn't read the expression on Gina's face. She just turned and left the room.

IT WAS EXACTLY midnight and I had just finished watching *Oz* on TV when I heard loud banging on the door.

"Who is it?" I asked hoping it wasn't that bitch cop from earlier.

"It's the pig that beat you up today," Darrel's voice replied.

"There were two of them," I said, undoing the locks and letting him in.

As soon as the light from the hallway shone on my face, Darrel's smile quickly disappeared.

"Holy fuck, they really fucked you up," he said, putting his hand to my eye.

"Don't touch," I said, locking the door behind us.

Darrel shook his head and headed over to the couch. "What are you up to?" he asked.

"Nothing, actually, I was just going to bed."

"Why so early? Come next door and smoke some bud with the boys."

"Not tonight."

"You want me to keep you company?"

I remembered the conversation Violet and I had had the other day at the restaurant about Darrel. I suddenly felt a little shy and wondered if he had talked to her about me.

"No, it's okay. You can go," I said, heading into the bedroom and crawling into my bed. Darrel came in and turned the lights back on. "I had a really bad day, man. I need to rest, I'm tired."

"All right, but I got good news."

"What's that?" I asked, turning over to face him.

"I'm taking care of my daughter this weekend. Amanda's actually letting me have her for two days. You gonna come over to my mom's for supper on Saturday?"

"If I feel better. Your mom is the best cook in the world."

"I want you to chill with Destiny and me on Saturday."

"I'll try," I said, rolling over.

"Good night," Darrel said, turning out the light.

I felt bad for punking him off. Maybe I did want his company; after all he was a very good friend. "Darrel, you still there?" I asked, not having heard the door close.

"I'm right here." His voice sounded soft in the darkness. "I wanna lie beside you. Is that okay? Just go to sleep," he told me and I did.

THE NEXT MORNING at nine, Darrel and I were awoken by Violet calling out for our attention.

"What the fuck?" Darrel said, rubbing his eyes.

"Get up, both of you. We need to talk right now," Roland commanded.

It sounded serious, so Darrel and I immediately got up and made our way over to the kitchen. We sat across from Roland and Violet. Violet was crying.

"Yeah, you're fucked," Roland said, looking at my face.

"What's the matter now?" I asked, looking at Violet.

"Roland doesn't want me to work no more."

"I thought you understood." Roland's voice sounded concerned.

"But these are my friends, this is my life!" Violet moaned.

"But now you have something more important to think about," he said, patting her stomach gently. He turned towards Darrel and me. "I think you guys are living foolishly, man, both of you, and the others are taking stupid risks."

"Like what?" Darrel asked.

"For one thing, you guys are living in this shitty apartment. What the hell for? It's not like you can't afford to get into a nicer neighbourhood. The cops know this building. They're here every other day. Why do you guys still want to live here?"

"I don't want to live here," I said.

"Good 'cause you guys are moving out of here, ASAP. Start looking for another place today. Another thing, I don't know how the two of you feel about it, but I'm sure you guessed that my leadership of the Diablos has been minimal these days. I don't have time to deal with gang bullshit. I'm only interested in making money and building a crew, with Diablos or not. I know Gina's pissed. I know Shawn doesn't like it either—don't worry about that goof, he's in jail. Cops found that knife."

"Shawn's an idiot," I added.

"You two don't get along?" Roland asked.

"No fucking way. I'm glad he's in jail, the piece of shit."

"Well, I heard Gina plans to do me in. It's not going to happen, because nobody knows where I'm staying, except of course my wife over here," he said, grabbing Violet's hand and kissing it. "I guarantee that I'll do her in before she gets a chance to do me and if she survives, she's as good as dead. That shit Gina and Shawn pulled with that Jay character was sloppy. The reason that cop beat on you yesterday was to get at Gina and they know she's behind it. One thing I know about Shawn is, he ain't no rat. Shawn wouldn't tell those cops Gina was there. Gina won't be selling for me much longer, but I don't want her to know. I gotta wait for her to make the first move. Then I'm gonna pounce. Violet will be outta the game soon, being my girl and carrying my baby puts her in a high-risk situation, especially with Gina. If she can't get to me, she might try to get to her. You understand all this?"

Both of us nodded.

"Darrel, you're my brother and I trust you. I know you wouldn't turn on your own brother. And you . . ." He turned his dark eyes towards me. "I always had a good feeling about you, ever since you were just a kid. I'm asking you two to watch over my girl. Protect her when I'm not around, be her guardians. If for any reason Violet gets in trouble and I'm not around, bring her to this address. She knows where the spare key is." He handed Darrel a piece of paper and motioned him to show it to me. "Think you can remember that?"

"For sure," I said, looking over at Violet.

"Don't tell anyone what we talked about, not even that other broad that lives here. Got it?"

"Yeah, of course, Darrel said. "We won't let anything happen to your girl."

"Good," Roland said.

"When do I have to quit?" Violet asked him.

"Baby, when I got my house all nice and set up for you, then you quit." He reached over and pinched her chin. "Violet, don't worry. I'll take care of you." He kissed Violet goodbye and headed out the door.

"Things are so fucked," Violet said.

"Gina's crazy," Darrel said.

I didn't know how to respond.

* * *

195

GINA AND JESSICA came home that afternoon while Violet and I were folding laundry.

"That girl's getting into Roland's head," Gina said to Jessica in the kitchen.

"Was I supposed to hear that?" Violet asked me as we sat on the floor of the bedroom folding clothes.

"Don't think so," I said, throwing a thong at her to ease the tension. Jessica popped her head into the room. "You guys find my North Carolina sweater yet?"

"No, it's not here, Jessica. We've looked," Violet said lifting up a bunch of clothes.

"Shit," she said walking all over the newly washed clothes. "Are you sure? It's kind of breezy out."

Violet shrugged. "See for yourself." She continued to fold the laundry.

"Violet, you're showing already!" Jessica said. She turned to me. "Don't you think she's showing?"

"I haven't noticed," I said, watching Gina pass by us in the hallway, giving us a sinister look.

"I'm happy you're having a baby," Jessica said, sitting next to her and helping her fold clothes.

"Why?"

"Because babies are the best thing in the world. Tyson and I've been trying to have a baby for the past four months now. It's just not happening. I think there's something wrong with him or maybe I've had too many abortions. What's with everybody getting pregnant these days? Did you know that Francine, the one that moved to Vancouver is pregnant again?"

Gina came into the bedroom carrying a load of clothes from the bathroom.

"Will you guys fold these up for me?" she said, dropping them to the floor. "I'm gonna catch some sleep for tonight. You hopping on with me?" Gina asked me before heading out to the couch.

"Yep," I said, avoiding eye contact.

"Shit, girl, we got to go. There are fiends to see," Jessica said, tapping on Violet's leg.

I NEVER told Violet what her mother said to me that day, "Take care of my daughter. I can't help her now," but it definitely changed things, even before this whole "Take care of Violet for me" thing from Roland. I looked at Violet in a different light. I always thought of her as transforming herself into a little gangster bitch. But now I saw Violet more clearly. She didn't belong in the projects; she never did and never would. She could have lived a decent life if she hadn't met us. She could have finished high school, gotten a good job and met a guy who wouldn't be putting her in danger like Roland was. I felt guilty because I knew this was true long before we started to deal drugs. I shouldn't have let her get this far. There was no way I was going to let anything happen to her. I was going to protect her the best way I knew how. By sticking close.

The other two girls couldn't figure out why Violet and

I were becoming so close. I got the feeling Jessica was jealous. After all Jessica had known me the longest and probably valued my friendship the most. If only I could tell her what was going on. I wasn't trying to make her feel jealous but I was sworn to secrecy. As for Gina, I knew she felt in her heart that I was no longer her friend and that she had to watch out for me because I was conspiring against her.

GINA AND I never technically made up. In fact, I was beginning not to trust her. One night on the road, I told Gina I thought it would be better if Violet and I worked together.

"Why? We've always worked together," Gina replied.

"I know but I'd like to work with her just in case something happens."

"Violet's a big girl. She can handle herself. You know what? I think Violet's paranoia is rubbing off on you, G Child. Since when are you Violet's keeper?" Gina asked angrily.

"Who says I'm trying to be her keeper? I just look out for the girl, that's all."

"You don't want to work with me no more. You can't stand me. You want me out of the game."

"Don't tell me what I'm thinking. I'll tell you what I'm thinking." I had had just about enough of Gina's miserable attitude.

"Don't be getting lippy with me. I'll throw you out of the fucking car!"

"I'm just telling you like it is," I said, not backing down. I knew she was stronger and tougher than me, but I couldn't let her know that because she'd walk all over me that way.

"Things are good the way they are. That's how they're gonna stay."

"What if I refuse to work with you?" I asked biting my lip.

"Then you don't work at all."

We drove the rest of the way in silence.

THAT MORNING when Gina and I got home, Jessica and Tyson were having an argument.

"That's what they were telling me all night last night!" he yelled, grabbing ahold of her arm.

Gina walked passed them like it didn't faze her but I stood in the hallway watching.

"It wasn't like that!" Jessica pleaded but Tyson only pushed her away.

"I'll find out!" he said and stormed out the door.

Jessica stood helplessly in the living room, her eyes red from crying. I wrapped her in my arms. Jessica buried her head in my chest and sobbed. We sat together on the couch and Jessica wouldn't let go.

"Tyson and I went to a party last night and there was this guy there that I fucked a long time ago, when I was like fourteen. When he saw Tyson and me together, he started laughing and he asked him why he was going around with such a slut."

"What did Tyson do?"

"He sent me home and he stayed at the party all night. I know he cheated on me. I could smell her on him. I don't think he wants to be with me anymore!"

"Tyson should have defended you or left the party with you; he shouldn't have sent you home. That should be reason enough for you to break up with him yourself."

"I love him, I can't," Jessica lowered her head. "Another thing, I know there's something funny going on between you, Violet and Gina, something I don't know about," Jessica said.

"Jessica, don't worry about that."

"But I do worry. Does it have anything to do with me?"

"No, nothing to do with you."

"Who then?" Gina said, coming out of the bedroom still fully dressed and her black eyes almost piercing a hole through me.

"I should ask you that," I said, moving Jessica's head and standing face to face with Gina. She looked me up and down, smirked and walked back into the bedroom. Soon after Violet and Jessica headed off to sell crack.

I WAS SLEEPING peacefully on the couch when I was awakened by the apartment door flying open and banging against the wall. My first thought was police, so I jumped up and looked around but when I saw that it was only Violet and Jessica, I sat down relieved. My relief was short-lived, though. They looked frightened.

"What happened?" I asked.

"We were robbed," Jessica said.

"How much?" I asked.

"Six hundred dollars' worth."

Just then Gina stormed out of the bedroom.

"Why the fuck did you guys take fifteen rocks out?" she yelled. "I told you to only leave with five at all times. When you run out, you're supposed to come back here and reload!"

"We didn't want to bother coming back," Jessica said in her defence.

"Well, what happened?" Gina asked, trying to clear her head.

"We stopped at the gas station. There were three guys standing beside the gas pumps. When I got out of the car, I noticed them staring at me. I didn't think anything of it but when I left the store one of them asked me my name. I thought maybe they were trying to pick me up so I told them I had a boyfriend."

"'We're not trying to get with you. I just want to know if your name is Jessica or not.' As soon as he said that, I knew there was going to be trouble. I told him my name was Tammy but he knew I was lying. I got into the car and drove away but they followed us the whole way. I turned down different streets, trying to lose them, which I eventually did. I thought they were just messing around, trying to scare us. We got a call from Norton, so I turned the back lane and they rolled outta nowhere and blocked our car with theirs. Three of them jumped out, one had his gun and pressed it on Violet's window and told her to roll it down. He told us to give him our rocks.

"I told them I didn't know what they were talking about but they threatened to kill Violet if we didn't hand it over, so we did."

"They were driving an old beat-up brown Chevy Malibu," Violet said. "Roland's gonna flip out. I could have gotten killed." I stood beside her and she put her head on my shoulder.

"What are we gonna do about the crack?" Jessica asked me in a worried voice.

"You girls have to pay for it out of your own pockets," Gina snapped. "Jess, you gonna come with me to my brother's place and tell him what happened?" Gina demanded.

"I'll tell him," Violet said.

"No, I want to go to his place and tell him," Gina said.

"He doesn't live there anymore," Violet said.

"What do you mean, he moved?"

"Yes," she said.

"Where is he staying right now?"

"I don't know," Violet said.

I could tell this was going to get ugly, so I jumped in. "Gina, leave her alone. She's had a hard day."

"You stay out of this, G Child!" Gina said, pointing her finger in my face. Her eyes chased Violet again. "You must know where he is. Where is he, Violet?"

"I don't know," she said, looking down.

"You're not going to tell me where my own brother lives? Why are you fuckers doing this to me? I'm going to find out what this is about. I'm going to find out everything!" Gina stormed out of the apartment and Violet turned to me with fear in her eyes.

"I don't think you should stay here anymore. Actually, none of us should," I said.

"What the fuck, why the fuck is everyone against Gina?" Jessica asked.

"You girls better cough up that six hundred," I said, changing the subject.

"No!" Jessica said angrily. "I demand to know what's happening around here. I'll lose my mind if you don't tell me."

"Gina is not herself anymore, Jess. She's the one losing her mind," I said.

"She's our friend. I'm not turning against her."

"I'm warning you, Jessica, if you get in her way, there's not a thing she won't do to get you out," Violet said.

"This is scandalous," Jessica said, reaching into her pocket and handing me three hundred dollars. Violet did the same.

"Don't worry. Everything is okay," I told them. I wanted to console them but I was too tired because our shift at nine last night ended at ten this morning.

"I'm going back on the road. Violet, are you coming or what?" Jessica asked.

"No, I think I'll stay here," Violet said.

"I guess I'm going by myself." Jessica walked out.

"Do you care about your life?" Violet asked me. I didn't answer her right away but she repeated the question.

"I care," I whispered.

"I want out of this crazy lifestyle. I'm only hustling now to save up money. I want to provide good things for my baby. Haven't you noticed that ever since we started hustling, we've grown apart, all of us? Things just aren't the same anymore. Don't you want to be around decent people, have a respectable job or go back to school?"

"Yes," I said, lying down.

Violet covered her face with her hands, her shiny gold rings glistening from the sun shining through the blinds in the window. She was right. I didn't like the way our friendships were turning out and I thought about where I would be in a few years if I kept at it: jail or dead. Unlike Violet, I didn't have a loving family to go to, a boyfriend that loved me and a baby in my gut.

I WOKE UP at 9:30 with a killer headache. I took some Tylenol but it didn't help. I heard a knock on the door.

"Ouch," I said, holding my hand to my forehead.

"Open the door. It's me, Darrel. Why is it so dark in here?" he said, waltzing past me searching for the light switch.

"Violet must be asleep," I said, turning the light on for him.

"I found a place in the South End," Darrel said, turning to me.

"When you moving in?" I asked him, getting a drink from the fridge.

"In two days. Have you been looking for a new place yet?"

"No I . . ."

"Wanna stay with me?" Darrel asked.

"Oh, I don't know," I said, pouring Pepsi into a glass.

"I just came from my mom's. Destiny's over there for a few days."

"How are they doing?" I asked him, noticing concern in his face.

"Destiny's doing great. It's Mom I'm worried about. She looks down, not herself. She's always in bed and always looking so sad. She went to visit Dad in the pen today. Doesn't look like he'll be getting parole anytime soon."

"Maybe she's lonely," I said, turning to face him.

"She's depressed. She had to put up with so much being married to my dad."

"Maybe you should spend some more time with her."

"That's what I'm going to do. Destiny got registered for kindergarten today."

"Baby girl is growing up fast."

"How's Amanda?" I asked him, wondering if he had had a confrontation with her.

"I don't know. She's not going to be moving after all. She and that geeky boyfriend broke up. She's saying that all I care about is my bitches, not my daughter. I don't care about any bitches. There's only one woman I care about."

"Who's that?" I asked.

"I lied. There are two women I care about." Darrel walked down the hall and into the living room. "Where's my sister?"

"I don't know," I said, following him.

"Who's on the road?"

"Jessica, by herself"

"Doesn't Violet work with her?"

"Didn't you hear?"

"Hear what?"

"I thought you knew. Violet and Jessica got jacked earlier this morning. They got robbed—six hundred bucks. Gina thinks Street Ryders did it."

"Roland know about this yet?"

"I imagine he does."

"Is Violet okay?"

"Darrel, she's gotta hop out of the game soon. Gina asked her where Roland lived and Violet wouldn't tell her. I know Gina's your sister but she's fucked in the head, man. She's not the same anymore."

"I know, she's a snake." Then abruptly he changed the subject. "I went to Red River today . . ."

"Red River College?" I asked, surprised.

"I am gonna get my General Education Diploma. I figure I might as well. You know, I'm not getting any younger. I wanna have something behind me. One day I want a normal job if I can get one."

We heard the door open, and Gina and Shawn walked in.

"Good thing you're here," Gina said to Darrel. "Where does Roland live now?"

"What do you mean, 'now'?"

"He moved," she said. "I don't know where he is. I didn't even know he'd left that apartment. Seems like no one around here knows where he is." She paused, watching Darrel, but he didn't say a word. After a minute, Gina turned to me. "Can you go on the road tonight?"

The thought of going back on the road nearly made me vomit. I was so exhausted. "I'm dead tired, man. I just worked two shifts. I gotta get some sleep—there is no way I can go on the road tonight," I answered. "Why don't you go?"

"Can't. Me and Shawn are gonna look for Roland. Why don't you go out with her tonight, Darrel?" Gina said, running her fingers through her thick black hair.

I watched Gina's face. It had changed. She had aged but it seemed to have taken place overnight. Maybe I only noticed it now because I'd been trying to avoid looking at her since we'd been fighting so much. The slight bags under her eyes that she'd carried from childhood drooped lower than usual. The creases over her face were more prominent. She looked so much older than twenty-one.

"Fuck. I guess I can go. I'll just have to drink seven gallons of coffee, but hey that's okay."

"I can go with this good girl," Darrel said, winking at me.

I looked back at him. There was a different connection between us that had never happened before. The feeling made me uncomfortable but I couldn't figure out why I felt this way. He looked the same—tall, young, perfect skin and incredibly handsome. Still, there was something strange that lingered between us.

"Hmm," Gina moaned while she noticed the looks we gave each other. "I did some research today and found out who jacked the girls. The owner of that Chevy Malibu is a clown named Lester."

"He's a Street Ryder and we're going to get him," Shawn added.

"Know what happened last night?" Darrel asked Shawn.

"Huh?" he asked, his mouth still open.

"T. J. and Sparks got shot at last night. T. J. said he saw Silas Flett behind the wheel."

"Anything happen to them?" Gina asked.

"Naw, Silas missed but T. J.'s car has a few bullet holes in it. This game's gonna start taking lives soon."

"I never leave the crib without my gat in my belt," Shawn said showing us his nine mil.

I DECIDED I'd better get ready if I was going out with Darrel. On my way to the bedroom, Gina stopped me in the hallway.

"Sit down for a sec," she said as she motioned me to the couch. "You don't mind going with Darrel on the road, eh?" she asked.

"Nope."

Gina sat back and stared at me for a while and let out a little laugh.

"Fuck, you used to be a downass bitch," she said, flashing her infamous smile that I once marvelled to see but now I couldn't care less. "You're still mad at me over that shit with Jay, huh?"

"That happened a while ago," I said.

"But it did still happen. You know how I am when I get mad—there's just no self-control. I'm sorry I freaked out on you that night. I've been a bitch to you lately, but it's just that I feel you're against me all the time. I want things to go back to the way they were. I know it scares you that I tried to kill Jay but it doesn't bother me at all. What does bother me is that the cops are looking for me and Shawn. Those stupid cops are trying to pin me down with anything they can think of. Anything to get Gina McKay off the streets of Winnipeg.

"I talked to my mom yesterday and she was giving me shit about the cops harassing her, asking her where I was, where I lived, if I was still a Diablo, just a bunch of shit. Damn, I miss Shawn. He's taking the rap like a true gangster."

Darrel came out and sat down beside me again. "Everything all right?" he asked.

"Things are fine," I answered.

"Good," he said, putting his hand on my leg.

"All right then, you take care of yourself tonight," Gina said. We both stood up and exchanged the Diablo handshake.

Darrel and I were getting ready to leave when Gina blurted out, "Hey, you might need this." She pulled out a revolver and offered it to Darrel.

"I got mine." Darrel lifted up his jacket and showed us his gun tucked in his belt.

"You take it." She handed it to me and I shoved it in my purse. It made me feel a bit better that Gina cared about my well-being but it didn't mean I trusted her.

CHAPTER TWELVE

GANGSTER LOVE

The night was young. We had sold twenty-five rocks in two hours and our phone was just banging off the hook. I thought about how I had left the apartment on good terms with Gina, something that hadn't happened in a long time.

"You think Gina's straightened out?" I asked Darrel as he headed back to the apartment to reload.

"She knows better than to fuck around. Gina loves Roland, she loves us. She wouldn't do anything to us."

"Just like the days of old," I said as I gulped down a mouthful of Old English Malt Liquor from the bottle we had brought with us. "So much for coffee. Yuck, that stuff's sick! I'm too old to be drinking this shit."

"You're a kid," Darrel said.

"I'm still a year older. Show me some respect, B.G."

"Oh, so I'm a baby gangster now, eh? I ain't no baby. I'm a man, a grown man."

* * *

WE MADE three more stops but it was dead for the next two hours. Darrel and I were both pretty drunk and began to talk nonsense.

"Why don't we just call it a night?" Darrel said to me with a sly smile.

"Are you sure?"

"Positive."

"Well, where are we supposed to go? We can't go back to the apartment."

"We could go to my mom's"

"Naw, I don't wanna wake her."

"She won't wake up. C'mon, I'll take you there."

Darrel parked in the back lane near his mother's house. I staggered out of the car while Darrel fumbled with the keys. We tiptoed into the house and headed downstairs. He closed the basement door and gently grabbed me by the waist and put his lips on mine and gave me a soft kiss. I smelled the alcohol on him and wondered if I smelled as bad and if he noticed or even cared. He took my hand and we walked into the den.

"Remember this place?" he said, sitting on the single bed in the middle of the room.

"Yeah," I said, standing next to him.

Before I could say anything else, he gently pushed me on the bed and lay on top of me. In my fog, I couldn't find words to tell him to stop and I wasn't sure I wanted him to. He ran his fingers through my hair and touched my face as we kissed. I felt Darrel's body tense up as our tongues darted in and out of each other's mouths.

"Hey!" a voice in my subconscious yelled. "This is

Darrel McKay, Gina's younger brother, your childhood friend." The butterflies began flying around my stomach and that strange but enjoyable sensation filled my breasts and the depth of my being. His soft lips swirled around the base of my neck and gave me goosebumps all along my spine. I rubbed his back and he whispered my name softly between his deep moans and heavy sighs. I wanted him, I wanted to feel all of his masculinity. My body ached for more but that little voice in the back of my head shouted, "No." I wanted it to happen. I loved this feeling but as his hand reached up to cup my breast, it was as if a siren went off in my head. I gently pushed him away and rolled to the side of the bed.

"What's wrong?" he asked.

"We can't do this."

"Why not?" he asked as his fingertips glided over my shoulders.

"We're both drunk; we'll regret this in the morning."

"I know exactly what I'm doing. Doesn't this feel right to you?" he said as he came up behind me and wrapped me in his arms.

I turned to face him and planted a seductive kiss on him. This time the urge was stronger than before. We got more physical with each other and the voice was beginning to fade away. He ran his hands up and down my back.

"I've wanted you for so long," he kept saying to me over and over again. All of a sudden he stopped and said, "I'm sorry. I didn't mean to pressure you."

"Huh?"

"I want you, trust me I do, but I think you're right; we should wait till a better time."

He kissed me lightly on the forehead and placed my hands on his chest and lay next to me.

I had no idea in the world how Darrel could shut off his hormones in the middle of that love scene, but I dared not question it because I knew he was right.

"We're pretty drunk," I added.

"Yeah, I'm not used to drinkin' no more." He sat up and took off his shirt.

I could see his skin in the moonlight that shone through the window. I licked my lips; damn, was he ever sexy. His creamy brown skin rippled up with abs on his flat stomach. I could only imagine what his skin would taste like.

"Aren't you going to get comfortable, take your clothes off?" he suggested.

"Why not?" I said, feeling brave.

"Why won't you give me a chance?" he said, lying back down.

I turned to face him. "What do you mean?"

"I want to be with you, more than one night. You probably think I would fuck and leave. But I'm not about that," he said.

"Where is all this coming from, Darrel? Damn, you're just trying to get laid but why are you trying to get it from me?"

"I'm not trying to get pussy. I could get that from anyone. I've known you for a real long time. You've been one of the few people and the only girl that kept it real, ya

214

know? I'd never use and abuse you like that. I care a lot about you but you don't see me that way."

"It's not that."

"What then?"

"You're Gina's brother. I've known you since we were little kids."

Darrel took ahold of my chin and melted my eyes as he looked into them. "Sexy, don't you know that friends make the best boyfriends?"

"That's what Jay told me and look how he turned out," I said, remembering how he had hurt me.

"Jay, that fucking cracker. I hated that goof. C'mon, don't change the subject. You'll never know if you don't take the chance. Don't you want a boyfriend?"

"I do and I don't. I don't really think about it. I try not to at least."

"Sounds to me like you're lonely and you don't even know it. There's no need for you to feel like that. G Child, I need somebody I can trust, someone that will be there for me, someone that makes me feel happy when I see her. I can't think of any girl who makes me happier than you."

We were both silent for a moment. I was overwhelmed. It was kind of like when a little girl has a crush on a boy in elementary school and she finds out he has a crush on her too. I was confused because something inside me told me Darrel and I weren't dating material, but could I be wrong?

"Is it okay if I hold you?" Darrel asked as he moved closer to me.

"I guess it couldn't hurt," I said as I crawled into his arms. I felt at peace.

"Darrel?" I broke the silence.

"Yeah?" he said, taking ahold of me tighter in his arms.

"Are you really gonna get your General Education Diploma?"

"What?" He let out a laugh. "Where did that come from?"

"Are you?"

"Everyone will be surprised when I show 'em my diploma."

"Does your brother know?"

"No, he wouldn't care. He's too busy thuggin' but he's been slowing down, you know, with Violet being pregnant and all."

"Are you gonna hop out of the game?"

"I want to. That's the whole point of taking my GED, so I can get a decent job. I'm gonna try to get custody of my daughter."

"I want out of the game too." I quickly covered my mouth with my hand. I couldn't believe what I had admitted.

"You shouldn't hop out right away. Do something with that money first."

"Save it?"

"Yeah, then hop out."

"That's what I'm going to do," I said, before closing my eyes and falling into a deep sleep.

DARREL AND I went for breakfast early the next morning. I was terribly hungover and wasn't able to eat much. Darrel then dropped me off at home and kissed me goodbye.

"Aren't you coming?" I asked, waiting for him to shut his car off.

"No, I want to spend some time with my daughter."

"All right," I said, walking away.

"Hey, I meant everything I said last night, I wanna be with you in every way. You're the one for me," he shouted out his window. He smiled and drove away.

I ENTERED the apartment strangely lighthearted with a feeling of newness and wonderful beginnings. Gina was pacing the apartment with Jessica right behind her. Jessica was holding on to her stomach tightly. "I feel sick, G Child. I think I got food poisoning."

Gina stuck out her hand, meaning she wanted the money Darrel and I had made, a total personality swing from last night's apology. Then she threw a piece of paper at my chest.

"What the fuck?" I asked angrily.

"Read it!"

> To Whom It May Concern:
> I don't like what we've become. I have sat back for months now watching us drift apart, yelling at each other every night. That's not

what our friendship was about before. We would die to protect each other and now all we care about is money. This damn, dirty money is ruining us, it is ruining me. Do you think people really respect us? They're just afraid of us. Is that the kind of respect you girls want? People look down at us. The type of people that look up to us are lower than the dust. What happened to me yesterday has brought me to the final edge. I don't want this life for myself anymore. I have a baby to think about now, so I have to be extra careful with my life because it's not only my own, it's my child's as well. I am better than this and so are all of you. I know that you girls will be mad at me for a while, but maybe one day you will see things the way I see them and if you don't, I understand. I only ask that you understand my situation.

I love you and will always miss you.

Sincerely,
Violet Marino

Gina tore the paper out of my hand. "What kind of bullshit is this? What did you put in her head?" Gina said to me.

"Nothing, I didn't tell her anything." I was glad Violet had come to her senses

"Yeah, right. You did and I know it." Gina began to pace around the room.

"Violet has a mind of her own. I think she made the right decision, she's thinking like a woman. Jess, relax for a bit," I said, noticing her face turning pale.

"So you want out then too?" Gina asked me.

"I never said that, but if I did want out, you'd be the first to know."

"Hurry up and get ready, Jessica," Gina said, turning to her.

"I can't believe you'd ask me to get ready when I feel this sick," Jessica complained.

"Fuckin' Violet should have let us know at least two weeks in advance. She can't just leave like that!"

"What's the big deal? It's not like you can't get someone else," I said, hoping Gina wouldn't retaliate against Violet.

"That isn't the point, you know. Like what the fuck is wrong with you?"

"I don't want to work today, Gina," Jessica insisted.

"Why don't you do it?" Jessica said, looking over at me.

"No way, I'm not a fucking machine. I want and need sleep."

"This isn't fair. Why should I be forced to work when I feel like I'm gonna throw up?"

"Stop acting like a little kid," Gina screamed.

"No, Gina, I am sick of you bossing everyone around. I am not working today. Fuck you." Jessica stomped out of the room.

Gina followed her and slammed the door behind her. I could hear some thumping and crashing. I rushed into the room. Gina was pounding Jessica's face.

"AH!" Jessica screamed at the top of her lungs. I grabbed Gina by the hair and pulled her off Jessica. I gave Jessica my hand and helped her up.

"Aw, look at these two fools," Gina said in her gangster voice. I gave her a dirty look and held Jessica in my arms. "You went soft on me, didn't you!" she said, stepping up to me and giving me her classic mad-dog look.

"Your role just turned sour," I said to her.

"Jessica Fox, you're nothing but a hood rat bitch," Gina screamed. "If it wasn't for me, you'd be nothing—nothing, you hear me? All you'd be is some damn hoochie, just like your alcoholic mother. You would have never met Tyson, the love of your pathetic life. You're not good enough for my cousin, you fucking skanky bitch!"

Jessica struggled to get away from my grip. "Stop!" Jessica cried.

"Stop!" Gina mocked her.

"Shut the fuck up and leave her alone!" I told Gina with a stern voice. Gina laughed as Jessica cried.

"Shut up!" I yelled, not sure if I was yelling at Gina or Jessica. Gina stuck her tongue out at us.

"You're pathetic," I said, grabbing Jessica by the arm and heading for the door.

As we went by, Gina pushed at us and we fell into the wall. I didn't let go of Jess. Gina charged at us both but I had enough time to pull out my knife. I stuck it in front of her face. She stopped dead in her tracks. Her jaw dropped as she stared at the knife and then at me in disbelief. Then as I watched, her eyes filled with intense rage, and she pulled out her gun and pointed it at my face. My heart raced and jumped into my throat. I had never had a gun aimed at me before. I had seen Gina point her gun at people, and now I knew the fear and anger that was felt on the other side. We remained in the same position for what seemed like an eternity. Our eyes were fixed on each other and I watched as Gina's expression changed. The corners of her mouth trembled and her angry eyes began to water. She's going to pull the trigger, I kept on thinking, and for the first time in a very long time, I thought about my parents.

Gina took a few steps back, put her gun down and stared into our dresser mirror. She looked at her reflection like she was seeing it for the first time. She ran the barrel of the gun along the tattoos on her arms, then up and down her chest. She let out a blood-curdling scream, raised her gun and shot at her own reflection. The mirror shattered into a million pieces and she ran out of the apartment.

For a few minutes, Jessica and I just hung onto each other without saying anything. Then finally I said, "We gotta get out of here, Jess."

We quickly gathered up some of Jessica's things and jumped on a bus to Tyson's. He didn't say much when we explained what had happened, only that he wanted some time alone with Jessica, so my visit was short. I promised Jessica I'd see her soon.

* * *

WHEN DARREL found out about the confrontation with Gina, he begged me to stay with him at his new apartment. Since I had no other place to go, I agreed.

"I'll talk to her," Darrel said as he helped me carry my bags into the apartment.

"Don't bother."

"She'll come around," he assured me.

"No, Darrel, I don't want her to come around. I want nothing to do with her."

"Yes, you do. Y'all are just fighting, it'll be all right."

"No, it won't. There's no going back. Actually, you know, I'll stay at a motel for a while, until I find my own place," I said, picking up my bags.

"Why?"

"I feel uncomfortable," I said. Something in the deep pit of my gut was telling me not to stay with him. I was frightened.

"Listen, Gina is my sister and I don't want anything bad to happen to her but everyone is sick of the way she throws her weight around. You know you're not the only one that's pissed off at her right now, don't you?" Darrel took ahold of my hand.

"I know," I said, rubbing his hand with my fingers.

"Please stay," Darrel said as he gazed into my eyes.

"Why do you want me to stay? I pulled a knife on your sister. She was like my best friend, I . . ."

"You were defending yourself."

I couldn't help myself, tears began rolling down my cheeks. It was the first time anybody had seen me cry.

"None of that," he said, wiping my tears away.

All of a sudden it hit me like a ton of bricks: I felt vulnerable. I felt like I needed his touch. It seemed like the only thing that could make me feel better.

"Thanks," was all I could manage to say.

DARREL AND I spent the entire day together. We went to the mall and bought stuff he needed around the apartment—a new shower curtain, pots and pans, etc. I couldn't help but stare at him in the checkout line. It was almost as if I was seeing him for the first time. His hands were beautiful: they were strong and masculine, and I wondered what they could do to me if I let them.

"I'M BEAT," I said, plopping on the leather couch in his apartment.

"Me too," he said, lying on the loveseat next to the couch.

He lifted up his white T-shirt and began to fan himself off. At that moment, I just wanted to jump on top of him, and it took an incredible amount of control to stop myself. I was getting hot just looking at him.

As if he could read my mind, he looked over at me. "I'm going to bed."

"Guess I'm sleeping on the couch?" I slid down the cushion.

"Lie with me, nothing will happen."

An open invitation. I couldn't control myself any longer. "What if I want something to happen?"

"Do you?" he asked.

"Yes," I said.

Darrel melted my heart with his sexy gaze. I got up, feeling like a cat in heat, and sat beside him, putting my hand on his leg. He took my hand and began to kiss my fingers, then the palm of my hand and finally, tiny little kisses on the inside of my wrist. I'd never felt anything so outrageous.

"Take me to the bedroom, Darrel," I said letting my mouth speak before my brain could catch up.

I kissed his mouth as we moved into the bedroom together, our mouths never leaving each other. I lay down and felt his body press against mine and that was about enough to send me into ecstasy. His kisses were long and deep and wet. I felt absolutely blissful as he kissed, licked and caressed every curve of my quivering body and tasted all of my juices. I needed Darrel, my body ached and my femininity throbbed. Our bodies were finally together, in union, in sync, and the feeling was like nothing I had ever felt in my life. His words edged me closer and closer to orgasm: there was no holding back now. Any inhibition or fantasy no longer existed; we were living it now. Between our voices that sounded like song and our jerking, sweaty bodies, Darrel's excited voice told me that he loved me. In the heat of the moment, I realized I felt the same way.

IT HAD BEEN five days since the fallout and nobody had seen or heard from Gina. Jessica and I weren't hustling anymore. But in spite of wanting to change my life, I felt the emptiness of my pockets grow day by day. Darrel and I were continuing our love affair with a fiery passion. We talked about making our own clique. He thought it was a good idea until he went back to school again.

"So, is this a promise?" I said, rolling on to my stomach and putting my head on his chest.

"G Child, I'm serious. You and I should work together, save enough money and both go to school. I don't wanna be selling crack and worrying about studying at the same time."

"Yeah," I said, contented.

"This is what you want, isn't it?"

"Oh yes. Darrel, you have no idea." I held him tight.

CHAPTER THIRTEEN

A DEATH IN THE FAMILY

It was the fifth night since the fight and I had just gotten back from the gym. I was looking forward to coming home because Darrel had promised to cook me some El Salvadorian food. I was in the shower getting my body nice and clean for later that night when I heard my cell phone ring. I jumped out of the shower and looked at the call display but it read only "private name, private number." I usually didn't answer unknown calls but then I thought of Violet; maybe she needed my help.

It was Darrel. "I'm picking you up right now," he said, his voice cracking.

"Darrel, is everything okay?" I asked.

"It's my mom—she's in the hospital."

DARREL WAS buzzing the door within a few short minutes and I rushed outside to meet him. We held each other's hands tightly as he drove to the hospital.

"What's wrong with her?" I asked.

"She was shopping with my Auntie Linda and all of a sudden she collapsed in the mall. I hope it's nothing too serious 'cause I don't know what I'd do without her," Darrel said, turning into the hospital's parking lot.

He ran through the doors of the emergency room like a madman and rushed to the nurse at the front desk. "Lenore McKay, my mom, is in here. What happened to her?"

"Next of kin?" the nurse asked without looking up at him.

"I'm her son."

"The doctor will be right with you."

Darrel and I sat down and waited nervously for the doctor.

"There's my Auntie Linda," Darrel said as he got up and met her at the end of the hallway.

I couldn't hear them but I could tell by Darrel's reaction that it was bad news. He buried his face in his hands while his aunt held him.

The emergency room doors flew open and Roland came storming in. He headed in the direction of his brother and aunt. I read Roland's lips as they formed the words, "Oh Lord."

I headed towards the family but before I could approach them, Aunt Linda had led them into a hospital room and shut the door. I peeked through a little rectangular window and saw Linda, Roland and Darrel standing over their mother's lifeless body.

"She's dead," I whispered to myself.

* * *

IT WAS a full hour before anybody came out of the room. Darrel was the last to leave. Aunt Linda's and Roland's faces were wet with tears but the look on Darrel's face sent a chill down my spine. He had obviously been crying as well but he looked much worse than the others. Darrel looked empty, darkened with despair. He slowly dragged himself towards me, never taking his eyes off the floor.

"Take the car. I'm going with my aunt. My mother is dead." He didn't look at me, only past me, as if in a trance.

I wanted to ask what happened but held back.

"Darrel, I'm sorry, so sorry," I said as I reached over to hug him but he pulled away.

"I've got to go," he said as he walked away.

I stood in the emergency room dumbfounded. I was about to leave when I saw a nurse leave Lenore's room.

"Excuse me, I'm a friend of Mrs. McKay. Could you tell me what's happened to her?"

"Sorry to say, but Mrs. McKay had a massive heart attack. The doctors tried reviving her but she didn't pull through." The nurse put her hand on my shoulder, probably expecting me to cry but I didn't. I just told her thanks and went home.

I STAYED UP all night worrying about Darrel. The last time I looked at the clock it was already 6:30 a.m. and he wasn't home yet. I called everywhere but Darrel was nowhere to be found.

I was in the laundry room later that day when Darrel surprised me by opening the door with full force.

"I've been worried," I said.

"Gina's in jail. She got caught drunk driving and gave the police a hard time."

"That's why Gina wasn't there last night," I said, slamming the dryer door shut.

"She knows but she's still in the remand centre. They're letting her out on the day of the funeral. I gotta go right away—I only came back to change. I'm taking the car," Darrel said coldly.

"Darrel, wait, where are you going?" He ignored me and walked out of the room, leaving me wondering in silence.

I DECIDED to pay Jessica a visit and let her know what was going on. I hopped on a bus to Tyson's sister's place. Tyson came to the door of the little white house but he didn't look too happy to see me. He stood silent, wearing nothing but a pair of black track pants with his hair tied up in a braid.

I dug my hands deep into my pockets. "Is Jessica here?"

"She's inside," he said, staring at me without moving.

"Well, can I come in?" I asked, giving him an odd glance. Tyson gave me a last look and walked away inside, leaving the door open wide.

I stepped inside. I made my way to the living room

and sat on the armchair, expecting Tyson to tell Jessica that I was waiting. I heard footsteps slowly walking down the stairs. Jessica came around the corner, her blond hair tousled all over her face. She forced a smile and sat down.

"I got some bad news," I told her.

"I already know. Tyson told me this morning. How's the family doing?"

"I don't know. I haven't seen any of them yet."

"Give Darrel my love," she said, curling herself up in a ball.

"What's wrong?" I said, noticing she looked very tired.

"Bad night," she whispered, her voice trembling.

"Are you crying?" I said, walking up to her and kneeling by her side. She stared at the blank television set and ignored my question.

"Isn't this a warm welcome," I said, teasing her. "First Tyson bites my head off and now you're ignoring me. Did I come at a bad time? Were you guys doin' it?" I asked, with a smile, trying to cheer her up.

"No, I'm sorry. It's really nice to see you," she said, sniffling.

"Think you weren't going to see me again? Uncover your face, Jessica."

"No," she said, her voice trembling with fear.

"Jessica don't be an idiot. What are you hiding?" I got up and attempted to brush her hair from her face but she pushed my arms away. Not before I saw her two black eyes and a fat lip.

"What the hell happened to you? Is this from Tyson, Tyson beats you?"

"Shh!" she put her finger over her mouth. I turned around and walked towards the staircase. Jessica jumped up and grabbed hold of my jacket. "What are you gonna do?" she asked.

"Take him out myself," I replied, still walking with her pulling on me.

She jumped in front of me and pleaded, "You can't do that. Please don't go up there!"

"He should learn to pick on somebody his own size," I said, feeling my blood boil.

Poor Jessica, she was just a tiny little thing. Tyson was a monster compared to her. Only a coward would do a thing like this.

"Don't do this to me. It will only make things worse!" she continued begging.

"I'm not doing anything to you. He's the one that's hitting you. What the fuck is wrong with him?"

Instead of answering, Jessica grabbed me by the arm and took me outside. We sat on the front step.

"It started a few days after I moved in here. One day, I wanted to go out and chill with a girl I met at a party but he didn't want me to. He told me he was coming home early, so I didn't go out and I waited for him. He left me at home all day and he came back at 3:30 in the morning and he was drunk on top of that. I asked him where he was and he got upset. He told me I was being too controlling and started pushing me around. He pulled my hair and slammed me into the wall. He

231

started to say all these mean things to me, like he never loved me and all he cared about was his money and his hoes and I was a worthless piece of meat to him. That was what hurt me the most. Once he realized that he'd hurt me, he was really sorry and he promised to never be mean to me again. Another time he starting pushing me around and scared me by putting his brass knuckles to my head. Just like the first time, he realized what he did and was sorry . . ."

Jessica paused and looked at me. She looked lost.

"Jessica, you don't have to stay here. We'll get a place, you, Darrel and me"

"Darrel?" she asked.

"Darrel and I, we're, you know . . ."

"Together?"

"Pretty much." I smiled.

"He always liked you, but what about Gina?"

"She's in jail right now." As soon as I said that, Tyson opened the front door, hitting me in the back.

"Sorry, didn't know you were sitting there," he said.

"I'm going to the store, want anything?" he asked Jessica as he lit up a cigarette.

"I'm fine," she said.

He walked up to her, lifted her face up, kissed her on the cheek and left.

"I'm glad Gina is in jail. Maria, Tyson can be really sweet," Jessica said, watching him as he turned the corner.

"What happened this time?" I said, looking at her bruised face.

"He was in a bad mood. He took it out on me."

"Jessica, you have got to get out of here," I said, knowing her life was in danger.

"I can't leave him. I love him, he's my life."

"But if you stay you might not have any life left!"

"What would I do? Where would I go?"

"Don't worry about that. I already told you that you could stay with us. We'll make our own clique again."

"This wasn't supposed to happen," she said as she walked over to the fence.

"Of course not," I said, standing next to her.

"No, you don't understand what I mean. I had my whole life planned out. I was gonna model for a while, make it big. My face was gonna be in magazines all over the world, they promised me. But I gave it up for this."

"For what?"

"For this fuckin' trash-ass ghetto life. All I cared about was being cool, fitting in, getting a man. I forgot about my dreams. Now I have nothing."

"I am telling you that you can get outta here, that we'll hustle again . . ."

"I can't work with you," Jessica frowned.

"Why not?" I said, sure she would have jumped at the chance.

"I'm working for Tyson."

"You're what?" I grabbed her arm and pulled her towards me, resisting the urge to slap her myself.

"I go out every night, under the bridge. I wait with Tyson, watching me and a few other girls working the track. Then I get picked up and I make my money, he takes half of it. I am not the Jessica you knew before. I am a different person now. It's like everything in the past is just a distant dream—it feels like it never happened. I know I can't go back to the way things were."

"When did all this start?"

"When I moved in."

Tyson appeared less than a block away with a slurpie in hand.

"I'm not leaving without you, and you're still Jessica, my friend!"

"You've got to go," she said, walking back towards the house.

"If you care about me, you'll leave."

"Do you think I'm gonna leave you here with this monster?"

"I don't have a choice."

"Yes you do, you can come with me. I'll take care of you. You don't have to do this anymore."

Tyson was coming closer and I became desperate.

"Why are you working for him? You were so against that!"

"He loves me!" Jessica said with such strong faith.

"But he wants you to go on track? Like that really makes sense. Open your eyes. I don't want you having an early funeral. I'm talking about the streets and the streets are fucked up. You could get killed out there or in here if you don't stop all this!"

"I could get killed selling crack too!" she said.

Tyson opened the gate and we both fell silent.

"What's the big secret?" Tyson asked us, his eyes squinting as the sun's rays hit his face.

"She was just leaving," Jessica said looking at me.

She didn't want my help. It seemed like she didn't want my friendship anymore either. I looked at Tyson and wanted to beat the living shit out of him but I knew it would only make matters for Jessica even worse, so I turned and left.

CHAPTER FOURTEEN

PAIN IS LOVE

I headed back home to find Darrel sitting in the dark with only the light of a single candle and a picture of his mother beside it. He didn't acknowledge my presence at first but then looked up at me with his dark eyes.

As I reached for the light switch, Darrel said, "No, don't turn it on."

"I went to see Jessica. Rough day."

"Funeral is in three days. Are you going?" Darrel asked me without taking his eyes off his mother's photo.

"Of course."

"I'm not. I don't want to see her like that."

"It might make you feel better."

"How would it make me feel better? You think I want to see my mom lying in a coffin?"

"I'm sorry. I meant that maybe it would give you some closure, you know?"

He got up, went into the bedroom and slammed the door.

I knocked on the bedroom door but there was no answer, so I decided to leave it alone.

ON THE DAY of Lenore McKay's funeral, Darrel was nowhere to be found, so I made my way to the church alone. The church was full and when it was time to pay our final respects, I saw the whole McKay family, including Lenore's husband, Ed, and Gina, Roland and Violet close by his side. As I walked past the open casket, I saw Lenore's body in a black dress adorned with all the best jewellery. She didn't look like the same woman at all, and I was glad in that moment that Darrel wasn't here to see his mom like this.

Even though I couldn't see her, I knew Gina's eyes were burning holes right through me. Maybe she thought I had no right being there.

After the service, I walked out of the church and headed to the parking lot. I was about to open the door to the shitty Tempo when I felt a hand on my shoulder. I turned to see Violet standing behind me with tears in her eyes as she reached over to hug me.

"She was so good to me. She took me in when I had nowhere to go."

"I know, you were close to her," I said, holding her.

"Where's Darrel?" she asked me, wiping away her tears.

"He didn't want to come."

"The whole family is worried about him," Violet said.

"I don't even know what to say or do about him, Violet. He's so angry all the time and he disappears in the middle of the night and doesn't come back until the next day."

"Be there for him. He needs you right now," she said as we watched Lenore's coffin being carried out by Ed, Roland and four of Lenore's brothers.

"Are you coming to the burial?"

"No, I'm going to try to find Darrel. I'm worried about him."

"I'm staying at my parents' house. Come see me soon, okay?" Violet asked as she hugged me goodbye.

"I will."

THE FIRST PLACE I went to search for Darrel was his mother's place. I didn't see any sign of him, so I went to the Latin Gardens, a place Darrel sometimes stopped to have a couple of drinks, but he wasn't there either. I searched everywhere I could think of but he was nowhere to be found. I went back to the apartment only to find Darrel just opening the door.

"You weren't at the cemetery," he said.

"I was looking for you. You were there?"

"Nobody saw me but I was there."

"Come here," I said opening my arms to him.

"No, don't, I just need to be alone. Amanda had the nerve to show up with my baby girl at the funeral," he said, sitting on the couch, lighting a cigarette.

"Why is that surprising to you? Your mom is Destiny's grandmother."

"Mom didn't have respect for her. That scandalous

whore fucked with my head. Bitch is always gonna be in my life. Girls are fucked—you can't trust them."

"That's not fair. You know me better than that," I said, putting my hand on his shoulder but he pushed it off.

"I thought I knew her too. I should just be alone. I don't need anyone anyway."

He got up and walked into the bedroom, slamming the door. I lay on the couch and couldn't help but feel sorry for myself. What could I say or do to make Darrel feel better? I felt selfish though I didn't know how much longer I could put up with his bad behaviour because he was starting to take his hurt out on me. It was like my whole world was a windstorm and the people I loved were being blown away from me. For the first time in a long time, I cried myself to sleep.

I WAS awakened an hour later by Darrel tugging on my underwear and trying to slip them off of me.

"I'm glad you're feeling better," I said as I helped him take them off. He then pushed himself into me hard and reached so far up that it hurt.

"Ouch! You're being too rough!" I said, trying to push his shoulders but Darrel yanked my hair back and didn't let up. "Stop!" I yelled but he kept on. Finally he stopped and climbed off me.

"What?" he asked annoyed.

"That hurts," I said, sitting up and holding my stomach.

"You liked it," he said, forcing me down and climbing back on top of me but I closed my legs so he couldn't get inside me.

"What has gotten into you?" I demanded.

"Stop freaking out. Don't act like you don't want me to fuck you, I know you wanna get fucked."

I tried speaking but his hand was pressed too hard against my mouth.

"C'mon girl, tell me how you want it."

I bit his hand and he quickly yanked it away from my face.

"Damn bitch, you bit me!" he said, slapping me across the face.

I slapped him back and rushed to the bathroom and shut the door behind me. This was a nightmare. I couldn't believe what was happening.

"Open the door," Darrel said quietly.

"No."

"C'mon, I'm sorry. I didn't mean to hurt you. I'm really sorry, baby, open up."

"Darrel, what the fuck is going on with you?"

"I'm going through a lot right now; please can you open the door?"

I sat in the bathroom, curled up in a ball against the door. I held my stomach. It was terribly sore. It took twenty minutes of him begging me to open the door and when I did, he took ahold of my hand and led me back to bed.

"I'm sorry," he said as he held me and we lay in silence.

DARREL SEEMED to get better over the next few days. He even laughed once in a while. We started hustling with some new non-gang-affiliated guys who were working under Roland. I didn't like them much. They were rude and obnoxious and I overheard one of them saying that girls didn't belong in a car selling crack; they belonged in a car selling head.

Darrel asked me if Jessica wanted to hop back into the game but I told him that her slanging days were over. Selling crack was becoming more dangerous by the minute. There were more and more shootings on both sides, and two of our dealers had been killed in the North End. The game was coming to an end for a lot of people and I felt it was time that it ended for me too. But when I mentioned this to Darrel, he became upset.

"You can't. I need you on my team," he said counting his wad of cash.

"You told me you wanted out of this shit too. Remember telling me you wanted to go to school and all of that?"

"Things are different now. You're basically the only one I trust. You can't leave." Darrel had become so much like Gina that I even noticed a physical resemblance I hadn't seen before. It totally turned me off.

AS THE DAYS went by, I was beginning to feel that Darrel and I getting together was a mistake and I felt stupid for having put faith in love again; I felt even more stupid for having tried it with Darrel McKay. After his mother's death, Darrel's affection for me subsided so quickly that I didn't know him anymore. I began to wonder about Destiny, and I hoped he wouldn't be abusive towards her as well.

I STOPPED at a party one night in Central with three homies from back in the day: Omar, Francine and Nathan. I had a knot in my stomach, a bad feeling, but I ignored it and walked in behind my bros. We stepped inside and people rushed to greet us right away. I recognized a few faces but two stood out immediately: Darrel's and Jessica's. Jessica was drunk and busy mingling, and Darrel was laughing it up with a couple of guys I didn't recognize.

"Your boyfriend's here," Omar said to me as he reached over and put his arm around my shoulder.

"Should we make him jealous?" Nathan asked.

"I should leave."

"No way, who cares what he thinks? Let's all just have a good time," Omar said and trotted off to talk to a group of girls.

"Hey, girl!" Jessica waved, hugging me like she hadn't seen me in years.

"How ya doin?" I asked her, noticing that she was skinnier than ever.

"Not bad. Drunk!" she said, kicking her leg in the air.

"I can see that."

There was a short little white girl giggling behind her. Jessica turned around and pushed the girl towards me.

"This is my good friend Nadia."

I said hello without smiling.

"Isn't she cute? I'm gonna get a beer—you want one?" Jessica asked, slurring her words.

"No, thanks," I replied and Jessica sped off, leaving me with Nadia.

Nadia didn't look like she could focus on anything. "Got any crack?" She asked me.

I wasn't used to people asking me for crack with such a loud voice; the girl was obviously slow. "No," I said sharply. I didn't like selling crack to people who seemed intoxicated already.

"Shit, we've been looking for some all day."

"Who's we?"

"Jessica and me," she said with a goofy smile.

"Jessica, you mean Jessica the girl who was here just a second ago?"

"Yeah, she and I are pals."

I walked away and began to look for Jess. I found her struggling to open a beer case. I put one hand on it and she glanced at me and smiled.

"Can you help me open this?"

"You're smoking rock now?"

"Says who?"

"Says your little friend Nadia. Apparently you were looking for some all day."

"Don't freak out. I just did it a couple times. It's not a big deal."

"If it weren't a big deal, you would have called me for some, you wouldn't have tried to hide it!"

"I'm not trying to hide!"

"Then why didn't you call me for any?"

"Because I didn't want any."

"I don't believe you! What's happening to you, Jessica? Your life is fucked already and now you're smoking crack, hanging around crackheads?"

"I came here to have a good time. I don't need you ragging on me."

"I saved your ass that morning Gina was gonna beat you. I pulled a knife on her to stop her from hurting you. Now none of us are friends anymore and this is how you repay me?"

"I'm not asking you to care about me. Just leave me alone."

She turned to leave, and I tried grabbing her arm but she yelled out. I didn't want to make a scene so I went outside looking for my three buddies. Instead I found Darrel in a cloud of smoke, talking to a couple of girls and Tyson. Darrel noticed me and flashed me the Diablos gang sign but I didn't flash it back to him.

"G Child," someone shouted to me as they pushed me into the circle in a friendly way.

"Who did you come here with?" Darrel asked me as we stood face to face.

"Nathan, Omar and Francine."

"Where are those fools?" Tyson asked, lighting up a joint. I didn't answer him.

"I'm going home," I said to Darrel hoping he'd come with me.

"Remember Justin Keeshond? He's here with his sister," Darrel said, dragging on the joint.

"I want to go," I said.

"I just got here, you go."

Tyson flung his arm around my waist. "C'mon, the party's just started," he slurred.

I pulled his arm off me. "Don't touch me."

"What's your problem?" Darrel asked.

"I just wanna go."

"Go ahead. I don't care what you do."

"Relax, take a hoot," Tyson said, putting a joint to my lips. I slapped his hand away.

"What happened in there, someone try to fuck with you?" Darrel asked.

"I think you better put your bitch in check," Tyson said.

"I think you better get yourself in check," I said, walking away and back into the house.

I passed Jessica in the hallway. She hollered out for me but I didn't look back. I walked over to the case of beer and grabbed six for myself. I hid in the bathroom and guzzled them down. I almost puked but got a wicked buzz. I opened the door and observed my surroundings. Now, that was more like it. When I was drunk I didn't give a fuck about anything and I felt like I belonged again.

245

An hour later, I had sold Nadia a rock, knowing that Jessica was going to get high with her; but I didn't care and with that in mind, I drank some more beer.

I felt a hand grab my arm and lead me out the door but I was too intoxicated to look at the person's face. I was now outside on the sidewalk looking down at my shoes. The person turned me around and held my face up.

"What the hell's wrong with you?" Darrel asked me.

"Nothing, I'm drunk." I tried to step away from him but he blocked my way.

"Where are you going?"

"Back inside."

"I'm taking you home."

"Oh, now you want to take me home. I wanted to go a long time ago and now that I'm having fun, you want to take me home. Fuck you, Darrel. Who do you think you are?"

"You better settle the fuck down." Darrel picked me up and I fought to get out of his arms but I was too drunk and I tired myself quickly.

"Get in," he said, shoving me in the car.

When we got home, I plopped myself on the bed wanting to sleep but Darrel had something else in mind.

"Get up," he instructed me.

"No," I moaned with a pillow covering my face.

Darrel yanked me up by my arm and stood me up against the wall and began to shake me, "You're weak man. You're fuckin' weak."

"Let go of me. I want to go to sleep!"

"Look at me when I'm talking to you."

"I'm going to bed!" I yelled and plopped back down on the bed.

"Get up," he said, yanking me by the arm and dragging me on the floor.

"Darrel, what's wrong with you? What the hell are you on?" I screamed, feeling the rug burns sting my legs.

"You fucking calling me a snifter?" Darrel asked me as he stood me up in the hallway and pushed me against the wall. He squeezed my shoulders and jerked me back and forth. "Why do you make me do this to you? Why?"

"Let go of me!" I said, pushing him away. I ran for the door but he caught me by my shirt and pulled me back with all of his strength, causing me to fall on my back.

"You're not going anywhere!" he said, standing above me with his foot on my chest keeping me from moving.

"I have nothing to say to you," I huffed. I tried to get up but quickly realized the fall had made me throw my back out of whack, and I yelled out.

"You have nothing to say to the guy that loves you?" Darrel bent over and slapped me across the right side of my face. My face stayed turned, as if I was in a trance, my eyes wide open. I was in shock. Darrel then grabbed my jaw and slammed my head on the floor.

"Don't you know you mean everything to me?" he said as his eyes swelled up with tears. He slapped me harder on the left side of my face and then again on my right. I struggled to get away but he only slapped me harder when I tried. I gasped for air as his knees crushed my lungs. He watched me gasp and then suddenly his anger turned into guilt.

"Fuck, I'm sorry," Darrel said, covering my body with his own. He held my face gently and his tears fell onto my cheek.

I looked up at him but didn't see Darrel McKay, my friend from the old school or Gina's kid brother who talked to me like he was my own. This was not my boyfriend, my lover and my confidant. I saw a savage gang member, a replica of his gang-member father who abused his wife for years. He was nothing more to me than a low-life Central piece of drug dealing shit. Whatever happened to being solid, I thought to myself. Crying over a girl? Crying over me? At that moment, I felt no sympathy towards him whatsoever.

"I don't know what got into me—please don't leave me."

I couldn't think of anything to say, so I just closed my eyes and hoped he would disappear.

"I'm so sorry. Fuck, I'm an asshole," Darrel pleaded.

"I'm going to leave," I said attempting to get up.

"No," he said, covering me once again with his body.

"You don't need me," I said. It wasn't like Darrel was an ugly kid. He could find another girlfriend if a relationship was what he wanted.

I attempted to get up again but that same sharp pain shot down my back once more. I had really thrown it out and screamed in pain. Darrel helped me up and sat me on the couch in the living room.

"Yes I do need you. I love you . . . beat me up if you want."

He sat back and waited for me to strike. As if beating him up would make it all better. Besides, I could hardly move, never mind being able to throw any punches.

I moved away from him and sat at the edge of the couch. Darrel wrapped me in his arms but I pushed him away.

"You don't understand," he moaned. "I've been through so much hurt in my life, so much hurt. When my mom died, I died with her."

I couldn't help but feel his pain at that very moment. I had never really gotten along with my mother but longed for a mother I could confide in. A mother that would understand me, a mother that loved me and accepted all the good and bad things that came with being me. I knew Darrel's mother was all those things to all of her children. They were blessed to have had her for a mother.

The Darrel McKay I'd known over the previous eleven years had been buried with his deceased mother. This stranger laid his head on my lap and cried hopelessly. I sat with him and stroked his hair but all I could think was, what the fuck am I still doing here? I remembered finding out for the first time that Tyson was beating up Jessica and thinking less of her because she stayed with him. But now here I was battling with myself, knowing I should leave but being pulled back by love. I looked down at Darrel's head in my lap and I felt the wetness of his tears on my bare skin. I felt an awkward smile come over my face and in that moment, I knew I was born to suffer.

* * *

I WAS EXHAUSTED mentally and physically and slept like a log. I awoke the next morning to Darrel giving me wet kisses between my legs and not long after, we made love but it felt empty. I was still emotionally and physically hurt from the night before. Darrel laid on his back when we were finished and I stared at the sweat rolling down his young face.

He turned to me and looked in my eyes. "Don't you like it when I make love to you?"

"You make me feel good," I said, reassuring him.

"It didn't look like you were enjoying yourself," he said awkwardly as he got up and got dressed.

"My back is sore, that's all."

"If your back is so sore, maybe you shouldn't be working today. Take the day off," he said, heading into the bathroom. Darrel came out wearing a beige T-shirt and a pair of black jeans that I had bought him for his birthday. "I'm getting picked up soon," he said as he leaned over and kissed me on the forehead.

"See you later."

I hated myself at that moment because I felt powerless. I had no control and it was eating away at my pride and self-worth, but worst of all, I felt like a statistic. I was just another young girl, stuck in an abusive relationship, not knowing how to get out. Staying cooped up in the apartment would just drive me insane. I needed to talk to someone, but who? I thought of Violet and her offer about visiting her sometime. It was time to take her up on it.

CHAPTER FIFTEEN

A FINAL GOODBYE

I rang the doorbell three times before Violet finally pulled the door open. She gave a little smile and invited me in.

We sat in the kitchen and she poured herself a cup of tea and sat beside me. She was seven months pregnant and her tummy was bulging out of her yellow maternity top.

"You look different," Violet said, looking me up and down.

"I feel different." The gangster inside of me was dying away.

"Jessica's cracked out," Violet said.

"I know about Jessica."

"Roland has ways of finding out about everyone."

"I'm almost afraid to ask you what's going on."

"It's Darrel. I don't know how to handle him. I don't even know him anymore."

"Darrel will heal with time. The situation can only improve."

"Darrel couldn't be worse—he's not himself, it's like living with a stranger."

251

"He shouldn't be ignoring his family at a time like this. They need him. Have you tried telling him that?"

"I can't tell him anything. He takes everything I say the wrong way."

"Being with someone like Darrel can't possibly be good for you."

"I want out, Violet. You don't know how bad I want out. One of the reasons I wanted to be with Darrel was because I felt that he was actually going somewhere with his life. Now he doesn't know whether he's coming or going. He's turning into a male version of Gina." Two fat tears rolled down my face.

"I've never seen you like this," Violet said, putting her hand on my shoulder.

"I'll be all right," I said, remembering that gangsters don't cry.

"Why don't you stay here for a couple of days? I know my mom wouldn't mind at all. She got a good impression of you the first time she met you. Just to get your head clear, to stop and think for a while."

"I appreciate it, but no thanks."

"I was meaning to ask you, what's up with Jessica?"

"I thought you knew," I said.

"No, I mean I tried to get a hold of her earlier to day and Tyson said she wasn't staying with him anymore."

"What?" I asked in shock.

"That's what he said anyway; did she go to her mother's house?"

"Jessica has no other place to go, I'm guessing she would go there."

"Hey, my offer to you still stands," Violet said as I left.

I didn't answer.

I TOOK a cab to Jessica's mother's apartment building. As I approached the steps of that grimy place, I had to laugh to myself because in my younger days, I remembered thinking this was a luxurious apartment.

I made my way to the third floor and knocked on Jessica's door.

"Who is it?" a groggy voice asked.

"I'm looking for Jessica. Is she here?"

"Who wants to know?" the voice asked back.

"Open the door and you'll find out." The door opened and a lady that reeked of cigarette smoke stood in front of me.

"Mrs. Fox?" I asked not being able to recognize her.

"In person," she said.

"Is Jessica around?" I asked surprised at how much Jessica's mother had aged. She was definitely not a vibrant petite blonde anymore.

"Jessica's not here. She lives with her boyfriend."

"She's not there anymore."

"Well, if she's not there, then I don't know where the hell that girl is. She's screwing up and if you're a real friend to her, you'll try to help her out."

I MADE my way back to our apartment and was surprised

to find Darrel sitting there with a bunch of our buddies from Central. They were smoking weed and watching *American Pie* on Darrel's fifty-two-inch TV.

"Wuz up?" Omar said, tipping his hat at me, and just like in the old days he got up and shook my hand. "So you movin' up in the world, livin' large, eh?"

"Yep," I said, trying to fake a smile towards him.

"I'm getting married," Omar said with a smile from ear to ear.

"To who?" I asked amazed.

"To Jasmine and she's sweet like honey, let me tell you. I don't wanna be a player for life. Sooner or later you gotta grow up and outta that bullshit."

"When are you getting married?"

"I haven't proposed to her yet. I'm going to do that tonight; I'm taking her to the revolving restaurant."

"What if she says no?" Darrel said, teasing him.

"She'll say yes. The bitch better say yes. I paid over a thousand for this ring right here," he said, pulling a box out of his pocket, showing me a very beautiful diamond ring. It was breathtaking and I could only imagine being in Jasmine's shoes.

"You're losing your touch," Cory said.

"Please," Omar replied, sitting back with a smile.

"So are you two gonna get married?" Cory said, poking Darrel in the arm.

"If she wants to," Darrel said, looking over at me with his dark eyes.

WHEN THE GUYS finished their beers and joints, they headed out, leaving Darrel and me alone. I went into the bedroom and slipped on a comfortable nightie and ran the bathtub. I headed into the kitchen to get a cold soft drink but when I tried to go back into the bathroom, Darrel shut the door and almost made me spill the can of pop all over my gown.

"What the . . . ?" I said.

"Just wait a sec," he said as I heard him move things around.

Just great, I thought. He picks now to go to the can. But just then Darrel opened the bathroom door. He had a look of passion in his eyes. I stepped inside and saw that the bathroom was completely lit by cherry-scented candles and the bathtub was filled to overflowing with bubbles and suds. The most impressive part of it all was the red rose petals on the floor, marking a trail that led to the tub with more soft petals lying in clouds of bubbles.

"I know it's not a ring but I thought you needed something like this," he said, wrapping me in his arms.

Darrel helped to undress me and held my hand as I climbed into the tub.

"I wasn't expecting this," I said, feeling happy and complete. I had seen this type of stuff in music videos and in movies, but I didn't think people did this sort of thing in real life. To Darrel, I must have been someone really special.

"I love you," he said as he began to rub my shoulders. "How's your back doing?"

"Better."

"That's good. I'll let you relax," he said.

"Why don't you come in here with me?" I asked.

"You want me to?" he asked kind of surprised.

"Yes, I'd like that."

He undressed and I watched his every move. Darrel may have became an asshole for a boyfriend but his body never failed to impress me. He slipped in behind me and our wet bodies pressed against each other.

"Mmm," he moaned as he stroked my arms with his hands.

"Do you love me?" he asked.

"Yes," I answered as I lay on his chest, at peace.

"Baby, I'm so sorry about yesterday."

"Let's just forget about it, okay?"

"Okay, but I want you to know I feel really bad, baby. I'd never want to hurt you. Besides my daughter, you are the only good thing in my life. I care so much for you. I want you to be with me for a long time, forever if you'll let me."

I TOWEL-DRIED my hair and went into our bedroom. I got out an old photo album and was looking at a picture of a young Darrel with Jessica hugging him from behind.

"What are you doing?" he asked as he reached for my hand.

"Looking at pictures. You know something?" I said, closing the album.

"What's that?" he said, crawling into bed next to me.

"Rumour has it that Tyson and Jessica aren't together anymore."

"Who told you that?"

"Violet. I went to visit her today."

"They'll get back together."

"I hope not."

"Why?"

"I just hope they don't."

"What do you know that I don't?"

I remained silent but Darrel knew not to question me any further.

"It could be a rumour. We'll go see them tomorrow," Darrel said, kissing me good night.

THE NEXT DAY we stopped at Tyson's place but he wasn't answering the door. We were just about to leave when we heard a gate shut in the backyard.

Tyson entered his yard from the back alley. Darrel called out to him.

"Oh hey, what you two doing here?" Tyson asked.

"Got any bud?" Darrel said.

"I'm out," Tyson said, his eyes fixated on me.

"Where's Jess?" I asked him straight to the point.

"Fucked off somewhere . . ."

"What does that mean?" I asked him.

"I don't know where she is," he said.

"What happened?"

"We broke up. I told her to beat it," he bragged, leaving the door wide open.

We followed him in. I knew Tyson was a dirty guy and I hated him for what he was doing to Jess. I also knew that if he broke up with her, it would be the end of her world.

"Fucking mess, I had a party last night," he said, stepping over empty beer bottles.

"Why don't you come work for me?" Darrel said in a joking manner.

"I don't do that type of shit. You know that." He stood over the kitchen sink and washed his hands.

"So what happened?" I asked him.

"Oh, nothing much, just a little get-together with some hos and shit."

"No, I mean with Jessica."

"I told her to pack her bags and go."

"Did she tell you where she was going?"

"Her mom's place."

"I went there already; her mom hasn't seen or heard from her."

"She's probably out getting high somewhere. She smokes rock."

"Thanks to you," I said, standing a little closer to him.

"What do you mean, thanks to me? I didn't put a gun to the bitch's head and say 'smoke this or die.'"

"You might as well have. She loves you, Tyson, and she would do anything for you."

"I didn't make her do anything. She has a mind of her own, right?"

"How 'bout working the streets?"

"Bitch, you better shut your fuckin' mouth."

"Relax," Darrel said to him with a stern voice.

"Fuckin' bitch is accusing me of making Jessica work. I didn't make her do anything she didn't want to do. Next thing you'll say is if she dies of an overdose, it's my fault."

"If I find out Jessica is hurt in any way, you better pray for mercy because you'll have to deal with me," I said, stepping up to his face.

"Oh, is that supposed to scare me? Time for you to get a reality check—you ain't nobody anymore," Tyson said, shaking his head at me.

"I might not be banging anymore, but don't think I don't have any gangster left in me," I said, storming out, feeling high on adrenaline.

EXACTLY A WEEK later I was at a Vietnamese restaurant with Omar and Jasmine, who was now officially his fiancée, when I got a phone call from Violet. Her voice was trembling and the first thing that popped into my mind was her baby.

"What is it?" I asked.

"Jessica, she's dead. They found her body in the river."

I couldn't speak. Omar and Jasmine stared at me in disbelief as I left the restaurant and waved over a cab while still on the phone with Violet.

"Tyson killed her, he killed her," Violet sobbed.

"Where are you?" I asked her.

"I'm at Roland's. Please come here right away."

AS I approached Roland's street, I saw Violet standing on the front step, watching for my arrival. I threw the driver twenty bucks and raced out of the car. Violet flung herself towards me and we embraced. She seemed to be hyperventilating.

"Violet, Violet tell me what happened."

"It's in the paper; didn't you read the paper today?"

"No," I said, grabbing the newspaper from her trembling hands.

It read, "The body of a twenty-one-year-old woman was found in the Red River last night by passing teenagers. The victim was identified as Jessica Lorraine Fox."

I couldn't read any further. I closed my eyes and felt an empty, hollow pain fill my body and tears blurred my vision.

"How do you know Tyson did this?" I managed to ask.

"Because I called Jessica's mom, and she told me. Cops are looking for him right now but people say he's left the city and nobody knows where he is."

"I don't believe this. I just don't believe this," I said, reading further into the article.

"Jessica is gone," Violet whispered.

A COUPLE of days later, police issued a Canada-wide warrant for Tyson McKay. An autopsy was done on Jessica and it showed that she had been suffocated to death.

Jessica's funeral was two days later and Violet and I went together. We spotted Janice sitting up front with some of her family around her. She must have seen us come in and waved us over, directing us to sit in the aisle behind her.

"But this is reserved for family," Violet said.

"You girls were her family," Janice said. "You were important to her. I know she loved her friends. Please sit here."

I stared at Jessica's shiny oak coffin with red roses laid on top. Janice had a picture of Jessica from back in her modelling days on top of her casket in a chrome frame. And there it was, that sparkle in her eyes, the one she had before she let the streets take her life.

"Look," Violet said over her shoulder. I turned around and saw at least fifteen Diablos from the old school wearing red shirts coming to pay their respects.

"And she thought they didn't have respect for her," I told Violet.

Standing alongside them was Gina, dressed in red from head to toe. Violet and I were shocked. Gina made eye contact with us and sat at the back with the Diablos.

"Gina almost looks . . . embarrassed," I told Violet, noticing how she kept on looking away from me.

"I bet she feels bad about what happened."

* * *

THE PRIEST started the service by talking about Jessica and God. He told us about how Jessica fulfilled her purpose here and how many lives she had touched in her short life. With Violet continuously sobbing on my right, I took a look around the church. There was such sadness on people's faces, some I recognized and some I did not. It hit me then: I was at Jessica's funeral, the girl who had the prettiest flowered dress, the one I had met in the sandbox. The girl that had been with me my whole life, the girl who was my best friend, the girl that lived for love and who died for it. Jessica Fox was gone. I covered my mouth with my hand and began to cry.

When the priest was finished, he asked Janice to come and say a few words and she walked up to the podium. She was wearing a faded black blazer and a navy blue skirt. She gazed over the people assembled and began to speak.

"It pleases me that there are so many people here this morning. I thank each one of you for taking the time to come honour the memory of my beloved daughter. Jessica was a strong person, although she didn't exactly have the easiest life. Jessica never knew her father. He died the day she was born, but it comforts me to know that they are now meeting each other for the first time and that my little Jessica will be taken care of. When Jessica came back to live with me, I looked at her and thought, 'How did I ever let his sweet little girl get away?' Soon my little girl grew up to be a beautiful woman. I didn't set a good example for her but deep down I always wanted the best for her. My daughter, Jessica Lorraine

Fox, was killed by the coward she loved, beaten to death by her boyfriend, Tyson McKay. I want to let everyone here know, and Jessica, my baby girl if you can hear me, I will not rest until this man is convicted for his crime against you, against your family and against everyone here today. May you rest in peace, my darling, we will always love you and miss you."

VIOLET AND I drove to the cemetery in silence.

As we approached the black iron gates, Violet hung back a little. "I can't do this," she said.

I felt sorry for myself and even though my heart ached, I knew that I needed to be strong for my friend.

"Will you be okay?" I asked her, knowing that this stress was not good for her pregnancy.

"I'll do my best," she said.

Violet and I stood close to each other; we listened to the priest say his final prayer and prepared ourselves to see our dear friend lowered into the ground.

"Why didn't anyone call me?" Gina said as she crept up behind us. Violet jumped.

"Nobody knows how to get ahold of you," I said, looking into her red and puffy eyes.

"I'm around," Gina said, choking back tears.

She stared into the distance and slowly put her head down. I'd never seen her look so weak and vulnerable.

She looked up at me with no sign of hiding her emotions. "Did you think I wasn't going to care? Did you

think I wasn't going to miss her? I know I was wrong."
She held me tight, my face deep in her long black hair. I
hugged her as hard as I could.

The priest finished his prayer and the coffin was
slowly lowered into the ground. Everyone looked so
grim and many were crying.

The three of us stood near the edge and watched. Violet walked away from the grave but Gina and I remained.
Out of the corner of my eye, I saw Gina take something
out of her pocket. It was a picture of us: Jessica, Violet,
Gina and me standing outside our apartment. I remembered the picture well: it was the first day we moved in.
We were surrounded with garbage bags full of our clothes
and cardboard boxes full of junk. We looked happy. The
excitement of starting this new life of money, power and
independence fulfilled us, but most importantly, we were
starting it together. Gina admired the picture and tossed
it down the six-foot hole with the picture landing face
up. The first shovel of dirt hit the picture. How ironic, I
thought. It's all gone, just like Jessica was gone and the
dream was gone; it was all being buried with her.

VIOLET AND I rode in silence all the way back to the city.
As we approached my place, she spoke up, "Why didn't
Darrel come?"

"He doesn't deal with death very well."

As I got into the apartment, Omar zoomed past me.
"What the fuck?" I said aloud, wondering what was

going on. I stepped inside to find Darrel pacing. "What happened now?" I asked.

"One of our runners got shot. Vernon, he's in the hospital."

"Who shot him?"

"Ryders did it!" he said angrily.

"What a mess," I said, looking around at some broken glass on the floor, regretting at that moment that I didn't go with Violet back to her place.

"Shut up, man, can't you see I'm stressed out?" he hollered while frantically pacing.

"I don't need to hear this. I came from my best friend's funeral. I wanted to come home to some peace."

"Get out of here then!" he yelled.

"How can you be so cold-hearted, Darrel? Jessica was your friend too!"

"I don't have time for this right now."

"Fine," I said, heading into the bedroom to get a change of clothes. I wasn't planning to come back that night. I was about to reach into the closet and pull out a shirt when I felt Darrel's hands turn me around. He punched me across the jaw and I hit the ground on impact.

"C'mon!" he yelled as he punched me again and again. He got off of me and yelled at me to get up.

"C'mon, you solid bitch, get up off that floor!"

It took all my strength to get up from the floor and when my eyes met his, it was as if somebody kicked me in the back of my knees. My legs couldn't hold my body weight, and I fell to the floor. The room began to spin. Darrel rushed to my side and held me to his chest. He was speaking in a remorseful tone but I couldn't register what he was saying. My head was in excruciating pain and I couldn't see straight. I knew that he broke my jaw. Darrel became frustrated and began to shake me.

"Hey, I'm talking to you. Answer me!"

I couldn't answer him: my jaw didn't move, I couldn't talk! Darrel picked me up and laid me on our bed.

"Baby, I'm so sorry. I didn't mean to hurt you, please!" he said laying his head on my chest.

I knew in that moment that it was over between us. Everything was over—the Diablos, the drug money. I never wanted anything as badly as I wanted out at that very moment. He looked up at my face and his eyes widened as he looked at my jaw.

"Please baby, I can make things better!" Darrel said as he blocked the door with his body. I got up, trying to ignore the piercing pain I felt in my jaw. I took ahold of him by the shirt, pushed him aside and ran out of the apartment down the hallway to the stairs with Darrel close behind me.

"Wait! Baby, please!" he called after me, but I just kept on running down the stairs and finally out the door. Darrel chased me down the street but stopped after a while. He wasn't about to take the chance of getting noticed by the cops. I had fifty dollars in my pocket and took a cab to the nearest hospital.

AT THE HOSPITAL the nurses begged me to tell them what had happened.

"Do you need somewhere safe to stay?" a young nurse asked me. "There are plenty of women's shelters."

Oh my god, is this what I've been reduced to? A suffering, speechless woman with no family or home and not even her gang standing behind her? I vigorously shook my head no and kept silent. They wired my mouth shut and packed me with painkillers. I worried briefly about where I was going to stay but then I remembered Violet's offer to let me stay with her a while back. I hoped the offer still stood. I had nowhere else to go.

Violet managed to understand me over the phone, in spite of my wired jaw.

"Of course you can stay with us. Mom said she'd pray for you."

CHAPTER SIXTEEN

TIME TO RETREAT

It was difficult for a long while, not being able to eat anything but cream soups and struggling to be understood whenever I spoke. The positive side was that I had time to think things out. I thought a lot about Gina and Darrel. A part of me wished things could be how they used to be between Gina and me. Deep down, I knew Gina wanted what was best for me, even if what I thought was best differed from what she thought. I tried to convince myself that I didn't miss Darrel, but I really did. I wondered what kind of woman would still miss a guy after he had broken her jaw. I decided to toughen myself up and was determined never to speak to Darrel again, no matter how much he begged. Darrel called almost every day but Violet always told him that I wasn't there or that I was asleep.

"I'll tell her you called," she would always say. I never made an attempt to call him back. I slept in Violet's room on an inflatable mattress. It was such a girly room, with walls that were sparkling white and about a hundred teddy bears sitting around.

I went back to the hospital to have the wires removed

a little over a month later. Because of my liquid diet, I lost seven pounds and felt great.

"It must feel good to have those wires and screws out of your mouth," Violet said as she bent down and picked up some clothes off the floor.

"Absolutely!" I told her as I helped her clean up.

"The swelling is gone completely," Violet said smiling. "You look as good as new."

"I feel a lot better. I can't wait to eat real food again."

"You've had a lot of time to clear your head, hey?" she asked.

"Yep, I know what I want and I know what I don't want. I want a normal life, not the streets anymore."

"Roland told me to tell you that he's stopping by to talk to you."

"He better not be bringing that asshole Darrel." Ever since the breakup, I felt this hate towards Darrel McKay. Violet thought it was because I still loved him, but it didn't feel like love to me.

"Don't worry. I wouldn't even let him inside this house."

The doorbell rang and Violet went up to answer it. Both Roland and Violet came down to her room in the basement and to my surprise Roland gave me a hug.

"You gonna live?" he joked.

"Sure," I said.

"I got something to ask you. It's something that I've been thinking about for a while."

"Okay," I said, not having a clue to what it was.

"I'm gonna be taking Violet to Calgary with me after

269

the baby is born. I'd like you to come out there with us."

"Calgary? Why Calgary?" I asked surprised.

"Winnipeg is too heat score. Cops are always on my ass for every fucking thing. The cops don't know me in Calgary. Me and a couple other guys are setting up shop out there. G Child, you're a good friend to Violet—she needs a good friend around. I'm gonna start up a crew down there. I already have everything lined up but I'd like to have a few familiar faces, ones that I trust, if you know what I mean."

"How about your brother? Is he coming too?" I asked, hoping that he wasn't going to be there.

"Don't worry about my brother. He has his own show out here. He's doing well for himself and to be honest with you, I haven't seen much of the guy these days."

"Gina, how about her?"

"How about her? Who knows what that broad's doing— she doesn't work for me anymore. Just think about it for now, but we're leaving as soon as the baby is born."

"Getting out of Winnipeg sounds pretty good but I don't know about setting up shop out there."

"Leave that up to me. If you wanna get involved in the drug business, you've got my okay. If not, that's okay too," he replied. I was relieved; I didn't know the sensible side of Roland. Getting away from this city and all its bad memories was just what I needed. I could still go to school, the only difference was that it would be in Calgary and there would be no Darrel.

"I don't need to think about. I'll go," I replied.

ONE MONTH later, Violet was in the hospital in heavy-duty labour with Roland, her mother and me by her side. She was in labour for almost nine hours and gave birth to a healthy baby girl they named Lenore.

A week after that, Roland, Violet and I were getting ready to move to Calgary.

"Where are my CDs?" Violet asked Roland as she sifted through boxes of her things.

"They're in the car," he said, holding little baby Lenore, who had been crying nonstop for ten minutes.

"What's wrong with her?" he asked Violet.

"She wants to be fed. Give her to me for a while," she said, her arms open wide. Roland placed their little girl in her arms and Violet went into the bathroom.

"Excited?" Roland asked me as I put the rest of my clothes into one of Violet's boxes.

"Oh yeah," I said.

"It'll be a fresh start for all of us," he said, pulling out his ringing cell phone.

"Oh what's up?" Roland asked the person on the phone.

Roland had a big smile on his face and I wondered who it was. Before I was able to ask, Roland passed me his cell phone.

"Hello?"

"What's up, girl? Where did you disappear to?" It was Omar's deep voice, a voice that was recognizable to me even if I was half deaf.

"I've been hiding," I said to him in a sarcastic tone.

"So, you gonna come out or what?"

"I'll come out, but only for a bit. We're leaving in the morning and . . ."

"And you can sleep on the way." Omar finished my sentence.

"All right. I'm over at Violet's. You can come pick me up in a half hour."

"I'll be there," he said, hanging up. I really wasn't in the mood to go anywhere but I figured one last night out with the boys couldn't hurt. I was just about to slip on a casual pair of jeans when Violet grabbed my attention.

"Wear this instead," Violet said, holding up a black-laced dress. "Roland bought it for me before I became pregnant, but I never wore it."

"It's really nice," I said, feeling the material.

"It's from Marciano. Wear it tonight."

"I don't know. Isn't it too short? It's winter and . . ."

"C'mon, it's not like you're gonna be rolling around in the snow. You got the legs for it anyway," Roland said.

I shrugged and took their advice.

I WATCHED out the kitchen window for Omar's white Honda. I was nervous about going out. I hadn't seen my homies in a while and I wondered what Darrel might have said to them about me. The thing I was most nervous about was running into Darrel. That would be so uncomfortable and I was afraid of getting all sorts of feelings back if I saw him again.

I saw Omar's car pull into the driveway and I hopped on out of there.

"I forgot where this place was," Omar said as I got in.

"What's up?" a voice asked from the back seat.

"Hey," I said, turning around and seeing Malcolm looking all G'd up and tipping his hat my way.

"You look like a real lady. I've never seen you wear a dress before," Omar said.

"There's always a first time. Where are we going?" I asked.

"Latin Gardens," Malcolm said from the back.

"Latin Gardens?" I asked as Omar pulled out of the driveway and zipped down the street.

"Why, you got a problem with Latin Gardens?" Omar asked as he drove.

"I don't wanna run into certain people."

"Like Darrel?" Nathan asked, laughing.

"What happened with you two anyway?" Omar asked me.

"Shit happens," I said, lighting one of his smokes.

"He's got a new girl now, Melanie," Nathan said.

"That's not his girl," Omar said, looking in the rearview mirror.

"He's fucking her or some shit," Nathan said.

"You probably don't wanna hear this," Omar said, looking over at me.

"Don't bother me," I replied turning the heat up in the car.

I lied. It did bother me, but I wasn't going to let them know that. I wanted them to remember me as the hard G Child, not the sissified one.

"You look beautiful," Omar said, looking over at me in the lace dress, black boots and suede winter jacket.

"Thanks," I said.

I don't remember getting so many compliments from my bros before.

WE PARKED right outside the club. There was a crowd of guys just chilling outside the doors smoking weed, most of whom we all knew. I was wondering if Darrel was in the club or if he would be coming later.

"C'mon babe," Omar said as we entered.

"Holy shit," Omar said as two white girls passed us and smiled over at him.

"Where's Jasmine tonight?" I asked him.

"At home, sleeping," he said.

The club was not as packed as it used to get back in the day. It looked rather dead actually, but I reminded myself that I had come out to have fun with the homies before I left, and that was what I intended to do.

"What are you having?" Omar asked me as a waitress stopped near us.

"Smirnoff," I said, grabbing a seat by the window. The other homies huddled around us and we formed a large group in the middle of the club. I downed four Smirnoff

Ices and was feeling a buzz when I saw Darrel walk into the club.

"Fuck," I said underneath my breath as I felt my heart race.

I watched him walk in and greet the others. Darrel didn't notice me at first. I watched him closely and saw underneath his smile that he was stressed out. He turned around quickly and caught me staring at him; I put my head down and shifted my feet. I looked up to see him still watching, but then he was distracted by a girl who flung her arms around him. So that's Melanie; she did look cute. She was aboriginal, about five feet tall, short dark hair and huge in the chest area. She wasn't exactly what I was picturing but good enough for someone like Darrel. I convinced myself that I didn't care and I ordered another drink. Throughout the night, we both caught each other's eye. I watched him as he sat with Melanie and laughed, and he watched me as strangers bought me drinks. I stood up to go to the bathroom and felt the effects of the alcohol in my legs. I felt his eyes watch me as I returned to my table. The atmosphere was different when I sat back down, though. Everybody had gotten out of their chairs and they were standing around looking like they were waiting for something. I saw my jacket lying on the floor with some grubby guy who was part of the crew standing on it.

"Excuse me, you're on my jacket," I said to him. He ignored me completely. "Move," I ordered him but he continued to look around. "This guy's an asshole," I said to Omar, who was nearby.

"There's gonna be a beef," he said in a concerned tone.

"Who cares," I said, bending down to get my jacket but a couple of screams filled the air and I stood right back up. The club lights were turned on and people ran out of the club, the guy who wouldn't get off my jacket included.

I quickly grabbed my jacket and rushed to the door. I stood alongside everyone else from the club in the middle of the sidewalk, not knowing which way my friends had gone.

Omar popped out of nowhere. "Let's go." He grabbed my hand and we ran down the street.

"What happened?" I asked him as a bunch of us, including Nathan and Shawn, ran towards a brown car and hopped in with Gina driving.

"Holy shit, back from the dead?" she asked me as I squished myself in the back.

"Hurry up!" Omar said.

"Fuck, did you see that?" Malcolm asked as Gina stepped on the gas.

"See what? I still don't know what happened!" I complained.

"Silas Flett pulled a gun out on Darrel."

"Oh my god, is he okay?" I asked.

"I don't know. I saw him run the other way. I don't think Silas got him," Nathan said.

"I didn't even know Silas was there," I said, looking behind me as Omar's white Honda zoomed by us.

"Who's driving your car?" I asked him.

"Darrel," he said, wiping sweat off of his face.

In the midst of it all, I was terribly confused and still didn't really understand what was going on. We all got out by a nearby crack house that the crew ran and hurried inside. Darrel wasn't there. I watched as Gina and the rest of them gossiped like a bunch of junior high kids about what had happened in the club.

From what I heard, Silas Flett and some hard-core Street Ryders came into the club and headed in Darrel's direction. Darrel and Silas began mouthing off to each other and Silas flashed him a gun that was in his jacket. Apparently a group of girls standing near them witnessed it and that's when the screaming started.

I looked at all the gangsters' faces and saw fear on each one.

"Things got this fucked up?" I asked Omar as I pulled him into the corner.

"What you mean?" he asked, peeking over his shoulder several times.

"Look at everyone, they're scared shitless of the Street Ryders."

Just then I heard a pounding on the door and it startled me.

"Don't open it!" I heard a voice say from within the room.

"Look through the window and check who it is first," another voice demanded.

Omar looked through the window and opened the door quickly. Darrel rushed in and zoomed past me.

"Somebody get me a towel!" Darrel hollered as blood

dripped down from his forehead onto his jacket.

"Are you shot?" Omar asked, searching him.

"No, I fell on some black ice, cut my eyebrow." He grabbed a towel from Nathan's grip.

"C'mon," Omar said as we made our way to the living room. Darrel stood next to the front door but I looked away from him as soon as I felt his eyes on me. I went into a bedroom near the front door and sat on the bed and realized how much I had changed. I didn't belong here anymore; this wasn't fun for me. It used to be that I enjoyed getting chased by the cops with the feeling of fear and anxiety mixed together all at once, but this stuff just seemed plain stupid.

"Why you sitting here all alone?" Nathan said, coming into the room and putting his hand on my shoulder. I tried to get out of his way but he stood in front of me and prevented me from moving.

"What's the matter?" he asked. "Everything is all right here. Relax, home girl, it's okay. Have a beer." He twisted open a bottle.

Omar must have seen my concern from across the room because he joined me inside the tiny bedroom.

"Don't worry, everything is good," he said, looking relieved.

"Is this place safe?" I asked.

"Oh it's real safe. Are you scared, G Child?" he asked in a surprised tone.

I sat back down on the bed and remembered that I wanted to leave a solid image with my childhood friends before I left the city.

"Scared? Fuck no, I just wanted to know, ya know? So I could be prepared."

I looked outside the room and saw Darrel walk by. He looked in and gave me the "I know you" smile. I felt uncomfortable because his smile said, "I love you still and I know you love me." I smiled back. He walked towards the room and stood tall in the doorway.

"Why you being antisocial?" he asked me.

"I'm not," I said, looking over at the fellas.

"Mind if I get some privacy?" Darrel said, stepping into the room. The two gangsters left us alone and shut the door.

"Your girlfriend might get jealous," I said.

"She's not my girlfriend. I'm just getting to know her. I don't want a girlfriend right now anyway."

"I see," I said coldly.

"How come you didn't answer any of my calls?" he asked sitting beside me on the bed.

"Dunno," I said, looking away from his chocolate eyes.

"Sorry about your jaw. I feel bad about it." He put his arm around me and just then the door opened wide. Melanie stood in the doorway with her hands on her hips.

"So you're gonna leave me out here all night or what?"

"I was coming out. I needed to talk to her," Darrel said, getting up and following her out of the room.

He turned around and attempted to smile but I raised my voice at him, "Pussy whipped," I said, slamming the door on their faces.

I was really upset. Omar and Nathan came into the room laughing their heads off.

"That bitch was so mad. She said she wanted to punch you out."

"Let's see her try it," I said without a hint of a smile.

"Do I sense a bit of hostility here?" Nathan said.

Everyone relaxed just a little but Gina still looked worried. She walked around the living room like a cop, back and forth several times, continually staring in my direction. Her stares made me feel uncomfortable as I sipped on my beer with Omar's arm around my shoulder.

"Quiet!" she yelled. "Did you hear that?" she said crouching on the floor.

"Hear what?" Omar asked her.

"Turn those fucking lights off!" she said, pointing at a little black kid that was sitting by the light switch.

"Turn the music off!" I heard a voice say.

"How the fuck do they know where this place is?" Gina whispered angrily.

"Shh, someone's talking," Omar said.

There was a loud knocking on the door. It made me jump, and without hesitation Omar, Malcolm and I lay flat on our bellies on the hardwood floor.

Bang, bang, bang, bang, bang, bang!

"Fuck!" Omar said in fear.

I was afraid, so I crawled into the closet and closed the door behind me. I sat in the dark with a smoke in my right hand and an empty beer bottle in my left. An awful picture came into my head of tomorrow's newspaper announcing that nine known Diablos were found dead in a crack house. Gun shots blasted the house and it sounded like someone was trying to kick down the door. I got out of the closet and found Omar and Nathan struggling to get the bedroom window open.

"Why don't we use the front door?" I asked as I pointed quickly at the door.

"Because there's guys at the front door too!" Omar said.

"Smash it!" I said, handing him a tall metal candlestick holder.

Omar smashed the window and at the same time, I heard the back door open and a dozen shots were fired into the house. Omar dove through the window and fell onto the snowbank at the side of the house. Nathan and I followed. I had left my jacket inside and noticed blood dripping down from my hands onto the snow. I had cut myself on the broken glass. All three of us were bleeding, but Omar was cut the worst. He had deep cuts on his hands, arms and face.

"Let's get out of here," I said, hoping there was still time to get away.

It was absolutely freezing out that night. Still, I tried to ignore it as we ran down the back alley, but Omar dragged behind.

"Ahh . . ." he growled.

"What's wrong?" I asked, rushing to his side as he leaned his body up against a wooden fence.

"I can't breathe," he said, holding his chest, his hands full of blood.

"Let's get to a pay phone," I said, tugging on his arm.

Omar fell down onto the snow. I took his hand away from his chest and saw a huge piece of jagged glass sticking out of his chest.

"Fuck, pull it out!" Nathan said.

I took ahold of the glass and yanked it out as Omar screamed in pain.

"Put pressure on it," Nathan said as he took off his sweater.

I did as I was told and Nathan helped Omar up.

"Heehaw!" we heard as a car drove past a crossing street.

"That's them!" Malcolm said as he put one of Omar's arms around his shoulder.

A set of headlights startled us from behind and we dragged Omar as fast as we could.

"Get in here!" Gina said as she poked her head out the driver's window. Without hesitation we hopped into her car.

"Thought you were them," Nathan said from the back with Omar leaning against the window.

"What's wrong with him?" Gina asked as she sped away.

"He got hurt when he jumped through the window," Nathan said.

"We should take him to the hospital," I told Gina as she ran through a red light.

"We'll do that later," she said.

"He needs to go now," Nathan told her.

"We'll take him in a while," she said.

"I want to go now," Omar moaned.

"Fine but first I wanna go get my guns and blast at these bitchass phonies."

"He's got to go right now!" Nathan yelled while holding Omar in his arms.

"Fuck, he didn't get shot. He'll be okay!"

I noticed a mysterious black van following us.

"It's them!" I said. Gina looked behind her.

"Hold on. Open the glove compartment and pass me the gun inside!" Gina said, looking at me wide-eyed and stepping on the gas.

"Omar's passing out. No man, hang on!"

"We're not going down like this!" Gina yelled as she rolled down her window and began shooting at the van behind us and driving at the same time. "It's a shitty fucking BB gun, man. I need my guns! I got to get my guns!"

We sped through downtown. Of all the nights, why did I have to come out on this one? But this was no time to feel sorry for myself. I turned to look back at Omar.

"How's he doing?" I asked Nathan.

"I don't think he's breathing anymore," Nathan said quietly while he held his blood brother in his arms.

"We'll get to a hospital," Gina said. "I don't see the black van anywhere, do you?" she asked me. I shook my head no.

A few minutes later, we rolled up to the emergency doors at City Hospital. With tears in his eyes, Nathan dragged his dying brother out of the car and before I had a chance to get out, she stepped on the gas and zoomed out of the hospital driveway. Just as we approached a stop sign, the mysterious black van appeared behind us.

Gina pressed on the gas and headed to an area that was unknown to me. "What are you doing?" I asked.

"Getting my guns. Isn't that what I've been telling you this whole damn time?" she said.

"Shit," I said, putting both hands over my ears, trying to escape my reality.

"I told you I was gonna blast at these punkass bitches." She stopped by the riverbank and searched frantically through some bushes. "Could you come out here and help me look? They're not here. Where the fuck are they?"

I got out of the car and looked through the bushes but there were no guns.

"Fucking shit!" Gina said, ripping out one of the shrubs.

A van turned the corner and the headlights were blinding us. I couldn't make out the colour but I didn't want to take any chances, so I ran through the bush and into an empty field. I heard guns blast off into the air and didn't dare look behind me. The deep snow was making it difficult to run any distance, but I stopped when I ran into a barbed wire fence.

My bare arms were ice cold and my teeth began to chatter from the cold and from fear. I slouched down to catch my breath and scanned the field for Gina's shadow, but I couldn't find it in the darkness. I watched my breath in the cold January air and listened to my pounding heartbeat.

Why didn't Gina run this way with me? Did she get gunned down?

I looked at my watch, it was 1:45 a.m. I'll wait ten minutes. I thought to myself, maybe Gina's just hiding out in the field somewhere. Suddenly I heard the spinning sound of tires screaming on ice. They must be leaving; I should get up. I rubbed my hands together, trying to get some feeling in them and was determined to go and find Gina.

I made my way to a lone tree standing in the middle of the field. I saw a mound of black on the white snow and knew in my heart that it was Gina. I ran to her but my excitement soon turned to harsh reality when I saw her. Gina was lying on her back, holding her stomach and gasping for air.

"I can't breathe," she whispered. I sat with her in the snow and put her head on my lap. "They shot me. I'm not gonna survive this one," she said, looking into my eyes.

"Oh yes you are," I said, trying to be strong.

"No, I've been beat but at least I died over something I believed in."

"You're not going to die," I said, searching for her cell phone in her jacket pockets.

"Where's your phone?" I asked.

"I dropped it," she said.

"Hold on," I said to her as I got up and searched frantically for the phone.

It was buried in a pile of snow but I managed to find it and called 911. I knew this meant that the cops were going to be on their way and that meant a whole night of questions in police headquarters.

As I turned around, I was startled by two men who seemed to come out of nowhere. They grabbed the phone and threw it in the snow. One covered my mouth and dragged me towards the street. I struggled but couldn't get away from his grip. They pushed me into the black van and one of them sat on me to keep me still. He flipped me over and I lay motionless on my back. The black-masked predator taped my mouth and hands together with duct tape.

"Your friend is going to die out there and you're next," he whispered in my ear.

Two others were sitting up front with black masks on as well. I sat up and tried to talk but the tape made me sound like I was only mumbling.

"Take the tape off," a guy in the passenger seat said. The asshole beside me ripped the tape off my mouth and I was finally able to talk.

"Who are you? Why do your have you faces covered up in those stupid masks?" I said, trying to show them they didn't scare me.

The guy beside me punched me in the face, and blood poured down from my nose onto my dress.

"Time for the blindfold. We don't want you to know where we're taking you," he said as he grabbed a black rag from his pocket.

He blindfolded me and I sat in silence. I felt helpless to save Gina and helpless to save myself but at the same time, I felt a little bit of hope. If they were blindfolding me because they didn't want me to know where they were taking me, that meant they weren't going to kill me.

AFTER WHAT seemed like a very long ride, I felt the van come to a jolting stop. I had a vision of them taking me to some deserted country road and shooting me in the back of the head, execution style. Street Ryders were known for capping people that way but I kept reminding myself of the blindfold. They dragged me out of the van, led me up some steps and pushed me hard onto a bed.

"Where am I?" I screamed.

I felt hands taking my blindfold off slowly.

"What you are about to see might shock you." That voice sent chills through my whole body. I opened my eyes and saw Jay's face.

Jay Sidhu, the same Jay that was my friend, the same Jay that wrote me all those long heartfelt letters from jail, the same Jay that Gina and Shawn tried to kill. I lay there without moving, my eyes wide and mouth open.

"Speechless?" he asked.

"Jay, how could you?" I asked in disbelief.

"We're after the McKays. I didn't think you'd be with Gina. I heard you two weren't even friends anymore. You were just at the wrong place at the wrong time, G Child. Just like the other time when Gina and Shawn tried to kill me and you just stood there like a stupid bitch. Welcome to my world."

"Where are the others?"

"They'll be back," Jay snarled.

"Jay, get me out of here . . . hurry . . . before they get back!"

"I can't," he said, looking away from me.

"Yes, you can. Just do it, quick!"

"Why were you with Gina tonight, huh? Of all nights you had to pick this one to make up! You know what? Fuck you, G Child! Why should I let you go? You didn't help me when your friends wanted to kill me."

"I wanted nothing to do with that. I tried stopping it, Jay! That's why Gina and I aren't friends anymore."

"You should have tried harder, look at me!" Jay lifted up his shirt and exposed three long scars across his chest. "If it wasn't for those cops that came down the street, they would have killed me and you wouldn't have done anything about it!"

"That's not fair, Jay. You have to let me out of here! Roland will pay you. I know he will. You loved me once, didn't you?"

"That doesn't make a difference . . . okay, so I did love you, but you never gave me a chance. Instead you went out with that small-fry Darrel McKay."

"You disappeared, remember? You're the one who brushed me off at the halfway house. Going out with Darrel was a mistake. People make mistakes, Jay."

"I would have treated you real good, G Child, none of this beating you up bullshit. Do you think I don't know the real reason you wouldn't go out with me? It's because I used to be a crack fiend! I'll admit it. I had a problem. That's past tense but you never could look beyond that. When you look at me, I remind you of those jonesers you serve. You know the type, the ones that crawl on their hands and knees looking for a morsel of crack that could have crumbled off of their crack pipe. You talk about mistakes! You never forgave me for mine, why should I forgive you for yours?"

The truth hurt and tears escaped my eyes. It never occurred to me that Jay could see right through me. All this time he was the one who really loved me, but I let his past get in the way of our future. My tears continued to fall, but this time I didn't care if I didn't look solid because I was tired of acting. Being solid got me nowhere in life. I wanted to be myself, I wanted to live.

"What the fuck are you doing? Crying? C'mon, I can't stand tears," Jay said, sitting next to me but I couldn't help it. I trembled with anxiety. "What are you doing without a jacket? You know what month it is? Jeez . . . put this on," Jay said as he tossed me a sweater that was lying on the floor. I lay there helpless as the sweater landed on my neck.

"Well, put it on. It's probably not clean but it's better than nothing."

"Jay, I'm tied up!"

"Right . . . oh for fuck sakes," Jay turned me around and removed the duct tape from my wrists. I stumbled to get the muddy sweater on and struggled to my feet.

"What about you? Aren't they gonna do something to you once they know I'm gone?"

"I'll deal with it. Go on, climb through the window and disappear. Oh yeah, you'll need these," Jay said, tossing a set of keys my way.

"What are these for?" I asked, catching the keys in mid-air.

"For the red Cavalier down the street. It's a piece of shit car that I was just gonna trash anyway but it'll still get you where you have to go."

"You're giving me your car?"

"It's not even worth five hundred bucks."

"But Jay . . ."

"No buts. C'mon, don't look at me like that. Get outta here before these guys get back." A single teardrop fell down the side of his face.

For a brief moment, I pictured us running away together and leaving all our friends and nightmares behind but it wasn't meant to be. So I did as I was told and got out.

It was still dark out but the moon gave off enough light that I could see a rusted Cavalier sitting across the street. The winter air was bitter, but I barely felt it as I ran towards the car and let myself in. I put the key in the ignition, started it and zoomed out of there. I didn't know exactly where I was or where I was headed, but I was out of there!

I kept my eyes open for the black van, but it was nowhere in sight. After passing a number of recognizable landmarks, I realized that I was on the Trans-Canada Highway heading west.

"I'm going the wrong way. I should turn around and head back east, back home," I said to myself. I pulled onto the side of the highway to gather my thoughts. I thought about Gina and wondered if I should go back for her. I figured the ambulance must have picked her up by then. I hoped she was alive; I had a feeling in my gut that she was okay. But did I want to turn around and go back to Winnipeg or did I want to keep going? I wasn't scared, I actually felt good. I felt free for the first time in a long time. I was damn lucky to be alive. I was getting a second chance to change my life around. Up until this point, my life hadn't turned out the way I had planned but that's a good thing, maybe a really good thing. I glanced at the gas gauge; thankfully it was full. I took a deep breath, pulled back onto the highway and continued westbound.

ACKNOWLEDGEMENTS

First and foremost, I would like to thank my mother for all her love and ongoing support. Without her, this project would not be where it is today. Secondly, I would like to thank Ray Blumenfeld for taking the time and effort required to get my work noticed. He has been a positive light in my life. A great big thanks goes out to Lynne Missen and Patricia Ocampo from HarperCollins Canada. They have helped me tremendously through the editing process from which I have learned so much. A final thank you to my father, Jose Maria Bernardo, my aunt Filomena Lafleur and my uncle Bert Bernardo for being proud of me and loving me.